Secret Dad

Timberwood Cove: Book 3

Liam Kingsley

© 2019
Disclaimer

Contents

Chapter 1 - Gavin

I looked at my reflection in the mirror with disbelief. When had I gotten so *old*? I had crinkles beside my eyes, a deep furrow in my forehead, and a patch of gray hairs near my temple, all of which said I was definitely past my prime and my playboy days were limited. Actually, my playboy days had been and gone, and it was really time to find a mate and settle the hell down.

I grumbled and took a step back, examining the whole package as I slicked my hair back. My reflection wasn't bad. I still had the broad shoulders from my high school linebacker days. Sure, I wasn't as trim as I used to be from too many nights programming and playing video games when I should have been at the gym, but I still looked good in a suit. If only I could get the damn tie on straight...

"Damn, Gav. You are looking *sharp*," my sister Nicole said as she burst into the bedroom behind me.

I glanced at her in the mirror and raised my eyebrows in skepticism before I turned my attention back to the tie.

"Did you see this?" she asked, holding up an envelope.

"Hm?" I didn't really pay attention as I continued struggling to tighten the knot.

"You need help with that?" Nicole put down the mail and came up behind me. She peered around my shoulders and stretched up on her toes to reach around my neck and straighten the tie. After a quick shake of her head she undid the knot and slipped it off my neck. I released a frustrated sigh as she rethreaded it through my collar, aligned the ends, and started to redo the knot.

"Thirty-three years old today, and he still hasn't learned how to do a perfect Windsor knot," she said as a cheeky grin spread across her face. "Big over little, take him through the hole, then loop-de-loop..."

I slapped her hands away. "Thanks so much, sis. I've been doing my own tie for over a decade, I'll have you know."

"Oh, sure." She patronizingly smoothed her hands over the shoulders of my suit jacket.

"It's just not second nature, yet," I mumbled.

"Maybe because you didn't do it as a kid, huh?" she asked as she sat down heavily on the bed. "Remember that skate wear you used to be into? All oversized and baggy and shit. Definitely no ties."

"I would have dressed better, if I'd had anyone to teach me how to do techniques like tying a tie," I grumbled.

"What? Daddy didn't teach you?" She looked up at me with her eyebrows raised.

"Did you ever see him wearing a tie? You ever see him in anything other than golf shirts and cargos?" I asked, then hissed as the collar bunched up too tightly and I had to start over again. "He said dressing smartly was *alpha stuff*. You know. Like, uh, everything else I needed help with."

I glanced at her in the mirror, but quickly looked away when I saw the pity on her face. That was not what I wanted to see on my birthday.

"He did his best as a single omega dad, Gav," she said in a quiet voice.

A growl grumbled up from my stomach. Nic was younger than me, and I figured that's why she saw our childhood in a kinder light than I had. I looked back at her and found her attention on the envelope in her hand. She ripped it open.

"Hey, is that for me?" I asked as I glanced over my shoulder and reached for a different tie from my nightstand.

"Yeah yeah." She waved me off, like privacy wasn't important.

I held up the silk ties to my face.

"Gav, you never told me about this!" she suddenly exclaimed.

"About what?" I asked absently as I judged the navy and the Persian blues, comparing the colors to see which one would make my eyes pop more.

Nicole started bouncing on the bed like an excited cub. "The gaming convention! Why didn't you tell me?"

I groaned as I suddenly remembered the invitation I got months ago. What Nicole held now must be a reminder to the convention being held next weekend.

"Because I'm not sure I want to go." I went with the Persian and threaded it through my collar. Maybe the silkier material would make it easier to tie.

"What?" She slapped my ass with the envelope. "Why not?"

"I hate those things," I said. "Had to do a bunch of them when RuneMaze was first released, and it was hell. A bunch of weirdos and nerds."

"Uh, says the nerdy weirdo game *developer*." She slapped my ass again. "You have to go! You already accepted."

"Yeah, but I was thinking of cancelling."

"And upset all your fans. That's not like you."

I sighed. As much as I didn't want to admit she was right, she was. I didn't want to let down the organizers or those who wanted autographed pictures, but I disliked being the center of attention. I don't know what made me accept in the first place. Maybe because it was here in Timberwood Cove?

"I'll think about it," I said as an appeasement as I struggled with the loop-de-loop move.

"Well, I'm sure Cole would love to go." I knew Nic and her manipulative ways, and I threw her a look that told her I didn't like the idea of her using my nephew as inducement.

"God, you're such a party pooper," she muttered as she stood up, leaving the reminder crumpled on the bed. "But, at least you look good."

"I look the same way as I remember Dad did," I said with a grimace. "Old."

Nicole choked on her laugh, and then smiled sadly at me. "At least you remember what he looked like."

I nodded, but felt my guts cramping up. It was a lie. I couldn't remember what our alpha father had really looked like. He'd died in a fire before I was old enough to make real memories. The patched-together idea of him in my mind was based on photos I'd found hidden in the attic, stowed away by our omega daddy in an effort to put aside painful memories of our father from the house. All I had of Dad was these vague ideas of who he was—a strong man, in a suit, with a bright smile. While my memories were of how it felt to hear his voice and what it was like to feel his hand in mine. Other than that, the rest was stitched together into some kind of fictional hologram.

"Okay," Nicole said, drumming her palms on my shoulders and bringing me back to reality. "I'm not here to reminisce with you, I'm here to get you to the party on time. Can we just lose the tie? It's still crooked."

"You think I'd look okay without it?" I raised my eyebrows.

"Yes, honey. You look good in anything. C'mon, let's find you a birthday date."

***

We walked through the brisk October night to the Wolf Lodge where my party was being held by our closest packmates. Nicole kept up with my fast pace, even though I could hear her breathlessness as she prattled on. "I just think you should go to the gaming convention. Cole would love it if you went."

"I'm definitely not going," I told her again.

"You might meet someone there," she said as we passed through a small thicket of trees. An ache started in my chest, and my wolf pricked its ears up, just like it did any time I was reminded that I *still* hadn't found someone to share my life with.

"Yes, I'm sure I'll meet *someone*. A weirdo nerd... Or another one-night stand."

Nicole laughed. "Woah, hang on, do I detect a hint of exhaustion in your voice? You're finally tired of casual sex? Done with being the most notorious lothario of Timberwood Cove? Or have you just run out of eligible omegas in our little town?"

"God, you're so annoying!" I shoved her playfully as we ambled through the trees and onto the grounds of the Wolf Lodge. The lodge itself was lit up with party lights, and music blasted out of the doors.

"C'mon, we're obviously late." She grabbed my hand and dragged me forward.

As soon as we stepped into the crowded Lodge, I spotted Linc—Nicole's ex and the father of her nine-year-old son, Cole—standing by the dessert table. Cole was rifling through candy jars and filling up a paper bag with chewy candies when his dad nudged him and pointed to us. Cole spun around and waved happily at us.

"Do not say anything to him about the convention," I warned Nic.

"Alright, alright," she said, holding up her hands in surrender. "I'll wait until you've decided to go."

I shot her daggers before Cole rushed over and threw his arms around my waist. "Hey Uncle Gavin! Happy birthday!"

"Hey, kiddo!" I laughed and hoisted him up into a fireman's carry. He squealed and kicked, then started feeding me candy as we walked over to Linc.

"Hey, man." He smiled and give me an awkward hug around Cole's body. "Happy birthday."

"Thanks bro," I said through a mouthful of chewy candy, which set Cole off into a fit of giggles. I hauled him down and set him back on his feet.

"How're Samuel and Shawn?" I asked Linc.

"Both of them are good, just way too tired for the party." His smile brightened as he spoke about his new baby son and his mate. I don't think I'd ever seen a man so happy. Nicole came up and he quickly brought her in for a deep hug. Their relationship had ended shortly after Cole was born, but it was great how they'd managed to go from being lovers to being best friends. Linc then decided to remain single to bring up Cole, knowing how important it was for

Cole to be around his alpha father, and I'd admired him for it, but then he'd met Shawn, his fated mate, and now Linc had Samuel, and I was barely able to hold back my jealousy.

Attracting potential mates wasn't a problem for me. My problem was finding the right one. I actually wanted what Jaxon, our pack leader, and Linc had. I wanted to find a mate, my fated mate, and have kids and settle down. Both of the other alphas had made commitment and fatherhood look effortless, so it shouldn't be that hard, should it? But what omega would want to settle down with me when I had no idea how to be a father?

I socialized with the pack, downed glass after glass of whiskey, got on stage and sang Bruce Springsteen karaoke with Nic, and got into a playful tussle with Jaxon. By the end of the night, Cole was running around wild with his best friend Liam and the other kids in the pack. I watched as Linc called Cole over, who obediently came running into a hug before the two of them started to play a hand clapping game, coordinating their hands perfectly.

"How does he do that?" I asked Nic, my words slurring a little at the end.

"What? The hand clapping game? It looks more complicated than it is. I can teach you, if you want."

"No, not the stupid game. The fatherhood stuff," I explained, leaning against her and watching as Linc and Cole took off and raced toward the Lodge kitchen.

"If you remember he wasn't always so good at it," Nic said with a friendly nudge. "But he's turned out alright."

"He had a good dad to show him how to do it, though, right?"

"This is really eating you tonight, huh?" Nic looked up at me, her eyes filled with concern.

"Yeah, I guess. Whatever. Who cares? Family isn't for everyone."

"You wish I'd invited Daddy?"

"Hell no! You think he'd even realize it was my birthday?"

"Good point," she said with a laugh. "Remember when he forgot Christmas?"

"Who could forget." I knocked back the last of my drink. Our omega dad had shut down after our alpha father had died, and Daddy had become an absent and distant parent—to say the least. I was about to slip into a stupor of self-pity about it when the lights suddenly went out. My wolf kicked up in my chest, alert for danger. My breath stopped.

"What the fuck?" I whispered.

I heard a *thud*. Light streamed out from the open kitchen door, followed by a roaring blaze. I gasped and instinctively grabbed Nic's arm, ready to get the fuck out of there when I realized what it actually was—not a raging inferno after all, but the thirty-three candles on my birthday cake.

Linc carried the cake while Cole and his friends burst into a rousing rendition of *Happy Birthday*. I felt Jaxon put his hand on my shoulder, and I looked up to find him beaming down at me, singing along softly. His father, our old pack leader, Greer, sang in a deep baritone and gave me a huge smile as Linc put the cake on the table in front of me.

"Woah!" I forced a laugh as I took in the grandeur of all of those candles. "This fire's so fierce it's going to singe off my eyebrows."

"Make a wish! Make a wish!" Cole said, bouncing on his feet. Everyone was lit by the orange glow.

Jaxon gave me a wink and said under his breath, "Wish for someone handsome for the night…"

I closed my eyes and made a drunken wish; not for someone for the night, but for the rest of my life.

The candles were out. The room was dark. I heard cheering and a round of "Hip Hip Hooray," but it all sounded muted. I could only hear my own breath and the pulse of my blood rushing through my veins. I felt like I'd just cast a spell on myself. Or maybe I'd just had one too many whiskeys…

Suddenly, Jaxon tightened his grip on my shoulder. I tensed. My breath stopped. And I jumped out of my seat as the pack leader let out a soul-shaking howl.

The lights came back on and the pack began shifting into their wolf forms all around me. Jaxon let go of my shoulder and transformed into his big, buff wolf. I looked from the cake to Nicole and back again.

"We'll eat it after the run. Let's work up an appetite," she said.

Cole was jumping around in his young wolf form, prancing back and forth in front of his friend. The doors were thrown open and the pack started to pour out of the Lodge into the yard, sprinting across the lawn and into the woods.

I followed. As soon as I shifted into my wolf, my senses were sharper and much less affected by the alcohol I'd guzzled down. My footing was still a little clumsy, but I barely noticed as I bounded across the yard. The cool ground felt soothing under my paws, and I stopped at the edge of the woods to scratch at a tree, loving the feeling of my claws ripping through bark.

I was sniffing at the marking I'd made when I felt a nip at my flank. I spun around and found a handsome, young omega wolf with a sharp snout and long legs bouncing backward. He tilted his head to the side and blinked with long, thick lashes. I sized him up while he dashed back and forward, urging me to play. He wasn't anyone I recognized, and I supposed he may have been invited to run with the pack if he wasn't from around here. It wasn't unheard of, allowing other wolves to run with us, especially on full moon runs. Our pack, though traditional in a lot of ways, certainly wasn't unwelcoming.

The young wolf landed another nip, and I felt my attraction starting to grow. He was *very* cute. Though it was hard to tell the ages of shifters in our wolf forms, I guessed he couldn't have been over twenty-five. He sure had plenty of energy…

He was absolutely my type, and as I was in my wolf it meant I was working on pure instinct. The next time he lunged for my flank I nipped back, landing a sharp tooth against his neck. He let out a playful yelp, then bounded off down the path before pausing and looking back over his shoulder at me. I sniffed at the air, caught a hint of a light fruity scent, and then bounded after him. I liked him. I liked how he smelled.

He took off like a shot, but I pushed hard into my muscles and soon caught up. We ran together under the full moon, and with every synchronized lunge over fallen logs and dense clumps of brambles, I felt more attracted to him. I caught his scent again as he ran ahead, and I inhaled it as deeply as I could.

We broke through the dense forest into a moonlit clearing. The younger wolf stopped to lap at a pool of water, and I looked up at the glittering moon overhead. It wasn't the first time I'd run with a stranger like this. But it *was* the first time I felt like my heart just wasn't in it. I heard a change in the rustle of autumn leaves and looked over to find him shifted into his human form—a lanky, gorgeous young man with a shock of red hair, perfect cheekbones, and gorgeous hands.

I'd been through this dance with so many men, so many times before. On cue, he was unbuttoning his shirt and revealing his washboard abs. I was meant to shift into my human form, walk toward him, take his hands in mine and plant a hot kiss on his mouth. Or else I'd dodge his attempts at a kiss and direct his attention much further south until he was sucking my cock. Either way, it felt as rehearsed and as dull as I could imagine. Maybe turning thirty-three had really done a number on my libido. Maybe I was just ready for a new dance with different steps.

The guy bit his lip. I could tell he was nervous. Or impatient. I huffed out a breath, and then slowly back away, dipping my head in apology before I turned and sprinted back into the trees to run with my pack brothers.

After a few hours of running, howling and yapping, a few more whiskeys at the Lodge and an outrageous amount of birthday cake, I stumbled home—alone. I lived as close to the Lodge as you could get, but the trek across the manicured grounds and through the small thicket of trees into my yard felt like it took an eternity. I fell into my living room through the doorway, and then barely made it to my bedroom.

"Happy birthday, old man!" I said to the guy in the mirror before I fell backward onto my bed. Something sharp dug into my neck and I fished around to grab it. It was the reminder of my acceptance to the gaming convention.

I remembered her encouragement when we'd discussed it again at my party. *You should go! You could meet someone…*

I also remembered how I'd just met someone on the run, and I wasn't interested in *him*.

You could meet someone special…

"Yeah, I could meet *nerds*," I grumbled, then let out a frustrated sigh and admitted out loud what was impossible to hide. "*I* am a nerd. I am. I'm a *king nerd*. I made a video game, what's nerdier than that?"

I hauled myself up off the bed with the intention of getting some water, but I ended up at my computer. With another look at the reminder, I sighed, and before I knew it I was e-mailing the organizers and acknowledging the reminder, telling them I'd be there. I was going to the stupid gaming convention.

I poured myself another drink to celebrate, and then decided to spend some time indulging in my favorite hobby: playing RuneMaze, the game I'd developed, and helping kids on the live online version of it while I listened to my favorite guilty pleasure—a love song dedication radio show. I couldn't get enough of those romantic songs, and the host's voice was to die for. I felt like I melted into my chair whenever I listened to him croon on about pop ballads…

When I logged into the game, I laughed to myself. I loved the names that kids came up with for their avatars in the game. *FangHunter* was my favorite, though. I always ended up helping that kid with some real tricky puzzles. He was there that night and we went hard on some of the more challenging levels.

By the time I went to bed, I felt good again. I even felt young! I was *King Nerd* and I was celebrating *me* and all I had come to be. Successful, rich…and alone.

Chapter 2 - Kyle

My ten-year-old son sat on the edge of his bed as he stared at his television screen and danced his fingers over the buttons of his gaming controller.

"Brock Shannon! Get dressed! *Now*!" I stood in the doorway of his room, holding his school backpack in one hand and a packed lunch in the other. I'd been yelling at him all morning, and he'd ignored me just as long.

"I just need to get through this challenge, Dad," he said in a no-nonsense voice as he continued staring at the screen with total focus.

"How about you get through the *challenge* of getting to school on time," I demanded.

"Just one second."

"Brock. You need to get ready for school right *now*. I'm not going to tell you again. This is the third morning this week. If you give me any more resistance, you're not going to the gaming convention this weekend."

"Dad…" he said, but didn't finish what he was saying, just sat up and stared right at the screen.

"Brock!" I had enough, and made a move to switch off the screen.

My son suddenly bared his teeth at me and let out a blood-curdling growl. It wasn't the first time, but it scared me. For the last two years his attitude had been becoming more aggressive. From what I knew about his other…nature, it made sense. But it still didn't make it easy. And me? A human omega single dad? Well, heck. I had no idea what to do with a prepubescent alpha wolf shifter.

All I could do was put on a brave face and stay consistent. That's what all the parenting forums said to do. Just stay consistent. Give them a sense of safety.

"Don't you growl at me, you little monster," I grumbled, chucking Brock's backpack at him. He dropped his controller to catch it midair, and then let out a stroppy sigh.

"Get dressed now or we're not going to the gaming convention on Saturday. I mean it," I warned.

"*Fine*!" He finally gave in and got dressed. "I. Don't. Want. To. Go," he said with every reluctant, heavy step he took down the stairs.

"Good morning, Brocky!" my sister Britt called from the kitchen where she served up breakfast on the kitchen counter every day.

"There's nothing *good* about it." Brock hauled his heavy bag onto his back.

"Where'd you get that attitude? The grumpy boy store?" Kennedy, Britt's girlfriend, asked through a mouthful of bagel.

"Good one…not." Brock shook his head, but still gave Kennedy a big good morning hug. The two of them had a special bond. Namely, they both played video games.

I grabbed a cream cheese bagel off the bench for Brock to eat on the way to school, and Britt balanced another one on top of it.

"You need breakfast too," Britt said to me.

"Are you off this morning? Meet me for a coffee and records?" I asked.

Britt nodded and smiled. She was my younger sister, but she was also my best friend, and some time with her at the record store was exactly what I needed after a stressful morning. Which seemed to be most mornings, these days…

"Alright, Brocky. Let's hit the *long and winding road*," I sang, grabbing my keys.

"But, Dad. I'm being *bullied* at school. Why do you want me to go to school and get bullied all day long?" he asked in an attempt to negotiate with my while clinging to Kennedy's coat.

"Bullied, huh? You're too tough to be bullied," Kennedy said as she ruffled his hair. But she shot me a curious look as if to ask *is this for real*?

"It's a free world, Brock. You can stay home if you really want to, but there'll be no gaming convention for you on the weekend." I shrugged because if he wanted to negotiate, he had to understand the conditions.

"That's not a free choice! This is still an autocracy!"

Britt let out an impressed laugh. "Where'd you learn a word like that?"

"School," I said, guessing. I opened the door and motioned for my son to haul ass out of it.

"You wish. I learned it from RuneMaze, *actually*," he said as he stomped past with his nose in the air.

***

After I dropped off my bratty boy at school, I made a beeline for the June Cafe, a funky little record store that had added an espresso bar and a few couches to keep business afloat when people stopped listening to CDs and started streaming music. It had worked. In a small town like Timberwood Cove, people flocked to anything new that had a cosmopolitan flavor, like a cool record store cafe. Or a stupid gaming convention.

"I am *not* looking forward to Saturday," I said as Britt flicked through the latest pop releases on vinyl.

"Well, Kennedy is definitely excited about it," she said. "She's trying to talk me into cosplaying as some Rune princesses or whatever with her."

"Oh god, is it fancy dress?" I shook my head and groaned.

"Well, here's a hot tip I learned just yesterday—don't call it *fancy dress* or the cosplayers get really huffy."

I laughed and wrapped one arm around her shoulder.

"But no, don't panic. Brock told Kennedy that he doesn't want to cosplay, so that's good." Britt's started flipping the records a little slower.

"Good?" I asked as I frowned.

"*Mhm…*" she said flippantly as she released herself from my grip and wandered over to the heavy metal section. This was a classic avoidant Britt-move. She knew I was shopping for records and inspiration for my nightly love song dedication show on the local radio, so when she wanted to lose me, she'd head for genres that were as far from conventional romantic ballads as it could get. Too bad for her, I knew her games. I chased her and looped my arm through hers, pulling her close.

"Please explain why it isn't *good* that Brock doesn't want to dress up for this convention."

"*Cosplay*," she said, correcting me again.

"Britt…" I said with the same voice of warning I'd used all morning with Brock.

"Fine." She sighed in defeat. "Brock said he didn't want to cosplay because… Well, I quote… *'I'm already a freak.'*"

Freak? Fuck. Though my heart felt like it was going to break, I didn't want to show how much Brock's words hurt. "He's become so dramatic lately. I think it's the games. Maybe he needs a week off."

"Oh yeah, great idea." Britt shook her head. "The video games are the only reason he's not an anxious mess. Remember last time he went a weekend without playing?"

I did. He was so full of energy he'd driven us crazy, then he'd gone for a run in the woods, disappeared for five hours, drove me even more crazy with worry, then stumbled back inside covered in dirt and scratches and just as much as energy as before he'd left. Maybe a whole week of that wasn't such a good idea.

"What if he really is being bullied?" Britt asked as she chewed her nails.

I took a sip of my coffee and shook my head. "Have you seen him? He's really big for his age. There's no way anyone is beating him up."

"It could be emotional bullying." She raised her eyebrows as if saying I should have thought of that.

"Then he'd beat *them* up, right?" I asked, becoming a little unsure.

Britt just grimaced at me.

"God, I don't know, Britt," I admitted with heavy sigh. "This single parenting shit is *heavy.* I thought it was going to get easier as he got older. But fathering an alpha boy alone is way harder than I thought."

"Hey, you're not alone in this," she said, reminding me that both she and Kennedy were always there to help.

"No, I know. You and Kennedy are honestly my lifeline. And Brock's. Imagine how wild he'd be if we didn't live with you two. I just meant…"

"Alone without his *alpha* dad to help you?"

"Right." I nodded and swallowed heavily as a wad of shame threatened to well up in my throat. It was my own fault I was *alone* in parenting Brock, and always had been. He was the product of a one-night stand. An incredible, unforgettable one-night stand… Even though I'd been pretty drunk when it happened.

Britt bundled up her long auburn hair and tied it on top of her head in a high bun, which meant she was about to lay down some hard truths on me. I put both hands on my warm coffee cup and brought it up to my chest.

"You've done everything you can to find Brock's other dad. You hired that investigator. There was nothing else you could do. You're a *great dad*. Brock just needs…time or something."

"You're right. I did everything…"

There was that gnawing in my stomach again. The truth was…I hadn't. Yeah, I'd hired an investigator. But I hadn't given him all I knew about Brock's dad because who would believe me, except my friend Trevor…

Nearly eleven years earlier, my best friend Trevor had informed me I hadn't hooked up with a human, but with a wolf. A wolf…*shifter*. Trevor was an avid believer of cryptids, obsessed with the idea there were wolf shifters living in the woods that surrounded Timberwood Cove.

I recalled the conversation I had with him at the time:

"And you think they'd be drinking at the Cove Brewery? Waiting to hook to up with unsuspecting humans like me?"

"Well how the hell else do you explain the *knot* then?" he'd asked with pursed lips. The *knot* was why I'd come to him in the first place after the one-night stand, even before I'd realized I was pregnant.

"I don't know, Trevor. I don't know if it was a knot, I don't even know if there was even a swelling or if I imagined it. I was so fucking wasted."

"Well, I guess we'll just have to wait and see."

"See what?"

"If a wolf shifter knots a human in heat, you best believe that human is getting pregnant"—he cleared his throat—"and having a wolf shifter baby."

I'd stared at him blankly. "Don't joke."

"No word of a lie," he said. "It's a well-known *fact*."

"You're full of shit," I'd replied. Nine months later, I'd given birth to Brock. The moment I saw his perfect little face I'd dismissed Trevor's wolf shifter bullshit. My son looked as human as any other baby. But not long after he'd shown some characteristics that were distinctly *not* human, and I'd instantly known my son was…different. Just like Trevor said. Over the following years he'd developed, not only an alpha attitude, but signs of restlessness I attributed to his inner wolf, until without warning, he'd shifted into this beautiful little wolf pup, right there in the middle of our living room. To be honest, it had scared the crap out of everyone, and because of that he'd never done it again, except in his room. I'd told him it was okay for him to shift in front of us if he wanted to, but he'd refused, claiming he didn't want to scare anyone again. I'd tried to tell him he wouldn't, but I hadn't been able to persuade him. It worried me that I wasn't able to reach him the way an alpha father would, and I knew I was going to have some serious trouble trying to raise a wolf shifter without any practical help from anyone who knew how to handle one of his kind.

"Anyway," Britt said now. "We need to help Brock with his self-esteem. There's no reason for him to think he's a freak."

"Um, *wolf shifter*," I whispered before gulping down some more coffee.

"That doesn't make him a freak, Kyle, and you certainly shouldn't make him think he's one. *And* he's obviously not the only shifter because how else was he conceived?"

"I know, I don't. I love him to bits. I've tried to help him with his anxiety over his nature, but he needs a shifter's influence to help him understand who he is, but I can't find one." I didn't even know how to start looking.

Britt sighed. "Maybe one day you'll run into one."

"And how would I know? I didn't know Brock's father was a shifter. How the fuck does anyone ever tell?"

Britt smirked. "I think you'd know when you were fucking," she said, unable to hide her grin.

I nudged her none too gently. "Shut up, that's gross," I said before striding back to the other side of the store to buy a vinyl for tonight's show.

***

"And that track was, of course, *Love Story* by our girl Taylor Swift, going out tonight from my dear friend Trevor to…" I chuckled as I read the dedication. "From Trevor, *to* Trevor. Well good for you, my friend—a beautiful example of self love."

My producer nodded to me from the control room, and I glanced at the clock.

"And it's time for me to call it a night, folks. You've been listening to the Nightlight Love Lounge, and I'm your host, Kyle Shannon, signing off until tomorrow. May the love bug bite you tonight. Bye now," I crooned, and then I hit play on the next record.

"Good show, Kyle," the producer said as I hurried into the control room and grabbed my jacket. I smiled gratefully as he spun around in his chair and gave me a thumbs up.

"You on tomorrow?" I asked, wriggling into my jacket, and then throwing my messenger bag on over the top, which was overflowing with the records I'd brought in.

"Sure am. See you then," he said, turning back to the desk.

"Yep, and every weeknight until I die." I'd never missed a show in six years of doing radio.

I drove home with the windows down, taking in a deep breath and reveling in the sharp, October air. It was after midnight and the moon shone big and bright in the clear sky, just a little less than full. I normally went straight home, but tonight I decided to stop at the beach to take a moment to myself. I sat down on the steps from the boardwalk, pulled my jacket tighter, and took in a deep breath of the salty air. The wind blew off the water and prickled my skin with how cold it was, but I loved it. I felt the tension melt away from my shoulders and I was more in my body than I had been for days.

After a few minutes though, I knew I had to go home. It was late, and I had to get Brock ready for school tomorrow. When I got home, however, I found Britt chewing her nails.

"What's wrong?" I asked quickly as I closed the kitchen door behind me.

"Brock's still awake," she replied. "He's fine, he's just… He won't stop playing video games."

"Shit." I looked at the clock and saw it was nearly one o'clock.

"I'm sorry!" she called as I hurried up the stairs.

Brock was sitting on his bed, hunched over in the dark, lit by the screen. I stood in the doorway and watched as a smile burst across his face, but he hadn't noticed me. I stayed silent as he chatted into his headset about strategy with strangers, laughed at jokes I couldn't hear, and looked the most relaxed I'd seen him in a long time.

I knocked gently on the doorframe and he looked up. He quickly pulled his headset off and gave me a bashful grin.

"Bedtime, Brocky," I said, coming into the room.

"I know." He sighed before putting down the controller and switching off the screen.

"You have a good day at school?" I asked as he scrambled into bed. I pulled the covers up and tucked him in. I normally would have already had this conversation with Brock, but today I had to go into the station much earlier than usual, so Britt had picked him up from school.

"No," he mumbled, looking up at the ceiling.

"What happened?" I asked.

"It was really hard to…stop." He swallowed hard, and I saw the beginning of tears in his eyes.

"Your wolf?"

"Yeah," he said in a small voice.

I paused for a moment, then put my hand gently on his chest.

"I understand, Brock," I said quietly, rubbing his chest soothingly.

He bit his lip and looked up at me with wide, worried eyes. "You don't understand. It wants to come out all the time and it's getting difficult to stop it."

I swallowed nervously and nodded. I knew it was normally more difficult for Brock on a full moon, and I remembered the big silver moon I'd seen on my drive home, and my heart ached, knowing he must have been struggling more than usual. I kind of understood why he didn't want to go to school now, but he also needed to learn self-control, and if there was one thing Brock knew about being a wolf shifter, it was that he could tell *nobody* else.

There was nothing I could do. So I kissed my son gently on his cheek. "I'm sorry I don't know how to help you with this, Brocky," I said as I ran my hand over his hair.

"Do you think my other dad would know?" he asked quietly. It was like a shot through my heart.

When I'd hired the private investigator to look for the gorgeous guy I'd slept with after a big night at the Cove Brewery, he'd come up with nothing, saying that he needed more info to go on. But what was I going to tell him? That he should be looking for a *wolf*? So that led nowhere, and I was left with a huge weight of guilt and a son who I didn't know how to help.

"I'm sure he would," I admitted. "I'll keep trying to find him, okay?"

"Okay, Dad." Brock nodded then closed his eyes. "I really, really, *really* want you to."

I bit down on my bottom lip to stop from letting out a soft sob. "I'll do my best," I promised quietly, then watched as my boy quickly drifted off to sleep.

All I could do was my best.

Chapter 3 - Gavin

The backstage area of the gaming convention wasn't particularly glamorous, but that was par for the course. The warehouse on Silvercoat Way, was full of upholstered room dividers, a makeshift coffee station, and a lot of dust. As I waited for the event to start, I picked up on the smell of superglue, synthetic fabrics, and glitter. Cosplay stuff. The hoards must have been entering the arena. Soon enough, the place was filled with the squeals, cheers, and chatter of thousands of nerds vying for a photo op with their favorite gamers.

Luckily, I wasn't on my table until later in the morning. I had an hour to kill. I filled up a paper cup with thick, burned coffee and sipped at it while the opener—Carol, a British developer of a cute romance game—did her Q&A.

"What size shoes do you wear?" someone in the audience asked. I could hear the desperation in his voice and my stomach turned.

"Uh, I think I'm a UK nine," she answered in her adorable accent. "Next question?"

"Can we see them?" someone else asked.

"See...what? My shoes? Right here, they're Vera Wang." She giggled nervously, and I guessed this was her first convention.

"No, your feet!" a gruff man yelled.

"Can we see your feet?"

"Please, just a glimpse?"

The absolute lack of *game* these guys had was giving me severe second-hand embarrassment. I needed to get the hell out of here. I downed the rest of my coffee, grimaced at the taste, and then headed out into the arena. The best part about being a game developer is that most of the time no one knew who you actually were. Like most gamers I hid behind a handle, and though my game had made me rich, I was mostly anonymous. Yes, I'd had my photo taken, but it wasn't often posted online, and unless someone specifically brought me up into the limelight, I usually stayed in the shadows. So, with that in mind, I strolled through the aisles with the hopeful assumption no one would recognize me.

Just another middle-aged nerd.

I glanced around and found that I was right. Everyone was either over forty, or under twenty-one.

I stopped at a stall filled with custom made, glittered game controllers, and was browsing the colorful array when I caught a scent. It was faint and it faded quickly, but it was like nothing I'd ever smelled before... Floral... Sharp... With an edge of cottonwood trees.

"Excuse me," I mumbled to the stallholder. I turned and tried my best to chase the scent. I hurried along and pushed through a group of teenagers who were taking up space by standing in the middle of the aisle.

"Hey, man! Watch it!" one said as I knocked his backpack.

"Sorry," I said absently, focused on trying to find that cottonwood trail again. But as I rounded a corner and found myself back at the Q&A table, I realized I'd lost it. All I could smell was the hormone-filled sweat of the teens and the overwhelming stink of glitter glue. I let out a frustrated grunt and ran a hand through my hair.

"Uh, Gavin!" I looked over and found Carol waving to me. Her crowd turned to look at me, too. "This is my *friend*, Gavin Stanton."

A murmur of surprise rocked through the crowd. I glanced from Carol to the crowd. I gave everyone a short wave and was about to scurry away when she continued with my introduction.

"He's the developer of RuneMaze," she said, beaming at me. Now *everyone* was looking at me, and a loud cheer started up in the middle of the audience and spread throughout them.

"And I'm done." Carol quickly stood up and rush backstage. A few of the weirdos who had been heckling her let out some groans of complaint, but they were drowned out by people clapping and whistling and starting to throw questions at me.

"Woah, woah, woah!" I said, holding my hands up defensively. "No Q&A from me. Just signings. I'll be back here in a few of minutes!"

People were starting to get out of their seats and make their way over to me, so I did my best to race to the backstage area without being mobbed. I got through a shitty plastic curtain just in time, and gave the security guard a look that said, "You gonna do your job?"

He just grunted, but luckily most people who are obsessed with video games are also good at following the rules, and no one tried to bust into the backstage area.

By the time I went back out there, the majority of the weird crowd had dispersed. Or so I thought. I could only see a few people lining up for their meet and greet opportunity, but when I sat down at the table I had a better angle to see it was just the front of a very, very long queue. The line snaked down the aisle and through the convention center. I raised my eyebrows and let out a long whistle.

"Uh, hey buddy?" I asked the security guard. "I'm going to need another one of those nasty coffees from the backstage area. Would you mind?"

The guy just looked at me like I was asking for a major favor.

"I'll sign whatever you want," I offered.

A sly grin spread across his face, and he disappeared behind the curtain. When he came back, he handed me an oversized cup of that burnt black tar and dumped a pair of extra-large women's underwear on the table in front of me. My eyebrows shot up and I looked up at him with suspicion.

"Are these...what you want me to sign?" I asked as I cautiously reached for my sharpie.

He grunted and nodded.

"And to whom should I make them out to?"

"No-one," he said.

"Well, alright," I said, then scribbled *Dear No-One, Enjoy the puzzles herein! Gavin xo*

With the security guard pleased, I motioned for the organizer to announce that the table was open and I got on with the signing.

It was off to a good start. Half an hour in and halfway through my coffee, I'd realized the people who I thought were weirdos were actually really nice and just wanted to thank me for making a game they loved. As I took a short break to sip my coffee, I wondered why I'd been so resistant to doing these meet and greets. When the game had been released, I was hitting the booze pretty hard while I toured the gaming conventions back then, and my memory was more than a little hazy. Maybe I'd had a bad experience at one and painted the rest with the same bad brush.

I smashed through another hour of signings and was thinking about taking a break when I caught that cottonwood scent again. I looked up, intrigued. The line in front of me was full of kids in costumes—aliens, gladiators, three different Supermen, and someone dressed up as an entire games console. Kids, no adults. I frowned, not understanding why I was getting such an enticing scent when there were only kids around. I sighed but continued to search the crowd, spotting a kid who wasn't dressed up as anyone. He looked around ten but was big for his age, and he was holding an early copy of RuneMaze to his chest and staring at me eagerly. He looked vaguely familiar, and I assumed he was a friend of one of the kids from the pack.

"Make it out to *Lucas,* please," a girl in a warrior costume said as she slid a game controller over to me.

"L-u-c-a-s?" I asked.

"Yeah, it's for my brother, he's really sick…" She sighed softly, and I carefully signed her game controller.

"Want a picture?" I asked, glancing over her head to the search the crowd again. That's when I caught a glimpse of an adult's hand resting supportively on that other kid's shoulder. I craned my head, but couldn't see who it was.

"Nah, it's okay, I have to go now." The girl grabbed the controller and ran off.

I almost stood, wanting to see who that adult was, but another kid pushed a game across the table, waiting for me to sign it. Suppressing a groan of frustration, I quickly surmised if the adult was with the kid, and the kid was only a few people back…

I got through the next signings as quickly as I could, that intoxicating scent growing stronger by the second, and I suddenly had an inkling of what that scent meant… By the time the kid was up next, my heart was racing. I looked up and smiled at him, expecting to see an adult with him, the one I was positive I was getting the scent from, but the scent had practically faded, and the kid was alone. But, as our eyes met, I almost fell off my chair. The kid had my eyes, and that familiarity I thought I'd noticed earlier… It was because he looked just like me. At least before the gray hairs and wrinkles had set in.

For several seconds I didn't know what to say, how to react. My wolf nudged me, and I reflexively pulled his game closer to me to start signing it while trying to figure out how to get him to talk to me, to tell me who he was and who his father was because…

"I just wanted to ask, um… When you did the game, did you put the puzzles in first and then build all the walls and bad guys, or did they go in last?" the kid asked in an adorable, assertive voice.

"That's the best question I've heard all day," I told him honestly as I leaned forward, a fierce understanding blooming in my chest.

"Really!" He smiled and I couldn't help but grin back.

"Most of the puzzles went in after we built the walls, but the bad guys went in after that. Though some levels are different. The Castle Den, you know it?"

"Yeah! I was playing there last night!" he said excitedly. "It's really hard."

"It can be, but the more you play the easier it gets," I told him, loving his enthusiasm. "So, what name do you want on here?" I hoped the information would give me a starting point on finding out more about him and where he was from.

"Can you sign it to FangHunter? That's my name on the live game."

My eyebrows shot up. *The same FangHunter I'd often felt drawn to? Had to be.*

Just then, the cottonwood scent came back, hitting me like a shot of caffeine. Every single one of my senses kicked in, and as I looked up, I inhaled sharply. A gorgeous man in a band t-shirt stood beside FangHunter.

"Sorry, Brock, I didn't think you'd move up the line so fast," he said in an oddly familiar voice, as he ruffled the kid's hair.

"It's okay, Dad. This is Gavin, he's just signing my game."

Dad. So this was the kid's father, and he was definitely the source of that heady scent. As I gazed at him, taking in every detail of his hazel eyes and dark brown hair, to the little dimple on his right cheek, I could barely control my wolf. I felt its paws burrowing hard and fast against my skin, urging me to shift, to lunge, to get closer to this man.

Mate.

I couldn't shake the word from my mind.

"Nice to meet you," he said with a polite smile. "C'mon, Brock. We've been holding up the line."

"W-would you like a photo?" I managed to stutter.

"Yeah!" Brock cried.

"Are you sure?" The guy looked at me then at the restless crowd behind them.

"Of course, c'mon," I said, standing and urging them to join me. Brock rushed forward while his dad took out his phone and started taking snaps. We threw up some hand symbols from the game and did a goofy high-five like the characters do at the end of the harder levels. I did my best to focus on it, but my eyes kept roaming away from the camera lens and down the long, lean body of Brock's dad. I didn't know him or remember him, but we damn well had to have met about ten years or so ago, I was sure of it.

"Alright, we have enough for a whole photo book," Brock's dad said as he lowered the camera. "C'mon, Brock. Kennedy's waiting by the car."

Brock suddenly threw his arms around me and pulled me into a tight hug.

"RuneMaze is my favorite game ever," he said, a light shining in the exact shade of blue eyes as mine.

I awkwardly squeezed him back and looked over his shoulder to his dad, who was gazing at me with a strange look in his eye. Just as quickly as it had happened, the kid let go and hurried off. And then his dad was gone too.

No, shit, they couldn't go!

"Hey, buddy, you've got a restless queue, let's get this moving," the security guard said.

I shook my head. "I'll just... I need a break," I said, thumping the "BACK SOON" sign on the table and ignoring the groans from the line. I grabbed a bag of merch and games from the sales table and chased the scent, frantic about losing it.

I followed it out to the parking lot and saw Brock and his dad walking away.

"Hey!" I called out. The dad turned around and looked at me with raised eyebrows. He slowed down and came to a stop as I raced over.

"I, uh... I wanted to give you these," I said as I held out the stack of merch and watched as Brock's face lit up with unbelievable excitement.

"What? Oh my *god*!" He happily took it all from me, fumbling it as he tried to hold it all in his arms.

"Oh, we can't," the dad said as he took the t-shirts and guide books from his son before they spilled onto the ground. "It's too much."

"No, really. Brock had the best question I've heard all day, and it was really nice to meet you both," I insisted. "It's my pleasure."

The guy swallowed nervously and I caught his eye again. Human, of course. If he'd been a shifter, he would have felt this intuition too. He would have been all over me, wanting to mix our scents and mark each other... Instead, he just held out a hand.

"Well, thank you. I'm Kyle."

"Kyle huh?" I took his hand. "Gavin."

"Oh, I know," he said with a laugh. That same feeling of being hit with caffeine raced through me again, and heated tingles started from the place where our skin touched. They raced up my arm and landed in my chest where my wolf yelped, leaped, and howled. I clenched my jaw and took in a sharp breath as I resisted the urge to shift right there and then.

Just as quickly, Kyle pulled his hand away and I regained my senses.

"Do you have lots of cheat codes and stuff?" Brock asked. I dragged my eyes away from Kyle and tried to make out what Brock was asking.

"Cheat codes? For RuneMaze?" I asked.

"No, for other games. I like how hard Runemaze is, I wouldn't want to cheat at it," he said as he looked at the t-shirts he was holding in his arms.

"I have some cool codes for turning the walls different colors, and there's even one where you can turn the bad guys into donuts." I grinned as Brock's face lit up again.

"Well that actually sounds pretty cool," Kyle said, sounding genuinely impressed.

"Would you want to get some dinner tonight after the convention? We could chat more about the games..." I asked, internally grimacing at how damn nervous I sounded. Where was my game? I was sounding like one of the weirdo nerds. Next thing I'd know, I'd be asking to see his feet.

"Tonight?" Kyle asked, sounding very hesitant.

"Yes!" Brock said, bouncing on his heels. "Please, Dad? Can we? *Please*?"

"I have to prepare for work..."

"Don't lie! You don't have to do work on the weekends!" Brock remarked. "Please, Dad. Please. Gavin's my gaming *hero*!"

I gave Kyle an apologetic grin, but I wasn't going to back down. No way was I letting my mate walk away without getting a promise to meet me later.

"Oh geez, alright. How am I supposed to say no to that?" He laughed and ruffled Brock's hair like he'd done earlier. "What time?"

"I believe I get out of here at seven. Maybe eight. I'll check with the organizer and text you," I said, motioning for him to hand me his phone. He hauled the merchandise from one arm to the other then fished his free hand into his pants pocket while I held back a groan, wishing I could be doing that for him. Once he got his phone out we exchanged numbers, and I watched with both sorrow and elation as they walked away. I was sorry to see them go, but absolutely delighted by having secured a date for the coming evening.

Back inside, I found Nicole standing by my table, looking at her watch and frowning.

"I'm here! I'm here!" I said, holding my hands up

"Where've you been?" she asked in a tight whisper as she motioned over her shoulder to the restless crowd.

"I…think I just met my son," I admitted.

"Excuse me!"

I gave her a quick grin before I turned back to the crowd and called over the next person in line. My sister growled but disappeared, and I focused on the task at hand: getting through the line as quickly as possible so I could get the fuck out of that nerdfest.

After another hour I was at my wit's end, and my coffee had run out. When I went to ask the security guard for a refill, he was nowhere to be found. I threw up the "BACK SOON" sign again and raced to the back where I found Nicole waiting to ambush me.

"What do you mean *your son*?" she hissed as she grabbed my arm tightly.

"He looks just like me," I said. "But the thing is, I think his dad is my fated mate."

"What? Seriously, Gavin. You're telling me you have a son with your fated mate? Why the hell did you not know this?"

"I don't know. The kid is about ten years old, so I must have hooked up with his dad around then, I mean, I *kind of* remember him, but…"

"Ten years ago?" She shook her head. "Yeah, that would have been right in your prime drinking period, right?"

"You could say that." I scowled at her, but it just made her laugh.

"What I'm trying to say is that would explain why you aren't *sure* if you remember him. And if he's your fated mate… Well, you must have been *super* wasted to have let him just leave."

Not liking to admit she was obviously right, I shrugged. "Either way, the kid looks *just* like me. And Kyle is definitely my fated mate," I told her as I poured a cup of coffee.

"Is that what your wolf told you?" she asked as she raised her eyebrows.

"If prancing around in my chest, howling and whimpering for me to get closer to the two of them is telling me something, then yes."

"Shit," she said, finally sounding impressed. "What're you going to do?"

"I'm taking them to dinner, and then I'm going to claim him."

"What?"

"Tonight."

"Gavin, c'mon. Seriously, you can't just claim him, especially if you only hooked up with the guy ten years ago. You're going to have to talk to him, get to know him. Find out if you like him."

"I know that, but he's my fated mate, I'm certainly not going to let him go. I'll figure it out."

"Just… Take it slow, alright?" she warned me, pointing a finger in my face.

"I can't guarantee I'll take it slow, but I will be careful." That was about the best promise I could make to her right then. Until I knew more, I certainly wasn't making any other promises.

The rest of the morning sped by, my mind and body in overdrive, and it wasn't just from the extra coffees. A son… The idea gave me a thrill. Almost as much of a thrill as I'd gotten when I'd shaken Kyle's hand. My fated mate… I could hardly believe it.

After lunch, the rest of the day lagged like an overtaxed games console, and I felt like everything was moving in slow motion. I couldn't wait to get the hell out of there. Once seven o'clock rolled around I sent a text to Kyle, and then headed straight for Tony's pizza joint.

Kyle and Brock got there right after me, and I could barely keep myself sitting in the booth from how excitedly my wolf jumped and leaped around in my chest when I spotted them. Brock beamed as soon as he saw me. I smiled when I noticed he was wearing the RuneMaze t-shirt I'd given him. He rushed over and slid into the booth beside me before giving me a quick hug hello. As Kyle pulled up a chair opposite me his scent struck me again, and I had to bite down on my lip to stop from moaning. I'd never realized an omega's scent could be so amazing. Obviously it was because he was my fated mate, but still, it pressed every single one of my buttons is a good way. He was wearing a black t-shirt of a band I'd only heard of from the radio show I listened to at night, a group called The Feather Boats, and it fit his lean torso just right.

"Thanks for coming," I managed to say, and was met with a bright, charming smile.

"Thanks for inviting us. We love it here." Kyle glanced at Brock who was drumming his hands on the table.

"You want to look at the menu?" I asked.

"Nope, no thank you," Brock shook his head. "Pepperoni with pineapple, the best pizza on earth."

Kyle wrinkled his nose, but I gasped. "Are you *kidding* me?"

"Ugh, I know, everyone says pineapple is gross on pizza, but *I* love it, so the haters can just *back off*!" Brock said, karate-chopping the air in front of his face.

I laughed and shook my head. "No I mean, *I* love it too. Pepperoni with pineapple is my usual order."

"What? No way! Awesome!" Brock high-fived me.

"Are *you* kidding *me*?" Kyle asked. There was a hint of genuine suspicion in his voice, and I watched as his gaze scoured my face then looked over at Brock's. My intuition picked up exactly what was going on. The penny was dropping about who I was. I lowered my eyes to the menu and pretended to look over the drinks selection while I assume Kyle started putting two and two together.

"It's just the best pizza." Brock shrugged, responding to his dad's question.

"It's gross, but okay." Kyle laughed nervously, and I worried he'd get up and leave. Maybe I should have said something in the carpark, but then Kyle may not have agreed to meet me. When he reached for the menu, I sighed with relief.

The waiter didn't bat an eye when we ordered, and as she walked away I whispered to Kyle and Brock. "They should just put pepperoni pineapple on the menu, I bet we order it so often."

The two of them chuckled and I felt myself getting a little addicted to the feeling of making them laugh.

"How'd you like the conference?" I asked Kyle.

"It was pretty cool." He smiled at Brock. "We had a good time."

"*I* had a good time. Dad humored me," Brock explained in a very grown-up voice.

I chuckled and nodded. "You don't game?"

"Not like Brock does," he said, looking at me over the table. As our eyes met, I was once again struck by how gorgeous he was, and how very familiar even if I didn't actually remember him or much of the night we'd gotten together. *If* Brock was my son, but I didn't have any doubt at that stage, and I think Kyle had certainly figured that out too.

"I like some of the bright colored puzzle games, some of the romance roleplay ones, too. Not into the violence or gore, though."

"RuneMaze isn't gory," Brock told him. "That's what I like about it the most, that it's not gory. You have to defeat bad guys but it's more about the puzzles and the maze and using your head to get out of tough situations and get away from people who want to hurt you."

A heaviness settled over Brock. I looked at Kyle to see if he was picking up on it or if it was something only my wolf intuition noticed. I couldn't tell. Kyle seemed oblivious.

"Do you, uh, do you game?" Kyle asked me "I guess you do. That's a stupid question, sorry." He laughed nervously again, but he didn't seem as anxious now as he had been before.

"No, not a stupid question at all. Honestly, I don't play all that much. Creating the game took a lot of time and energy, and I had to play it over, and over, and over again to test it out. So I'm kind of tired of games. Still getting back into gaming in general. I do like going live and helping out kids who are stuck in tricky parts of RuneMaze, though. That's always cool." My heart fluttered when I noticed Kyle nibbling on his lower lip as his eyes scanned my face once more.

I cleared my throat. "What do you do for a living?"

"I'm a radio host," he said.

"Wait… Seriously? Are you Kyle *Shannon*?"

"I am," he said with a nod.

"The Nightlight Love Lounge?"

"That's the one."

"No shit," I said, bewildered.

"Is that… Not good?" he asked, his nervousness coming back again, which I didn't want to see.

"No! It's incredible. That's literally my favorite show. I listen to you almost every damn night. Don't tell anyone, though. Everyone who finds out makes fun of me." I laughed as I leaned forward and smiled at him.

"I love it when alphas tune in," he said with a chuckle.

Just then, the pizzas arrived. Brock and I split the large pepperoni with pineapple, but the kid ate most of it. I remembered he was an adolescent shifter who was probably due for another growth spurt in the next year, so let him go for it. I hadn't forgotten what it was like for me at that age. I'd been ravenous.

"Is yours good?" I asked, eyeing off Kyle's margarita.

"Mm! Of course it is," he said as he wiped his mouth with a napkin. "Because it doesn't have pineapple on it."

We laughed, and he shared his slices with me. I watched as his lips parted every time he took a bite, and I barely kept my wolf under control. It was already doing crazy dances because it was close to our mate. I didn't need it jumping out in an attempt to claim him.

We chatted about video games and music for an hour or so, until Kyle called it a night.

"Brock has lots of a homework to get done this weekend," he explained, almost apologetically.

"Oh, of course, no problem." I said, grimacing on the inside. I didn't want to let them go, not yet, and certainly not before I had a proper chance to talk to Kyle about Brock and who he was to me. As I got up out of the booth to see them off, I reached out and touched Kyle's shoulder. He looked at my fingers, and then right into my eyes.

"But we should talk soon," I said, hoping he'd understand why.

"We should talk really soon," he agreed, before turning to his son and urging him to say goodnight to me.

"Goodnight!" Brock said, and again threw his arms around my waist. I gave him a short hug while I grinned awkwardly at Kyle, then watched as they walked out.

"Night…" I said.

As the door shut behind them, my phone buzzed in my pocket.

We're at Kay's Diner if you want to join before your dinner. N & C.

I wrote back straight away. *Order me a shake. Be there in five.*

I drove right there, and Nicole looked stunned when I walked over to their table by the window.

"Uh, that was fast? Did you come from the convention?"

"I came from Tony's. I told you, I was having dinner with Kyle and Brock," I said while I gave a high-five to, Cole.

"The convention was pretty cool," he said, playing with a toy on the table.

"Yeah it was cool," I agreed. "What's that?"

"Some free toy someone was giving out. It sucks," he said, but kept playing with it.

"So, how was your dinner?" Nicole asked pointedly to grab my attention.

"It was very clear but also very *complicated*," I said, looking down at Cole and giving Nicole a pointed look.

"Hey, Cole can you go check on our order?" Nic asked. Cole nodded, and then happily wandered over to the line.

"Complicated how?" Nicole asked in a whisper.

"Well, I think Kyle put two and two together, but we couldn't talk about it while the kid was there." I glanced up as the waitress brought over my shake, and I gave her a big smile before she left.

Nicole just squinted at me like she was having a hard time accepting it all.

"Nicole. I have a son," I said before taking a sip of my shake.

"And do you think this is a good thing?" Nicole asked. There was a quiver in her voice that touched right on the bundle of insecurity that had sat in my gut since I left Kyle and Brock. If I had a son, that meant I was a *father,* and I had absolutely no idea how to be one of those.

"Sure… I mean… It can't be a *bad* thing, can it?"

"For some people, yes, but does Kyle have any idea that his son is a *shifter*?"

"Damn," I said, letting out a long breath between my lips. "I don't know. I mean… Shit. He had to. Brock certainly wouldn't have been able to hide his nature all this time. The kid would have shifted as a pup without even thinking about it. Cole was shifting at just a couple of years old, and it was sometimes hard to get him to shift back to human, remember? He loves being a wolf."

"Then Kyle must know, which means you need to tell Jaxon. We can't have a human knowing about shifters if he isn't part of a pack. Unless Kyle found another alpha shifter to help bring Brock up? Someone from one of the other packs in the area?"

I hadn't thought of that. Kyle hadn't mentioned he was with an alpha. God, what if he was? What if he didn't want me around Brock? Was that why Kyle hadn't acknowledged Brock was my son? Had an alpha shifter adopted Brock as his own?

I think Nicole must have realized what was going through my head because she placed a hand on my arm.

"Maybe you should speak to Kyle first. Find out what he wants to do," Nicole suggested gently as Cole came back to the table. We sat back in our chairs as the waitress brought over the food they'd ordered. I thought about Kyle being my fated mate, about Brock being my son. I didn't think I could let that go, continue with my life while knowing they existed and not do anything about it. Even if Kyle didn't want me, I still had a right to know my son, didn't I? After a few minutes I made a decision.

"Cole, want my shake?" I asked as I slid it over to him. "I have to get home and make a phone call."

Chapter 4 - Kyle

So I was a little slow on the uptake. But at least I got there, eventually. There was no denying that Gavin looked *exactly* like my son. Or rather, my son looked just like Gavin... And it wasn't too far a stretch to realize Gavin was my son's father.

As soon as Brock got his seatbelt buckled outside the pizza joint, he was out like a light. It had been a huge day for him. After our morning at the gaming convention, he'd spent all day playing the games that Gavin had given him before we'd headed out for dinner. As I drove us home, I wondered whether Brock had realized what Gavin was to him. As that whole concept sank in I shook my head. Brock *definitely* would have said something if he had.

After we pulled up to our modest home, I woke Brock gently and helped him stumble into the house. I would have loved to carry him to bed, but he was a big kid, and I was very much *not* a big dad. I couldn't help but imagine how easily Gavin could lift him with those thick tree trunk arms that had looked so good in the tight t-shirt he wore.

"Hey boys, how was dinner?" Britt asked from the living room. Brock mumbled something incomprehensible, and I gave Britt a quick wave before helping him up the stairs and getting him into bed.

"Did you have a good night?" I asked him as I tucked him in.

"*Mhm.* Gavin is so cool," he mumbled. His eyes were so heavy he was barely able to keep them open.

"Yeah, he seems pretty cool. You two have a lot in common, don't you?"

"He's such a cool alpha..." Then Brock's eyes finally closed. My heart beat hard, and I felt a gnawing sensation in my guts. Once he was out, I switch off his light and ran a hand over my face as I walked down the hall. What a fucking crazy day.

I headed downstairs to the kitchen to get myself a glass of water before bed, but Kennedy appeared out of nowhere, grabbed my wrist, and hauled me into the living room.

"Tell. Us. *Everything*!" Britt insisted.

I silently groaned, not wanting to say anything until I had it straight in my head first, but this was Britt, her hair was still in that high bun. She'd never let me rest until I spewed out the whole story, and she'd certainly know if I was holding something back.

"Oh man, I don't know where to start," I admitted, rubbing my hands over my face.

"Was it a hot date or what? Wait, was he a creep? A loser? A nerd? Was it disappointing? It was bad, wasn't it?" Kennedy asked, making me laugh.

"No it was actually really great," I said as I sat down on the couch between the two of them.

"So what's with this face?" Britt asked, pointing at me and wiggling her finger.

"There was just a strange...coincidence," I admitted.

"*Oh,* a synchronicity," Britt exclaimed. She glanced over at the bookshelf that was overflowing with her metaphysical books, so I put a hand on her knee to stop her from getting up.

"No, not a synchronicity," I insisted. "A very weird, very *strange* coincidence."

"That's what a synchronicity is," Britt said, then she slapped my hand. "Let me get my books so we can look up what it means!"

"I know already know what it means," I said quietly as I stared at the muted television.

Britt and Kennedy shared a look, which was impossible to miss it was so obvious.

I cleared my throat knowing it would be best to voluntarily offer the information instead of having it dragged out of me. "Gavin looks…exactly like Brock."

"Uh… Okay. So you think you're related to him?" Kennedy asked as she scratched her head. "Like a long-lost cousin or somethin'?"

I looked at Britt, who looked back at me with huge, shocked eyes.

"I know," I said to her.

"Oh wait," Kennedy said as she slowly cottoned on. "Wait… Wait! What?"

"I think he might be…"

"He's Brock's *dad*?" Kennedy asked none too quietly.

"He might be," I said, holding my hands up. "I don't actually know, *but…*"

"Does he look like the guy you slept with that night?" Britt asked.

"Maybe! I don't know, it was literally ten years ago and I was *so* drunk, you guys. I mean, totally off my ass."

"Which he got into."

"Britt!"

Kennedy giggled and I gave them both a glare.

"So he lives in Timberwood?" Kennedy asked with a frown. "And he never reached out?"

"Why would he? As far as he knew, it was just a one-night stand," I stated.

"Well, does he know *now*?"

I sighed. "I have to assume so, I mean, he was definitely looking at Brock in a way that made me think he'd guessed, and they spent the whole night talking about everything they have in common. They're both into games, they're both into gross pizza toppings… And… If Gavin is his dad then that means that Gavin is…" I didn't need to say any more because both Britt and Kennedy knew what that meant. It didn't take long before they reacted collectively with a gasp.

"Oh my god," he's a *shifter*, Britt said.

"Yeah."

"That's great." Kennedy smiled. "Now Brock will have someone to help him."

"I don't know. I've been a single dad for ten years. Brock's doing okay." Which was a total lie, especially recently. I remembered the other night when he'd almost cried with how hard a time he was having.

Britt raised an eyebrow. "You're an *omega* dad dealing with an alpha kid—"

"I'm not the only omega dad who had had to raise an alpha child…" I objected.

"I know that, but Brock is a shifter. He really needs specialized help with his wolf, and that's why you hired the private investigator to find his dad in the first place, remember?"

"Yes, but what if he just ditches us, though? What if Brock gets close to him, and he turns out to be a loony or just abandons us?"

"Alright, you're absolutely overthinking this," Britt said. "Take it slow but at least take the opportunity you've been given. Let him in."

"Let him *in*?" I asked, absolutely not willing to do that yet.

"Let him in," Kennedy agreed.

"You're a good dad. Gavin deserves the option to be, too. And Brock deserves the chance to meet his other dad," Britt insisted.

I bit my lip and let out a sigh of defeat. She was right, but I still didn't know if I was ready to let a complete stranger into my life, into Brock's life. And then my phone started ringing.

"Oh my god, it's him."

"Answer it!" they said in unison.

"I can't! Oh my god, what am I going to say?"

"*Answer it*!" they said, shoving me from both sides. I broke out in a nervous laugh, then jumped up and paced around with my phone in my hand.

"Kyle!"

I nodded, and then pressed the little green button on my screen.

"Hey," I said, then grimaced at how pathetic I sounded.

"Hi." His deep voice sent a shiver ran up my spine.

"Did you get home okay?" I asked, and then scowled when Britt and Kennedy shared a look about my conversation skills.

Gavin chuckled. "Yeah, I got home okay. Did you?"

"Yep, just got in really. I just… Hang on…" I covered the mouthpiece and motioned to the girls that I was going to my room, which was on the same floor level as the living areas.

Britt gave me a thumbs up.

I scurried off down the hall and quietly shut my door before I sat down heavily on the edge of my bed.

"Hey," I said. "Sorry, I just needed to get some privacy."

"Mm, good," he said, and I thought I caught a hint of sexual energy in his tone. I instantly felt my cheeks flush, and I was really glad he couldn't see me.

"Thanks for dinner tonight," I said wondering where the hell my aplomb had gone. This was not going well.

"You're *very* welcome, but I wanted to ask you something… About Brock."

Here we go.

"Oh?" My voice came out so high-pitched I sounded like a fourteen-year-old.

"I couldn't help but notice…"

I waited for him to continue, not willing to admit anything yet, not until Gavin actually *said* what he noticed.

"You remind me of someone I hooked up with about ten years ago," he said.

Well, that technically wasn't about Brock, but I guessed Gavin was leading up to it. He no doubt felt as odd about this conversation as I did.

"I was just thinking the same thing about you." Actually, as I vaguely recalled flashes about that night at the Cove Brewery and what happened afterward… I felt a mixture of embarrassment and arousal.

"Because of Brock?"

"Yeah. I noticed he looks exactly like you," I said.

"Yes, he does. Not as many wrinkles, though."

I let out a short laugh, and then a deep, anxious sigh. "I don't know for sure if he's…"

"Was there someone else?" Gavin asked.

"Actually, no. I hadn't hooked up with anyone for months before that, and I found out I was pregnant right after. So…"

"So it was me."

"If you were wearing some punk outfit with leather and spikes…" The memory of grabbing his spiked jacket and dragging him in for a kiss had stayed with me for a whole decade, that and a few other choice moments.

He laughed. "Yeah, not my best fashion choices."

"This is crazy," I said.

"Well, it's crazy we didn't have this conversation earlier."

"Are you…okay with this?" I asked, biting down on my lip nervously and bracing for the answer. I still didn't know if it was a good thing to bring Gavin into our lives, but like Britt and Kennedy had said, I should give him a chance, and it might help Brock.

"Yes, I'm okay. More than okay. Not something I ever expected to happen, but I'm glad it did."

"You never expected to have a child?"

"Um, well, I've been busy, and I haven't…" Gavin cleared his throat, and I immediately felt a little sorry for him. I hadn't expected to have Brock when I did, but the idea of not having him or any child certainly wasn't part of who I was. I probably would have had more children if it wasn't for the fact that Brock was a shifter…

"Look, I want you to know I hired a private investigator to find you, but all I had to go on was a groggy memory. Your DNA isn't in any system he could get access to, either."

"No, it wouldn't be. Um, Kyle, I need to know something about Brock."

I took a deep breath and braced myself. I was glad he was going to bring it up.

"Does he have any signs of uh… There's something that runs in my family and…"

"If you're asking whether there's a wolf inside his chest that wants to burst out of there all the time, then yes, there is," I said frankly.

"And is he okay? I mean, he seemed okay when I saw him today, but how are you dealing with it? It must have been a shock to you," he said, genuine concern in his voice.

"It was, and Brock isn't doing well. He thinks he's a freak," I admitted. "When he was younger it wasn't too bad, but as he's gotten older and his alpha tendencies have increased, he's finding it harder to stay in control. He's confused and worried, and so am I."

"I'm sorry. If I'd known about him, I swear I would have helped out. Does anyone else—" A hint of panic rose in his voice.

"My best friend is a conspiracy nut and has been talking about a secret community of wolf shifters living in Timberwood Cove since we were teenagers. When I told him about…that night, he immediately jumped to that conclusion. I originally didn't believe him, until Brock shifted for the first time."

"What did you tell him to have him figuring out I was a shifter?" Gavin asked, still sounding suspicious and a little anxious.

"Well, I needed a second opinion as to why your cock swelled up *so* big when you came."

"Oh, shit. That. It's called knotting. To be truthful, I don't remember much about that night either. I was pretty drunk, but I do remember it was some of the best sex I've ever had."

I'm positive I heard him release a soft moan, and my cock twitched at the sound. I wet my lips and ran a hand over my inner thigh. I suddenly evoked a memory of kissing him outside the brewery, his lips smashed against mine, his hands all over me…

"We should meet up to discuss this further. Without Brock. That way we can work out what you want to do going forward. I'd love to get to know Brock, and you, if you're not seeing anyone…"

"No, I'm not, I'm single." Shit, did I need to say that?

"That's good, so, can we meet?"

Should I meet with him? Should I let him have access to Brock?

"Please, Kyle. It's important to me." The plea in his voice was my undoing.

"Yes, okay. I'm free weekends, but during the week I work in the evenings—"

Gavin chuckled. "I know your shifts," he said.

"You do?"

"I listen to your show every night, remember? You have an extremely sexy voice."

"I do? Oh, well, um… I pick Brock up from school, and I'm usually with him until I have to be at the station a little before eight to get my stuff ready, but I can get my sister Britt to watch him on Monday, so I'm yours."

My heart thumped as silence descended on the line. Did I just tell him I was *his*?"Very good. You're all mine before eight on Monday." When Gavin spoke, I could actually *feel* the smooth sound of his alpha voice all through my body. Damn, he was hot. Definitely well practiced at seduction. Was he a total player? Was I inviting a real playboy into my life? I mean, Brock's life…

"Monday," he repeated.

"Monday," I promised.

After I ended the call, the air in my room felt like it was buzzing. I stared down at my phone and saw my reflection looking back at me in the black screen—and noticed there was a huge, silly grin on my face. I let out a laugh and fell back on my futon bed, spreading my legs and arms as wide as I could.

I stared up at the ceiling and took in a ragged breath. I could barely believe it. The whole thing felt like a dream. I'd woken up that morning with a heavy weight of dread about the stupid gaming convention and ended the day having found the father of my son, who happened to be incredibly hot and seemed kind of into me.

I closed my eyes and strained to remember what Gavin had looked like ten years earlier in the dim lighting of the Cove Brewery bar. I'd been six tequila shots in and he'd appeared out of nowhere, standing close to me at the bar. I'd been sitting on a stool, swiveling back and forth when he'd put his hand on my thigh. His grip had been firm and stopped me from moving. Then he'd leaned close to me and whispered in my ear. I don't remember what he said, but it must have been good because not long after he was fucking me senseless.

I opened my eyes and took in a sharp breath as my dick throbbed in my jeans. I hauled myself up off the futon and began unbuttoning my pants as I stumbled toward the door.

"Going to bed! Night!" I shouted down the hall to the living room.

"Wait, what happened with Gavin?" I heard Britt ask.

"I'll tell you tomorrow, bye," I said quickly as I shut the door and switched off the light. In the dark, I undressed and threw myself down onto the low bed. I knelt and closed my eyes, running my hands over my body. It felt good to be touched like that even if I was the only one doing it.

I remembered Gavin grabbing my hips firmly as we swayed on the dance floor. I grabbed my hips now, just like that. It wasn't the same, it was nowhere near as furious and demanding as his touch had been, but it still felt good. My cock got a little harder.

I now remembered his scent—whiskey, and something else like lilacs—earthy, green, and wild. I inhaled and imagined I could still smell him. My breath caught in my throat as my dick twitched and started to ache, demanding attention.

I sat down on my heels and took the base of my cock in my hand. I moaned and gripped it tightly as it firmed with a surge of blood. My cockhead swelled, and I teased the tip with the fingers of my other hand. Even though a drop of precum oozed from the slit, it wasn't enough, so I reached over to my bedside table and rummaged around for my lube, disguised as a bottle of moisturizer. I pumped up a huge amount of it into my hands. I loved it wet and sloppy, and I lathered it all over my cock before I started slipping both my hands up and down its length. My cock hardened even more, and a hoarse moan escaped my lips. My balls tightened. Fuck, it felt so good.

Though I'd tried several times to remember all of that night in detail and couldn't, it was suddenly easy to call to mind Gavin's hands on my hips, pulling me forward and grinding me against him, our dicks pressing together as we swayed to the music and urgently kissed.

I thought about what his mouth looked like now—full lips red and wet as he smiled at me at dinner. What if he'd kissed me goodnight? How would it feel to have him kiss me right then on my bed, with me kneeling in front of him?

Where else could I kiss him?

My breath caught again and I started to pump myself harder. My mind raced. It was easy to imagine tasting his cock on my tongue, but what I remembered with clarity was how big it became when he blew his load deep inside me. I wondered if would thicken up like that in my mouth. How much of his cum could I take before it dribbled from my lips and down his shaft?

"Fuck," I moaned, tugging my balls gently and sending a rush of pleasure through my body. I wanted to taste him. I wanted him to fuck my mouth, fuck my ass like he did before. I don't remember how we ended up in bed together, but I *did* remember him bending me over and shoving the head of his cock inside my tight opening.

I reached down and ran a finger over my hole. It twitched and an urge for more pulsed around the edges of my ass. I gave in, shoving two slippery fingers deep inside my aching hole and barely holding back a loud moan as my ass clenched down on them. I fucked myself as best I could, bouncing up and down on my hand as I held my dick in a loose grip. Everything was soaking wet. I gasped and breathed through parted lips, trying my hardest to stay quiet as shock after shock of pleasure rushed through me and buried itself deep in my groin, growing stronger and hotter by the second, threatening to explode. My cock leaked precum, adding even more fluid to pump over my shaft, and my hole dripped with slick, which ran down my hand.

That's when I unexpectedly remembered how wet I'd become the moment Gavin had thrust the full length of his cock in my ass. I'd gone into full blown heat, and sex hadn't become something I simply wanted, it had become something I frantically needed. I'd whined like crazy as he'd rammed his fat cock into my tight hole over and over, pushing me through multiple orgasms. By the time the base of his cock was swelling and locking us tight and I felt him flooding my ass with cum, I'd been seeing stars.

Now, my ass clenched down, desperate for that same feeling again. I knew I couldn't outdo how he'd made me feel that night—god knows I'd tried so many times to recreate that feeling on my own… But I could come close. I roughly shoved a third finger into my hole and started to fuck myself hard and fast with it. There was a light pain that joined the waves of pleasure, and I bit down on my lip to stop myself from whimpering from it.

I leaned forward to give myself more leverage and urgently tried to fit another finger and a thumb inside my hole. My eyes squeezed shut, and I barely moved my hand on my cock, but I didn't need to, I was going to come, and I was going to come *hard*. When my balls pulled up tight against my body I fucked my hole harder and faster, on the edge of being too rough, but I was so far gone by then I didn't care. My muscles tightened, and I managed only a few short, raspy breaths before my whole world focused only one thing; the intensity of my pleasure.

My cock pulsed and shot a heavy load of cum high into the air. I felt the splatter as it landed on my chest and stomach. I also felt my ass spasming, and each spasm squirted more slick over my hand and more cum out of my dick. It felt like I was literally coming front and back, and it was too much. I groaned, aware of how loud I was, chanting Gavin's name over and over but unable to stop as my balls emptied themselves and my vision grayed.

I collapsed onto my mattress with a heavy *thud*, face-down and panting hard. I could feel my slick leaking down the inside of my thighs, and it reminded me of Gavin's cum. He'd filled me up so much I hadn't been able to take it all. I shivered, a little lost in the memory of being face-down like this after Gavin had fucked me senseless. After his cock had shrunk back to a normal size, after his *knot* had released me, he slipped free and lay down right beside me. I'd opened my eyes and found him staring at me. The room had been spinning, but I'd been able to focus on his smile. He'd been panting just as heavily as I was, but he also seemed to be breathing me in.

"I think I love you," he'd whispered just before his eyes had closed and he'd sank into a deep, motionless sleep.

Now, my eyes flew open and I stared into the darkness of my bedroom. My heart was pounding so hard that I thought I was going to have a heart attack.

What the fuck?

Had Gavin *really* said that? It seemed as crystal clear as a sober memory, but had I just made it up? Did my subconscious just fabricate it to top off the sweet orgasm I'd just had?

"Oh god." I rolled over onto my back and put one hand on my chest and the other on my stomach. I tried to focus on my breathing instead of the panic that was racing through me.

So what if he'd said I love you in a moment of passion? He was drunk.

Sure, it didn't mean anything. But what *did* mean something was that now, ten years later, he was back in my life, I'd just jacked off over the memory of him, and when I thought about him saying those three words, it made me giddy and dizzy.

And he was a, uh… wolf shifter.

Chapter 5 - Gavin

"Everyone! Quiet down!" Jaxon shouted as he stood on the stage at the Lodge, with the pack elders standing behind him. The hall was jammed full of shifters—almost everyone in our pack and even a few neighboring packs had crammed themselves into the space to hear the last-minute news he was to deliver to us.

Instead of listening, everyone was chatting, catching up, and laughing. Even Nic was prattling on with Cole while I stood by them with my arms crossed. They'd brought Paco, their wild-eyed husky, to the morning's emergency meeting and he was weaving through legs, sniffing butts, and looking for treats. I kept an eye on him, even though I knew there wasn't much I could do if he decided to be a rascal.

"Paco!" I called as he tried to squeeze out of view behind Cole.

Of course he ignored me and was gone in a flash. I was about to take off after him when the energy in the room suddenly changed. Jaxon shifted, and the scent of our pack alpha in his wolf form made my own wolf stand to attention. My eyes were locked on him as he released a blood-chilling howl.

The room fell silent.

He shifted back to his human form just as quickly as he'd changed and addressed us all with a serious tone. "Listen to me. I called you here this morning for your own safety."

A murmur ran through the crowd. I glanced over and saw Jaxon's mate, Bryce, bouncing their ten-month-old baby girl, Lori in his arms. Her mouth was wide open in awe and she stared at Jaxon with huge eyes. A feeling of envy raced through me and I took in a deep breath to try and calm the hell down. Was this... Was I feeling clucky?

"As most of you know, there have been rumors of other shifters in the area," Jaxon announced. I pulled my gaze back to him and listened attentively. "But now we have confirmed sightings of these other shifters."

"Wolves?" someone asked loudly.

"Can't we make contact and bring them in to talk?" someone else asked.

Jaxon swallowed and shook his head. His eyes looked over the crowd and then came to rest squarely on Nicole and me. He looked stricken, and my stomach started to cramp. I knew what he was going to say before he said it.

"Not wolves. These shifters are...dragons," he said.

Nic glanced at me. Her face was etched with worry, but I couldn't tell if she was upset for *her* or if she was just worried about me.

Jaxon looked away from us. "A pack of dragon shifters have been seen causing havoc in the woods, and in nearby towns. And now, small fires have been set off in Timberwood Cove."

A murmur of concern spread through the crowd.

Greer, one of the elders and Jaxon's father, stepped forward. "There's no need to take action yet. In the past, dragon shifters have been migratory through this part of the country. They seem to be settling here for longer than usual, possibly due to weather patterns. They may soon move on."

Nic put her arm through mine and leaned her head heavily against my shoulder. At the contact I realized I'd been holding my breath. I let it out in a heavy sigh.

"I need you all to stay vigilant. If you see anything, tell me or a pack alpha immediately," Jaxon emphasized. "Be cautious in the woods. Don't run alone."

Nicole looked up at me as Jaxon took questions from the crowd. Her gaze pierced mine and a look of sibling love moved between us. I didn't know where I'd be without her. I wrapped an arm around her and pulled her in for a tight hug.

"Are you two alright?" Linc asked as he appeared out of nowhere. His mate, Shawn was right behind him with their new baby Samuel in his arms and his corgi, Lulu at his feet. Cole stood on tippy-toes to tickle the belly of his baby brother while Lulu sniffed at my legs.

"We need to get some air," I said quickly, not wanting to state how much I wasn't alright in front of everyone.

Nicole nodded, then wrapped her arm around my waist as we pushed through the crowd and found our way outside. Suddenly, Paco was right at our feet, walking in step with Nicole as if he'd always been a perfectly behaved dog.

"You okay?" she asked quietly as we paced across the lawn outside the Lodge, heading straight for the thicket of trees near my house.

"Well, that wasn't fantastic news," I admitted.

"Mm," she agreed.

We walked on in silence until we came to a fallen log at the edge of the tree-line and sat down, close together. The weather held the last clutches of an Indian summer, and a warm breeze blew across the Lodge grounds, carrying the scent of our pack with it. It was dense and muddy, and I took in a deep breath. It made me feel safe.

"I hate thinking about it," Nicole said in a quiet voice. She looked down at Paco who lay at her feet.

"About dragon shifters?"

"Yes, and about what happened to our alpha dad."

So did I.

Suddenly, I felt a buzzing in my pocket. I instinctively reached for my phone, just like I'd done all morning. Sure enough, it was Kyle texting me. And just like every other time I'd looked at that name, it gave me a little thrill of excitement. I grinned. I hadn't felt excited and giddy about someone like this for years, and it was nice to have something cut through the heaviness of the morning's news.

"Is it him?" Nicole asked with a sudden excitement in her voice.

I gave her a big smile and nodded.

She nudged me. "Big date today?"

"Big *talk* today," I said while quickly sending Kyle a message to confirm I'd be at his house by noon.

"Mm, a lot to discuss, I'm sure. Has he told you anything about the kid?"

"Not too much. Brock is having trouble with his wolf, with controlling him."

"That's not good, but kind of understandable considering he hasn't had a shifter around him to help out."

"I know, and that's what's worrying me," I told her.

"In what way?"

"Well, I was excited at first, to know about him, but…"

"But…"

"He's a ten-year-old alpha wolf shifter... I don't know if I have what it takes, Nic."

"To do what?"

"To be a dad," I said quietly. "To be an *alpha* dad... How would I ever know where to start with that?"

Nicole was silent. She looked out at the grounds and I followed her gaze to find the pack spilling out of the Lodge and mingling on the lawn, talking, laughing and playing. Cole and his best friend Liam, Jaxon's son, had shifted into their wolf forms and they were romping through the yard with their packmates, tumbling over each other and play fighting.

"Well... You would have a whole pack to help you," Nicole said as a reminder.

I swallowed and nodded as I saw Jaxon making his way through the crowd and walking over toward us.

"I wanted to apologize for not filling you in sooner," Jaxon said as he approached, lowering his head. "I know what happened to your alpha father, and the subject of dragon shifters must be a sore point. I wanted to tell you about the recent sightings personally, before doing it publicly, but time constraints made it impossible. My apologies."

"It's okay," Nic responded. "We're okay."

Jaxon scrutinized me and frowned. "I'm not convinced."

I laughed and shook my head. "It's fine. There's just a lot going on. In fact, I'm glad you're here. I have news and I need your blessing."

Jaxon nodded and urged me to continue.

"I've just found out I have a son," I told him as I looked at him, squinting into the sunlight that shone behind his head.

His eyes widened and a huge smile broke across his face.

"With a human," I added, and watched as his eyebrows twitched with a little concern. "The boy is ten."

"Ten? How did you not know before now? The boy would have shifted years ago, especially if he's an alpha..."

"He is, and he has, and I didn't know because I hooked up with his dad on a one-night stand."

"Did the human at least know about us before you put a pup in him?"

"Um, no."

"So we have a young pup out there born to a human, who didn't know about shifters until he gave birth to one. Do you know how dangerous that was?" Jaxon asked, anger now lacing his tone.

I understood his anger because as our pack's leader he was responsible for keeping us safe, which meant keeping us a secret from the majority of humans. Some knew of course, it was inevitable, but they were ones we trusted. No shifter was supposed to go around getting an unenlightened human pregnant. I dropped my head in an apology.

"He could have told *anyone*," Jaxon said, fuming. "*Did* he tell anyone?"

"I don't know. I mean, he told me of a friend who already knew about shifters, or at least he'd heard rumors. Kyle apparently found out from him when Kyle mentioned...the knot."

Nicole let out a loud laugh. "Sorry," she said as I jabbed her with my elbow. "Please, go on."

"But I believe that's the extent of it," I told Jaxon.

"You need to find out who this friend is," he said. "And ascertain if Kyle had told anyone else or if he knows of anyone who knows. God, this could turn out to be a mess."

I didn't apologize again otherwise I'd be doing it all morning.

"And the child? How's his temperament?" Jaxon asked.

"I'm not sure," I replied honestly. "I only met him for the first time on Saturday. I'm finding out more today."

Jaxon nodded, and then looked off into the distance, into the deep dark of the wood. I had a feeling he was calculating things or putting pieces together.

"And your relationship with the father…"

I glanced at Nicole, who put a hand on my knee and gave it a reassuring squeeze.

"I believe he might be my fated mate," I said.

"*Might* be? You slept with the man. How could you not know?"

"I was drunk at the time. Very, *very* drunk. He was too, and I guess I just didn't notice his scent then, but I met him again and his scent drove me crazy. I mean, it might have then, too, but like I said, I was…drunk." I didn't like admitting that. Not even to myself. I could have spent the last ten years or more with my fated mate, but I'd wasted that time because I'd been too busy drinking and getting laid while not particularly caring who I slept with; I was just out for a good time then. Now it was different. *I* was different.

Jaxon glanced off into the trees again before looking back at me.

"Sounds like fate. You have my blessing. And of course we'll welcome your son and mate into the pack," he said as he put a hand on my shoulder and squeezed it tightly. "However, take it slow, and be careful. Being part of a pack might take them a little getting used to, but at least your son will now have you as his alpha father."

I nodded, doing my best to have complete faith in what my alpha leader was saying. Easier said than done when I had a big pit of self-doubt grumbling in my chest. Young alpha shifters needed an alpha father, it was part of our nature, but they needed a father who knew *how* to be one.

"Tell me more information about his situation when you have it. And I'd like to meet the omega father as soon as possible," he said.

A yelp shot through the yard and Jaxon turned to look at the crowd. His son Liam, in his wolf form, was yelping as Cole bit down on his neck.

"Cole!" Nicole shouted as she got to her feet. "Be gentle!"

Paco immediately shot off and bowled Cole over. Jaxon was close behind and helped Liam to his feet as the boy changed into his human form. Cole also shifted as he tumbled backward. Paco immediately licked at his face.

Nic stormed over and started lecturing Cole about being gentle with his friend while Liam blushed bright red and insisted he was fine. I groaned and ran a hand through my hair as I watched the scene unfold. I sat still on the log and wondered how hard it could be to keep pubescent shifter boys in line. Very hard, I guessed. I was getting what I'd wished for on my birthday candles… But had that wish been a mistake?

My phone buzzed again.

See you soon :) - K.

It was almost midday. I pushed down my feelings of doubt, hurried home, and got ready to see him.

***

"You look…amazing," Kyle said with a smile as he opened the kitchen door for me. Actually, *he* was the one who looked amazing in a different Feather Boats t-shirt that had a low-cut neckline, revealing his lightly freckled skin across his chest and collarbones.

I brushed off his flattery and cautiously made my way into the house. He lived in town on the corner of Poplar Road and Silvercoat Way, right near the doggy daycare that Paco attended, and I could hear the odd bark from there until Kyle closed the door behind me.

The kitchen smelled like freshly cooked bread, punctuated by Kyle's scent. I took a deep breath as I stepped through the threshold and looked around the kitchen.

"It's lovely in here," I said, gazing over beautifully displayed pots, recipe books, and spice racks. The wooden countertops and kitchen island held bowls of fruit, cups stuffed with utensils, and a few piles of what looked like Brock's homework.

"I live here with my sister and her girlfriend. They're out during the day for work," Kyle explained before shrugging. "They have good taste in interior design."

"But I guess this is yours?" I made my way over to the living room then stopped in front of a built-in cabinet that displayed hundreds or possibly thousands of CDs, records and cassette tapes. Kyle let out a nervous laugh and nodded as he came up beside me.

"Yep, that's my contribution to the interior design."

"It's impressive," I said genuinely. The whole house felt impressive, to be honest. It wasn't big, but it was so cozy and well-designed I felt completely at home. I wondered how much of that had to do with Kyle's scent being all over the place.

I took in another greedy breath as I leaned closer to him. I could hear his breathing quicken before he pulled away and wandered back into the kitchen.

"Tea?" he asked. I caught a little quiver of nervousness in his voice, and it made me feel better about my own nerves.

We sat at the kitchen bench and Kyle poured me a cup of tea with shaking hands. He gave me an embarrassed grin as he placed the teapot back on the counter, and I gave him an understanding smile. This was a strange situation. How do you start talking about the kid you had from a one-night stand, ten years ago?

"So, Brock…" Kyle said, but he suddenly stopped as we both reached for the freshly poured cup of tea and our hands touched. A zap of excitement ran through me, and I felt a little dizzy from the pull I felt toward him. He slowly took his hand back and placed it on his lap.

"Sorry. So, we both agree I'm his other biological father?"

Kyle nodded. "I'm certain. We could do a DNA test if you—"

"No." I shook my head. "We couldn't."

"Oh, right. Because of…" Kyle waved his hand around as if indicating something beyond words.

"Because I don't want a DNA lab having my kind of DNA," I said. I smirked and took a sip of tea. It was hot and sweet, and just how I liked it.

"Right."

"And because it's unnecessary. My intuition says, very clearly, that he's my son."

Kyle let out a relieved sigh and nodded. "Okay. Good. We're on the same page. So, to give you some background… I was serious when I said I tried to look for you. I don't want to put any pressure on you, but you should know I've always wanted to find Brock's dad, and he's always wanted me to find you. You can be as involved in this as you want to be…"

"I want to be here for him. It's not right for him to grow up without an alpha, let alone without a shifter to guide him," I said sternly. I needed to get that across; that an alpha shifter child needed an alpha shifter father. That wasn't really up for debate even if I wasn't completely certain I was the *right* father for him.

Kyle nodded and took a sip of his tea. "That makes sense."

I liked how quickly he accepted my assertion, and I felt myself relaxing.

"You seem really positive about all of this," he said.

"Do I?" I shook my head and laughed. "I'm a little nervous. I didn't have an alpha father as I was growing up, and my omega father was, *is,* absent to say the least. I'm not exactly sure how to *be* a dad. But I know how to be an alpha wolf shifter."

"Hm," Kyle said, biting his lip.

"But that's why wolf shifters live in packs," I said, taking a moment to sip my tea. Kyle raised his eyebrows.

"Packs…"

"There are about one hundred shifters in Timberwood Cove," I explained, and then laughed as Kyle spat out his tea into his cup. "Some of us live in the gated community on the north side of town. We call it the homestead, and we call ourselves the Timberwood Cove Pack. Not very original but we've been here for generations. Other packs moved to the town, and that's fine. We get along really well, keeping mostly segregated but getting together for meetings when it looks like there might be trouble. Our particular pack is a tight knit family. We predominantly live with relatives, our chosen mates or…our fated mates."

"Fated mates? Sorry, listen, all of these terms are very new to me and it all sounds *wild.*"

"It's a phenomenon where our wolf instincts just *know* that someone is meant to be with us forever."

Kyle looked at my face as though he were seeing it for the first time.

"Like true love?" he asked quietly.

I nodded. "Similar to true love, but deeper. It's more of a soul bonding… When an alpha claims his fated omega mate—"

"Uh, *claims* his omega? That sounds a little antiquated," he said, sitting upright.

I grimaced. "The language is outdated. But it's an ancient ritual where the alpha imprints the omega by biting his neck. From then on the two of them have a deeply devoted bond that lasts through time."

"Are we…fated? Do you want to *claim* me?" he asked quietly.

Take it slow, Jaxon had said. But what was I going to do? Lie to my mate?

"Well… Yes, we are."

A shy smile touched Kyle's lips, and it struck me that he was a true romantic who loved the idea of being soul mates. His romanticism was undoubtedly why he played love songs all night long. Something I probably should have picked up on earlier.

"And if I was to claim you, you'd become a wolf shifter, like Brock and me." I hoped that would be Kyle's decider, that he'd want to share the same experiences as his son.

Kyle's eyes widened as he stared at me. "Wow. Okay. This is a lot to take in. But wait—how do you know? That we're…fated?"

"There's a certain scent I pick up from you and—"

"I *smell*?" He let out a loud laugh that made me smile.

"You smell *good*," I said. Without actual thought, I put a hand on his knee. A warmth spread through my fingers, and I squeezed his leg gently. Kyle grazed his fingertips across the back of my wrist, sending a shiver up my spine.

"It's a scent that's unique to you, that only I can smell. If you were a wolf shifter, you'd smell a unique scent on me too. And there's a feeling. An…undeniable attraction."

Kyle licked his lips and gazed at my mouth.

I took in a deep breath to try and relax, but his scent hit me harder than ever. I wanted to kiss him, hold him, assure him everything was going to be alright. I wanted to make him *mine*.

Kyle leaned back in his chair, shaking his head. "I need a minute to get my mind around this. Or a week. Maybe a year."

I nodded, accepting that he needed some time, but praying it wouldn't take that long.

"But we were together before…" he said, obviously still trying to join the dots. "Why didn't you want to *claim* me then?"

"I probably did. If I hadn't been drunk out of my mind I'm sure I would have stuck around." I reached for his hand and held it tight as I looked straight into his eyes. "And I want to apologize. I shouldn't have let you get away or raise our son on your own."

I felt Kyle resist with an almost imperceptible movement of his hand, as if he was about to pull it back from mine, but he let it rest there as he stared into my eyes.

"I need to take it slow," he said cautiously. "For my sake, and for Brock's."

I nodded, but I felt my wolf nudging me to say more. "But he does need his alpha wolf father in his life."

Again, Kyle almost pulled back from my hand, but I held it firmly and he slowly relaxed under my touch.

"You're right. He does need an alpha to help him. So do I…"

"Has he been lashing out?" I asked, remembering my own tantrum-filled adolescence of broken toys and shouting matches with Nicole. I imagined Kyle didn't just sit by and watch it happen like my passive, withdrawn omega father had done with me, but it seemed obvious Brock was feeling the same frustration I'd felt from not having an alpha father at home.

Kyle nodded and lowered his eyes. "He has some anger problems. But mostly he has anxiety. He plays video games to help release some energy, but then he's so worked up he can't sleep, and then he feels more anxious the next day."

"I think being with the pack will help," I said, agreeing with Jaxon's advice.

"Maybe, but that's what I'm talking about. We may both need help, but I'm not going to jump in with this pack thing or fated mate thing without taking my time to make sure it's the right thing to do."

"This *fated mate* thing?" I asked with a grin.

"Whatever it's called. I don't know if I'm interested in being *claimed* by you."

I think I would have believed him if I hadn't seen Kyle lick his lips as he dragged his gaze over my body and let it linger on my crotch. I slowly pulled my hand away from his and rested it on the exact spot he was looking.

To my delight, Kyle let out a soft whimper. I'm sure he didn't mean to, but to hear it caused my cock to swell. I sucked in a greedy breath, inhaling his scent once more, and that's when I noticed a slightly different fragrance—his slick.

Kyle's eyes widened as I leaned toward him.

"I'm sorry, I'm… Oh god. I'm going into heat… I'm sorry…" He swallowed, then shook his head slightly even as he kept his full attention on the bulge in my pants. "I wasn't due for another week."

"Another sign that I'm your fated mate," I said as I leaned even closer to him. "I can trigger your heat."

"You can?"

"Yes. It's probably why you unexpectedly went into heat when I was with you ten years ago."

Kyle let out a desperate moan and started to writhe on his seat. I expected him to say it was best if I leave, but he simply continued to stare at my half hard dick like a man starving. When he wet his lips again I barely held back a groan. I imagined how his slick would make it *so* easy to glide into his ass, and then I imagined how hot it would be inside him, how he'd squeeze my cock as I plowed into him. As if guessing what was going through my mind, Kyle looked up at me, desire flaring in his hazel eyes.

"I should… You should…" He shook his head again, but then groaned and shoved his hands between his thighs and ground them down on his cock. "Fuck."

"I could help with that," I said with a knowing grin.

"I haven't felt this way since… Since the bar."

"How much do you remember about that night?" I asked, my voice gone rough as I watched Kyle almost jacking himself off in front of me, his eyes wild, his lips parted as he panted heavily. I leaned so close to him now I could feel his hot breath on my skin.

"I remember you kissing me," he whispered.

"Like this?" I asked, right before I pressed my lips against his mouth. A shock ran through me, and I grunted as my wolf lunged in my chest. I immediately got up off the chair and pulled Kyle into my arms. Without being prompted, Kyle hooked his legs around my waist and his arms around my neck. I slid my tongue into his mouth and he instantly started to suck on it. My cock throbbed, wanting in on the action.

I slid my hands under his ass and hoisted him up, easily carrying his light frame. I headed into the living room, and Kyle started tugging on the hem of my t-shirt, trying to get his hands underneath it. I dropped him on the sofa and he landed with a grunt, then immediately started to take off his jeans. I was just as fast with my own, stripping off my tangled t-shirt before helping Kyle until he was completely naked. Desire surged through me and my mouth filled with saliva as I knelt between his slim thighs and inhaled the most delicious scent. Sweet, fresh, and utterly addictive. How could I have forgotten this? I spread his ass cheeks, revealing his sopping wet hole.

"Fuck me like last time," he begged.

"How did I fuck you last time?" I asked as started to pull on my cock.

"Nice and hard," he groaned, pulling on his own cock.

I changed position so I could press my cock against Kyle's. Kyle wrapped his hand around us both, barely able to close his fingers.

"You're so big," he said just before he started to jerk us off at the same time. I groaned and leaned my head back as I melted under his touch. The feeling of his dick beneath mine was incredible, and the sensation of his firm fingers made my cock harder still.

I growled with desire and grabbed his legs, pushing them back to spread him even more. He gasped, and then deftly squirmed his body so I lost my grip. He flipped over, pressing his ass in the air with his back arched, presenting himself.

I immediately grabbed his hips to drag him closer to me, but just as quickly he pulled away and scampered over the back of the couch. He turned to face me, his gorgeous lean body on full view, his cock fully erect and pointing straight up. I let out a warning growl and watched as he quivered in response, but a sly grin spread across his face. Suddenly, he turned and dashed down a hallway.

I loved to chase, so that's exactly what I did.

I bounded over the couch in one jump, and then I was right on his tail. He raced down the hall but I managed to snag his hips just as he was turning into a room. He yelped and laughed, then wrestled with me to try and get my hands off him. He had no chance. I moved him like he was a doll, twisting him around so he faced me, and then I planted a demanding kiss on his mouth. He relented for a moment before he pulled away again and gave me that same, naughty smirk.

I growled deeper this time, and physically felt his body react under my hands. He trembled, a look of surprise crossing his face. Now it was my time to smirk.

"Do you honestly think I'll let you go now I have you in my arms again," I said.

He didn't answer, just stared at me with wide hazel eyes that seemed full of both desire and mischief.

I stepped forward and he stumbled backward. He would have fallen if I hadn't held onto him. He put his hands on mine and strained to loosen my grip so he could get away, but I wasn't relenting. My cock was throbbing. My senses were overwhelmed by the smell of his slick. I was running on pure instinct, and my instinct was telling me to fuck.

His cheeks flushed, and I noticed his scent getting even stronger. He panted, his chest heaving, and it was easy to see he was playing a game. Though he had no idea of my proclivities toward the hunt, he seemed to have his own instincts on how to get the best out of me.

I spun Kyle around so he was facing away from me. He tried to wriggle out of my grasp again, but I propelled him onto a futon mattress where he instantly attempted to scamper away on all fours. I was positive I heard him giggle before I yanked him back by the hips and positioned him so his upper body was flat against the bed and his ass was in the air.

"Oh fuck yes," he moaned, and he tilted his hips so the tip of my cock skimmed across his slick hole.

"You're already so fucking wet for me," I growled, thrusting forward. In one motion, the head of my dick popped into his ass, sending a thrill straight to my balls. "You want this?" I asked, thrusting more of my cock inside his hole.

"Shit! Yes, I want it, I want your huge cock," he whined.

And I wanted to give it to him. I wrapped my arms around his waist and leaned over him so I could angle my cock in deeper. I fucked him with short thrusts until his ass relaxed and took more of my length. Kyle moaned but he was still tight, and I wasn't sure if it was because he was deliberately squeezing me out or if he just naturally had a tight hole.

"Take it," I groaned through gritted teeth. "Take all of my cock." I thrust harder into him. "How are you going to take my knot if you can't take my cock?"

"Oh fuck!" Kyle cried, as if he'd just remembered what was coming. "The knot!"

I reached down and took his dick in my hand. It was a nice, perfect size, and I loved how hard he was as I wrapped my fingers around him. I jerked his length just twice and his ass immediately loosened.

"Good," I said in praise, and he whimpered in response. I let go of his cock and straightened up so I could watch him take me. I pulled almost all the way out and then slid in with a deliciously slow thrust, all the way from the tip to the hilt.

"That's it," I moaned appreciatively as my balls hit against his.

"Shit! That's so fucking good! You're so fucking good!"

"That's right, I am." I smoothed a hand down his back and he wiggled his hips side to side. I loved how it felt to be balls-deep in his tight, wet hole and I shuddered with pleasure as I felt his ass clench around my length.

I started moving again, nothing but the thought of filling him entering my mind as I became overwhelmed by the clenching, throbbing sensation of his ass trying to milk my cock. Instinct once again took over. I pulled out and slammed back inside him in one strong thrust, pushing a guttural groan out of his mouth. I did it again, and again, pulling his hips back to meet mine. Soon, I was fucking him hard and fast, grunting with every thrust. My eyes started to shut and I began imagine how it would feel spilling deep inside him, flooding him with my cum. It was only then that I remembered we'd been so swept up in Kyle's heat that we hadn't used condoms, and considering his heat was early, he probably wasn't on any form of suppressant or pill.

I knew in that instant I should pull out, but that was the exact moment my knot swelled, and then I had no choice. I couldn't pull out until I came; I was locked tight in his perfect, wet ass.

"Fuck!" Kyle shuddered and began to grasp at the sheets.

I let out a barely human growl as I tried to shove more of my knot deep into Kyle's sopping hole. My balls tightened, and I couldn't hold back. I began saturating his insides with spurt after spurt of thick semen.

"Oh my god, it's so much." Kyle whimpered deep in his throat, and then let out a loud, desperate cry. "I'm coming!"

His clenching, twitching, pulsing ass felt like it was sucking me in. I couldn't believe how fucking good it felt. My knees began to buckle and I could barely hold myself up. I collapsed onto him as waves of pleasure continued to rock me. Kyle moaned and pushed back with his ass, writhing beneath me until I had to grab him to hold him still.

"It's okay, Kyle, relax."

"Still coming," he groaned. He shuddered, and I snaked a hand beneath him to feel his cock throb in my palm. His cum coated my fingers, and I grinned, squeezing his cock just a little until he groaned again.

By the time he'd stopped coming, I'd managed to roll us to our sides. He lay panting in the circle of my arms, his back to my chest, still locked tight. My knot throbbed, and it was sensitive as hell. Every small movement Kyle made sent a shiver of pleasure through me.

I don't think I'd ever experienced anything like it. Not like that, not so powerful, intense, or with a sense of complete contentment.

Eventually, I opened my eyes and glanced around.

"Is this your bedroom?" It was kind of obvious with the band posters adorning the walls and an oversized stereo sitting in the corner.

"Mm," he mumbled.

"What's with the stack of sheets?" I asked as I spotted a huge pile of clean laundry beside the futon mattress.

Kyle twisted his head slightly to look up at me, an amused grin on his lips. "I've had to keep changing them since I met you at the convention."

I laughed, but then immediately groaned as the movement caused my knot to jostle inside Kyle. He groaned too, and we tried to remain motionless for a while.

"Did we do this last time?" he asked after a moment.

"I don't know."

"It would have been nice if we did. I probably fell asleep. I know you were gone when I woke up."

A deep regret twisted my heart at that. "Sorry. I didn't know you were my mate. I honestly wouldn't have abandoned you if I'd known."

"It's okay, what's done is done, but..."

"But what?"

"Now we're not both drunk..." That sly smirk spread over Kyle's face again, and he started to move his hips back and forth. I gasped as a rush of pleasure shot through me. My knot was still not letting him go, but Kyle had enough leverage to fuck himself on my cock.

We spent the afternoon like that—fucking, coming, recovering, and then repeating until we finally collapsed and couldn't come anymore. We ended up in a puddle of his slick and an outrageous amount of my cum, and thoroughly sticky, we hazily dragged ourselves to the bathroom.

The hot shower helped me come back to earth. Kyle lathered me all over with a grapefruit scented shower gel that he said would wake me up. He was right. By the time he was done rinsing me off, I felt almost normal.

I looked down at him as he as he handed me a fluffy white towel and felt an intense surge of love for him. I wanted to take him back to the homestead with me. In that moment, I wanted to claim him and take care of him for the rest of my life.

"You are incredible," I told him as I cupped the side of his jaw.

He looked up at me with wide eyes and a huge smile. "So are you. That was most definitely the best sex I've ever had."

I wasn't actually talking about sex, but I smiled anyway. He pressed his body against mine, but then bit his lip and looked down at my chest. He ran his finger through the wet hair there as a little frown crossed his face.

"But I meant what I said before. I need to go slow... Which means you should go before Brock gets home."

My wolf instantly growled. I pulled back, put a finger under Kyle's chin and tilted his face up so that he was looking right at me.

"I'm your alpha," I told him. I felt him eagerly surrender under my gaze and my wolf was appeased somewhat. "And I meant what *I* said. I'm going to be part of Brock's life, but for the sake of argument today, I'll do as you requested. As for *you*. I'm happy enough to take things slowly between us, but I won't wait forever."

Kyle quickly nodded, and a grateful smile crossed his face. "I want you to be part of our lives. I promise. Come by tomorrow and we'll talk more about it."

Chapter 6 - Kyle

I felt so high after sex with Gavin I wasn't sure if I should drive. I figured a walk would do me the world of good, so I set out on foot to pick up Brock from school.

Fated mates? The whole concept sounded absurd. But every experience I'd had with Gavin sure did sound a lot like what he was talking about. And that *sex*. I was going to be sore for days from the pounding he gave me.

But fated mates or not... Things were moving at a crazy fast speed. If it was just me on my own I'd have fallen head-first into something serious with Gavin. But it wasn't just me. I had Brock to think about. Gavin's alpha energy was so intense I genuinely wanted to do whatever he said. It felt so good to have him take control when I was with him, and I could certainly see how he would be a help with Brock. But when I was away from Gavin, I started having second thoughts...

I was getting so caught up in my head, I knew I had to talk to someone to stop myself from going crazy. I sent a text to Trevor, to catch up before work.

Juicy gossip? - T

Trust me. You're going to love it.

I'm in. Stop by the shop before your shift? - T

Ok, I'll be there at about six.

I looked up from my phone as I heard the school bell ring.

"Hey, Brocky!" I called when I spotted my son walking out of the doors. He raced across the yard with his head down and his backpack high on his shoulders. I thought I caught a group of boys laughing at him, but when I looked at them, they were just laughing at their phones.

"Where's the car?"

"Nice to see you too." I gestured to take his bag, and he slid it off his back and passed it to me. It was way heavier than I was expecting, and I realized how exhausted I was from my day's...activities as I hauled it onto my shoulder.

"Why didn't you drive?" Brock asked as we started walking home.

"I thought a walk might be nice," I replied cheerfully.

"Wrong. I want to get home so I can talk to Gavin on live chat."

My chest tightened and anxiety bubbled in my gut. "Hm, I don't know how I feel about you talking to strangers on that thing."

"Ugh, *Dad*. Gavin isn't a stranger. And it's just a normal part of the game, get over it. No one knows who I am."

I shook my head, feeling like a completely out of touch parent. And a worried one. "Gavin knows who you are. You told him your gaming handle at the convention."

Brock fell quiet for a moment, and then said in a quiet voice, "Gavin's different."

"Different how?" I asked quietly as I wrapped an arm around his shoulder.

Brock just shrugged and didn't say another word until we got home. He grunted his way through dinner conversation with the girls, and even Britt noticed he was being especially quiet.

"Ice cream for dessert?" Kennedy asked as she cleared away his plate.

"No thanks." Brock shook his head, and we all turned to stare at him. "I'm just going to play a game if that's okay?"

"No ice-cream?" Kennedy asked again to clarify.

"No thank you," he said in his most polite voice.

"That's very suspicious, Brocky," Britt said, leaning forward and peering at him.

"Have you finished your homework?" I asked.

Brock let out an exasperated sigh, and I was about to lecture him about his studies when he shook his head again. "I have, I finished it hours ago. I told myself I could have a treat *later* if I finished my trees and animals poster for class. Come and see it if you don't believe me."

"Oh, I want to see that!" Kennedy said. "Even though I already believe you."

"Me too," Britt and I said in unison. We followed him upstairs to his room where, sure enough, he'd created a huge poster that detailed the trees, plants and animals that were found locally to Timberwood Cove. He'd included plant samples he'd taken from the woods and the beach, and he illustrated mini-ecosystems that existed in the area.

"Brock, this is amazing," I said genuinely.

"Thanks, Dad." He smiled, and I felt my heart swell with pride as I took him in my arms.

"Seriously, Brocky, this is so cool," Kennedy said as she traced her finger on the lines between trees.

"I based the layout on a map from RuneMaze," he said. "But all the details and drawings are mine, I didn't steal that."

"Very cool," Britt said in praise.

Brock craned his neck to look up at me and asked quietly, "Can I play the game now?"

"Sure, Brocky. Just don't stay up too late, okay? Bed by ten."

"Ten thirty," he said in an attempt to bargain as a playful grin crept onto his face.

"Ten ten," I said as a compromise.

"Yes!" He fist-pumped the air.

I hurried to get ready for work, and as I was about to leave I stuck my head in his door to find him engrossed in the game, headset on.

"That's so *cool*, Gavin!" he said, then he let out a loud cheer. "Thank you so much, oh my *god*, I had no idea how to get through the bad guy, it was so hard. The cylinder! Of course it was the codex combined with the crystal coil, *duh*. It makes sense now but I couldn't have figured that out without your hints. Thank you thank you thank you, oh man I'm so excited for this next level!"

He may as well have been speaking another language for all I understood, but the look of joy on his face was clear to me. I knocked on the door and he looked up.

"Just a sec, hang on," he said to his headset, and then he quickly yanked it off and beamed at me.

"Thanks for letting me play tonight, Dad."

"You did great on that poster," I said, praising him again. He jumped up to give me a big hug. I closed my eyes and held him close, my heart warming. I lived for these moments of affection with him.

"Have a good show tonight, Dad." Then he added quietly, "I love you."

I stopped into the lounge room on my way out. Britt and Kennedy were on the sofa watching their favorite show on television.

"Hey guys, can you keep an eye on Brock tonight?" I asked.

"Uh, yeah of course, what do you think we normally do?" Britt asked with a roll of her eyes.

"I mean, *more* of an eye, while he's on his game. He's talking with Gavin."

"Oh my god, that's right, you saw him today. How was it?" Britt asked. I realized she was sitting right where I'd been writhing around on the couch under Gavin's hot, strong body, and I felt myself turning bright red.

"It was *good*," I said, my voice rising in pitch at the end. "I'll fill you in later. Can you just... I don't know? Make sure he doesn't make any long-term plans with Gavin?"

Kennedy stood up and smoothed down her cargo pants. "I'll go get on the game with him and do a spot of chaperoning."

"Oh how selfless of you," Britt said as she slapped her girlfriend's ass. "Any excuse to get on that game, huh?"

"No way, I hate that nerdy stuff." She winked. "I'll take care of him."

Relieved, I turned to leave for work but Britt stopped me.

"Was it?"

"Was what?" I asked as I doubled back into the living room.

"Was it good?" she asked quietly.

I nodded. "It was really, really good. I think."

"You *think*?"

I glanced at the clock and saw it was almost six. "I'll fill you in. I gotta go meet Trevor."

"Ugh, that guy gets all the best gossip out of you." Britt sighed and slumped back against the couch.

She was right. Trevor had been my best friend since we were young, and he was still my greatest confidant. We'd been talking about our love lives for as long as I could remember, and we had promised to be each other's best man at our future, imagined weddings. I couldn't wait to fill him in on what was going on. He'd know what to do.

I pulled up to Trevor's business, *Pampered Paws Doggy Daycare*, as a corgi and a husky were walking out of the front doors with a cute guy who reminded me a little of Gavin. I did a double-take, but on second look, I realized he looked nothing like him.

The door swung open with a ring of the bell, and I found Trevor leaning on the counter in his usual get-up; bright pink shirt over a Taylor Swift tour t-shirt, pastel capris, and white boat shoes. He insisted the white shoes made the dogs more comfortable, though he never ventured to explain why, and I sure hadn't noticed a difference.

"Oh my *god*, look at you!" he cried as he rushed over and locked the door behind me.

"Look at *me*? Look at you. Nice shirt."

"You look exhausted," he said as he flipped the sign from *"Open To All Puppies!"* to *"Closed. No Mutts Allowed."*

"I am a little tired." I smiled to myself.

"*Mmmm-hmmm...*" Trevor looked me over as he squinted his eyes, then he led me through the shop to his office area. I fell down onto his red velvet sofa and he took a seat opposite me in his oversized floral armchair, and then I started to fill him in on the last twenty-four hours.

"What are you going to do?" he asked after I explained how Gavin wanted to be a part of Brock's life.

"I have no idea. I've been parenting on my own for over ten years. I don't know how I'm going to adjust to sharing it with someone else."

"But isn't it exciting, finding a long-lost lover who wants to claim his son?"

"And speaking of claiming… Gavin told me I'm his fated mate."

Trevor's loud squeal was enough to have Bonnie and Clyde, his two huskies, barking from the outdoor play area. "Oh. My. God! Are you serious!"

I sighed, not sure if I wanted to actually talk about what all that meant even though I'd brought it up. "Yes. He said I gave off a unique scent, and his attraction to me meant I was his fated mate. It's something to do with him being a shifter, and—"

"Oh, I know all that! What I want to know is, what are you going to do?"

"I don't know." I ran a hand over my face. "I wasn't looking for a relationship, but according to him, I don't have a choice."

"Of course you do." Trevor dismissed my statement with a wave of his hand. "From what I've heard, you don't *have* to be with your fated mate. You'd just be a fool to pass up the opportunity."

I let out a short laugh, and then sighed. "Thanks."

"Wait. Are you seriously thinking of letting this go?"

"I'm just thinking about Brock. I agree that Gavin should be in his life. Obviously I need help with the alpha stuff that Brock is going through…"

"And the *wolf* stuff."

"That too."

Trevor crossed his legs and looked at me with concern. "So what's the problem?"

"If things between Gavin and me don't work out, then where does that leave Brock? What if Gavin just disappears again?"

"First of all, give the guy some credit," Trevor said, pointing an accusing finger at me. "He disappeared after a one-night stand ten years ago. That's different. And if things don't work out, there's no evidence he won't still be in Brock's life. If anything, it sounds like their bond is already very strong."

I thought back to the way Brock had said Gavin was "different" and how happy he seemed on the game with him. "Maybe you're right," I admitted.

"Oh, honey. Of *course* I'm right. I'm always right."

***

I kept that in mind while I started my shift. If Trevor was *always* right, then that meant I should open the show with a Taylor Swift song and spin another one every hour.

Halfway through the show, the producer gave me the report. "Huge listenership tonight, Kyle," he said through my headphones, and I let out a short laugh.

As I was starting the final hour, a call came through the line for a dedication. As soon as the producer hit play on the prerecorded request, my heart started racing.

"I'd like to dedicate this to the new man in my life," Gavin's voice stated over the airways. "And the son I didn't know until now. This one is for both of you."

The producer hit play on the record, and tears started to well up in my eyes. I leaned back in my chair, letting my tears flow as I listened to the lyrics of devotion, adoration, and true love.

This I promise you / I'll be with you / Until the end of time
No need to hide / Let's dance all night / Let's make it right
Together / Together / Together

As the song faded out, I took a sharp inhale and wiped my tears before pressing my lips close to the microphone.

"Another beautiful love song dedication on the Nightlight Love Lounge. What a lucky man and what a lucky son. Next up, you guessed it, a little more Taylor Swift. This one is going out to the biggest *Swiftie* in Timberwood Cove—the one and only Trevor of Pampered Paws. Thanks for the advice, my friend."

Two verses into the song, and I felt my phone buzzing. I grinned and reached for it, expecting to see a cheesy text from Trevor. Instead, my heart fluttered when I saw Gavin's name.

Glad you liked the song. I love that I can hear your voice even when we're apart. - G

You're too sweet. Thank you :)

I'd like to come over tomorrow. - G

I had to get back to work before I could reply, and the dedications started coming in hard and fast in the last hour. After I wrapped it up and said goodnight to my producer, I pulled my phone back out, ready to text Gavin back. Instead, I found another message from him.

Sleep well tonight. I'll come by your house tomorrow. I'm going to have sweet dreams before I even get to sleep while thinking about you and remembering what we did today… You really are incredible. - G

I sucked in a sharp breath and felt a thrill rush through my body. I hadn't felt so adored in…years. If *ever*. I strained my memory to try and find a time when I'd felt so wanted, and I couldn't. It was sad, really, how woeful my life was. Yes I'd had Brock, and I loved him with all my heart, but having him, being a single omega dad to an alpha wolf… It didn't really allow me to have a love life. And now Gavin had dropped into my life like a tornado, blowing aside the barriers and walls I'd built up over the years, and like anything with that much power, his presence could be destructive.

As I drove home I felt myself re-building a barrier against the fear that all of this, all of *Gavin*, was too good to be true.

Take it slow. Take it slow. Take it slow. I used the mantra each time I laid a brick in my new wall, but I couldn't help recalling the text he'd sent me and thinking back to the afternoon we'd had together.

By the time I got home, I was completely worked up. I was about to jump straight into bed and take care of myself when I realized my bed was bare. I'd stripped the sheets—I'd had to, given how much we'd both come… But I hadn't had the time to put fresh sheets on yet.

I glanced from the pile of linens, to the bed, and back again. I let out a frustrated groan as my cock ached in my pants. I immediately stripped and ran a hot shower.

All of the tension melted out of my body as I stood under the warm water and ran a hand over my cock. It was already half erect, and it bounced into a full hard-on as soon as I touched it. I leaned back against the wall of the shower and wrapped my hand around my length. My thoughts immediately went back to the feeling of Gavin pushing inside me, and my ass twitched. I'd felt so *full* with his knot lodged deep in my hole.

But as I started jerking off, my mind wandered away from the furious fucking he'd given me. Instead I began thinking of other things he'd done to me. I couldn't shake the memory of his lips pressed against mine, the soft touch of his hand on my face, the look of adoration in his eyes when he stared at me.

I gasped as a rush of pleasure pulsed through my cock. I jerked harder and faster, and each of my thoughts kept coming back to that beautiful moment when he'd first kissed me, and when he'd held me close in his arms. I imagined what it would be like to hold hands with him as we walked through town. I thought how it might feel to have him pick me up and literally sweep me off my feet.

As I realized where my thoughts were taking me I frowned and tried to bring my mind back to the intense fucking from this morning. There was no way I was going to come while I thought about the way his eyes crinkled when he smiled at me… Or the way his laugh made my heart soar…

"Oh god." I gasped as my balls pulled up and a shot of heat raced down my spine.

I squeezed my eyes shut and desperately searched for hot, horny, x-rated memories of his thick cock taking me from behind, but my balls relaxed and my excitement faded. I bit down on my lip… And thought about his fingers tracing over my jaw, his eyes gazing into mine. My balls drew close to my body once more, and my cock throbbed with such *need*. I moaned, lost in a romantic bubble where Gavin whispered soft, sweet words to me like that night all those years ago, when I heard him saying *I love you*.

Suddenly my body jerked, and I moaned uncontrollably as my release finally took me from thinking to feeling. My mind blanked out with intense bliss, all thoughts gone as my cock pulsed in my hand and sprayed its load.

I fell back against the tile wall with a heavy thud, but that's when I was once again flooded with old memories, new fantasies, and worst of all, the realization that Gavin had already woven his way into my heart.

Chapter 7 - Gavin

So much for taking it slow, but I couldn't hold back. Kyle was in my head, and there was nothing I could do about it. I'd had to jerk off twice before I could get to sleep that night, and I was shocked that I was able to come at all, given how intense each of my orgasms had been with him that afternoon.

I slept like a baby, and the next day I woke up at sunrise with a huge grin on my face. My wolf was excitedly jumping around inside my chest so I sprung out of bed then quickly dashed outside into the woods where I ran until my legs were tired and my lungs burned from the exertion.

After stumbling back into my house I took a shower, and then played a round of RuneMaze to try and keep myself distracted, but I kept gazing at my phone, wondering if Kyle would cancel our plans. Surely he wouldn't. Granted, he was a sassy omega, but he seemed to be going with my lead, which was a good sign. However, I couldn't shake the feeling that I'd need to woo him a little more if I was going to have any chance of making him mine. Of claiming him.

On my way to see him, I stopped at Petal Pushers, a local flower shop run by a packmate and good friend of mine, Jason Meredith. The heavy scent of blooms hit me as I walked into the store, making me a little lightheaded. The bright color practically smacked me in the face, and I had to blink a few times to adjust my vision. It was hot and humid in here, and I was shrugging off my long black overcoat when Jason came out from the back of the store.

"Hey! Gavin! Never thought I'd see you in here," he said as he brought me into a familiar hug.

"Hey now, I'm as romantic as they get," I protested as I gave him a firm thump on the back before letting him go.

"Hm, not exactly what you're not known for."

I rolled my eyes. The playboy reputation I had earned was warranted, but it was getting old. And so was I.

"Well, I need some new tactics now the gray hair is coming in," I said as I motioned to my head.

"Sure, I get that." He laughed, but I didn't exactly feel like he understood. The guy was still in his late twenties, when life seemed to stretch on forever, and he still had a model-perfect face. I'd take his empathy after he'd hit thirty, and not a minute before.

"How's Stacia?" I asked, mentioning Jason's daughter.

"She's wonderful, but she's become obsessed with the dogs at the doggie daycare next door," he replied with a frustrated grunt. "I knew it was only a matter of time until she noticed them. She loves animals so much. But god. *That place...*"

"Still having a rivalry with the owner?" I asked as I looked at a display of bright peonies.

"*Mhm*, you could call it a rivalry. Or you could call it what it is... A disgusting, stinky, *loud* business that should be shut down," he grumbled as he craned his neck to look out the window toward Pampered Paws.

I grinned to myself. "Oh of course. Nothing to do with the cute owner."

"Cute!" Jason exclaimed. "He wears gaudy bright pink almost every day, and he has the sassiest mouth I've ever heard from an omega. That's not cute."

"Sounds kind of cute," I insisted.

Jason let out an exasperated groan and started tugging at his hair.

"C'mon," I said. "Admit it."

Jason shook his head, but then sighed. "Maybe. But those dogs are heinous. Ugh. Horrible."

"Strange that you, a canine, can't deal with dogs," I commented.

"You try getting bitten by one at the tender age of ten, and then talk to me about it."

"Hm. Fair point." I remembered how horrible his wounds had been, and a shudder ran up my spine.

"Anyway, what can I do for you?" he asked as he picked up a spray bottle and started misting blooms around the shop.

"Flowers. But while I'm here, I could use some dating advice."

"*Dating* advice?" He raised his eyebrows, and I nodded. "From me? *Gavin*, the playboy of Timberwood Cove, coming to *me* for advice? You realize I haven't been with anyone for years, right?"

I chuckled and nodded. "I do. But as it turns out, we have more in common than I thought."

"Oh?" he asked as he spritzed a big leafy Monstera Deliciosa.

"I just found out I also have a child from a drunken night at the Brewery..."

Jason's jaw dropped and he froze in place, mid-spritz. I laughed at his expression.

"Tell me everything," he insisted as he lowered the bottle.

I filled him in on the basic details, and he let out a long, impressed whistle.

"Ten years ago! Well, that's a whole different scene to what I have with Kiefer and Stacia. You know Kiefer was already my best friend before we hooked up that one night and I got him pregnant. We've remained friends the whole time, so I'm not sure I can give you much advice," he admitted.

"You didn't want to claim him?" I knew Kiefer was human, and because of him falling pregnant he was now one of the few who were aware of shifters in general and specifically who belonged to the Timberwood Cove pack.

"No. We never should have hooked up, but he was in heat and... Well, you can guess the rest."

Oh, yeah, I definitely could guess the rest. I sighed. "How did Kiefer react when you told him you were a shifter?" I remembered there being a bit of a fuss when Jason told Greer, which was not too different from the way Jaxon acted when I told him about Kyle.

"He was surprisingly okay with it. To be honest, I kind of think he'd suspected something was different about me and Jaxon, who Kiefer is also friends with."

"And he kept the secret about shifters?"

Jason nodded. "Is that your biggest worry? That the secret will get out?"

"Oh good god, no." I laughed and shook my head. "My biggest worry is suddenly being a dad when I've spent my life being irresponsible and reckless. I don't know how to do father...stuff."

"Well, from where I stand, you've always been smart, strong, honest, and capable. That's a good combination for fatherhood."

I pursed my lips as I let that wisdom sink in. Maybe I did have what it took. Or at least, a little of it...

"I'll take the peonies," I said.

***

"Peonies? Are you kidding?" Kyle looked me over with suspicion as I stood on his doorstep, holding out the bouquet.

"Wrong choice?" I grimaced, and he let out a loud laugh.

"No! The right choice. They're my favorite," he said, admiring them with wide eyes. "How did you know?"

As I passed him the bundle our hands grazed, and I felt a shot of excitement thumping in my heart. His eyes looked up and met mine.

"I just looked for the flowers that reminded me of you," I said softly.

"You did, huh?" He grinned then motioned for me to come inside.

I sat at his kitchen bench on a bar stool while he hurried to get a vase for the flowers. I couldn't keep my eyes off him. His long torso looked so good in his black band t-shirt, and his small ass was perfectly framed in his tight black jeans. There was a rip in the denim across his upper thighs, and it gave me thoughts about ripping the rest of it off him with my teeth.

Kyle leaned over me to place the vase of peonies on the kitchen counter, and his arm brushed across my shoulder. Before I knew it I'd reached out and I slid my hand over his hip. I cupped his ass and squeezed it firmly as I looked up at him. He let out a delicate moan, and then wrapped his arms around my neck and leaned down to press a soft kiss against my lips.

"Mmm." I relished the sensation of his mouth against mine. I took a deep breath, hunting for the scent of his slick, but didn't find it.

He pulled back and searched my face for a moment, and a look of worry shot across his eyes. It was as if he wondered why I hadn't already dragged him off to bed.

"You are gorgeous and incredibly sexy," I told him, running my hand up his back. "But I didn't come over for sex."

"Oh?" He sounded genuinely surprised and a little relieved. "What did you..."

"I was hoping we could talk about Brock."

Kyle bit his bottom lip and nodded. He pulled up a bar stool and scooted it close to me.

"He seems really happy to be talking with you on the game," he said. "And, I mean, it's been *one* day but he seems to be calmer since he met you. That sounds weird, but I think something's changed for him."

"Have you told him that I'm—"

"'No," he said quickly, shaking his head. I nodded in understanding.

"We can work up to that," I said.

"Yeah," he murmured, but he looked down at the counter and I could tell he was having some doubts.

"Listen, I missed so much. I want to know what happened. What was your pregnancy like?"

"Horrid," he replied, and then let out a short laugh that made me smile. "The morning sickness was pretty bad, and kind of strange. I was only a little nauseous, but mostly dizzy. I had to keep lying down. My sister Britt was a godsend, of course. She took great care of me."

"I'll have to thank her," I said, and shocked myself by how much sadness came through in my voice.

"She'd love to meet you," he said. "Her girlfriend, Kennedy will too. She loves your game."

"It *is* a good game."

Kyle laughed nervously. "That's what they say. I don't know anything about video games. To be honest, I feel it's a bridge Brock and I can't cross."

"Really? I could teach you some things," I offered.

"Me?" Kyle raised his eyebrows skeptically. "Who doesn't know one end of a controller to the other?"

"Well, at least you know what a controller is," I said with a laugh.

Kyle laughed too and he visibly relaxed. "Oh, hang on, let me go get something," he said, hurrying off into the living room. I spun around on the stool and watched him go. My wolf whimpered as he left, and I sniffed at the air again, trying to catch a scent that just wasn't there. I wondered what had happened; he smelled so different from yesterday.

When he came back carrying a stack of photo albums, my heart soared.

"Here we go," he said as he dumped the photo albums on the kitchen counter. The weight of them made the bench shake, and water sloshed in the vase of peonies. I pulled my stool closer in a hurry to open the first album.

The first page was a huge photo of Brock as a baby, his button nose and bright blue eyes were a spitting image of mine, while his chubby cheeks and pink lips looked exactly like Kyle's.

"Wow."

"Cute, right?"

"Adorable," I whispered. Protective energy rumbled in my chest, and I felt my wolf go on high alert. It was ridiculous, it was just a picture of a kid I didn't even know. But still, I recognized him as my kin, my cub... I should have been there for him, to guide him, protect him.

I let out a pained sigh as Kyle flicked through the photos. With each page, Brock grew bigger. More of his personality started showing. At first he looked like a shy, unsure kid, but by the time he hit seven or eight, his muscles started filling out, and he suddenly got taller. He had my wide shoulders with Kyle's long torso, and an air of mischief started showing on his face.

"Is he about eight years old here?" I asked, pointing to a picture where he had a deep furrow on his forehead, looking almost pained.

"Yeah, that's right," Kyle said.

"Is that when he became more...aggressive?"

Kyle nodded, pulling back and looking at me.

"I should have been there," I said softly.

"You couldn't have," he said with a shrug.

"I know but... I know what it's like... I grew up without an alpha father," I told him. I felt tears pricking my eyes and bit back the urge to break down. "You're far, far better than my omega father was. But even if he'd been the best omega dad I could have had, there were things I still needed an alpha's help with. Especially at Brock's age. Especially as a shifter. His wolf is getting stronger and it takes more to control him."

Kyle's own tears had started to well up, and I watched as his bottom lip quivered.

"I don't know how to do those things for him," he whispered.

"I want to help you. I want to help Brock," I said, my voice breaking. "I'm so sorry I missed so much of his life. I want to be there for every moment from now on. I don't want to miss anything more."

My wolf started whining, and I felt a deep, heavy regret sitting like a stone in the pit of my stomach. Kyle ran his hands over my back, no doubt to comfort me. I appreciated it, but in reality I wasn't the one who'd had to worry and stress over the last ten years, who'd had to raise a child on his own. Because of my omega dad I knew exactly how hard that was. What Kyle needed now, what *Brock* needed now, was for me to start taking charge along with a huge dose of responsibility, and I suddenly had a great idea.

"There's a kids baseball game on Saturday afternoon run by our pack leader. Would you bring Brock? Some of our kids play on the team, and Brock could meet them, and then you could come home with me to see where I live."

Kyle hesitated. I held eye contact with him and silently urged him not to look away.

"Alright," he said. "Saturday."

I internally gave a shout of joy, but obviously didn't cover it very well because Kyle smiled. "I'll come by to pick you up after lunch," I said, smiling myself now.

We spent the next few hours going through the rest of the photo albums. Kyle continuously touching me, letting his fingers linger on the back of my neck while he caught me up on all the major events in Brock's life. A broken leg from climbing a tree, an award he won for doing an incredible painting of fish at the aquarium, and every Christmas with Kyle and his sister Britt, exhibiting elaborate decorations and Brock with a massive smile on his face. By the time we finished, it was almost time for Kyle to pick up Brock from school.

We left together, and as we stood in the driveway I placed a soft kiss on Kyle's lips. "Saturday," I said as reminder even though I know Kyle hadn't forgotten.

"We'll be here," he promised.

***

The week dragged on and I kicked myself for making plans that were so far away. I kept in touch with Brock through the game chat and was able to enforce an earlier bedtime for him by signing off after dinner. As much as I wanted to keep leading him through the mazes and showing him ways to combat the bad guys, I knew it was more important for him to get sleep. Especially if I wanted Kyle to see I was a good influence.

On Saturday morning, I headed over to Nicole's to help Cole get ready for his big game. I found him in the backyard doing catching practice with Liam. Nicole, Jaxon and Bryce were also there with Lori, sitting on the porch in their Timberwood Cubs letter jackets. Paco was dashing between the players, trying his best to snatch the ball out of midair.

"You should recruit that dog," I told Jaxon as I bounced up the stairs.

"He's a good runner, but not so good on the bat," he said with a warm smile, then he shouted at Cole. "Wider grip on that mitt, Cole!"

"Yes, sir!" Cole said with an unusual respect for authority. He was obsessed with baseball, and it helped that his coach, Jaxon, had been a world-famous pitcher for the Timberwood Wolves major league team.

"I'm going over to pick up Kyle and Brock after lunch," I said. "They're coming to the game."

"Yes!" Nicole clapped and smiled at me happily. "I can't wait to meet them."

Jaxon raised his eyebrows, and I was quick to explain, "This *is* me 'going slow'."

Bryce choked back a laugh and Jaxon slapped me on the back. "Good for you, buddy. I'm looking forward to meeting them. So, how is everything going between you and Kyle?"

I chuckled. "We...reconnected."

Nicole and Bryce choked back another laugh, and I shot them a cheeky grin while Jaxon cleared his throat to remain as professional as possible.

"He seems a little hesitant, though," I said.

"As he should be. He has his boy to worry about. Stay consistent. Show him you have what it takes to be a good father," Jaxon said, then he let out a whistle and applauded a good catch by Liam.

"*Do* I have what it takes?" I asked quietly.

Jaxon nodded. "Of course you do. You're an alpha. Cole, hit him with a spin on the next few! Liam, go outfield for this."

I might be an alpha, but a father? I wasn't so sure.

***

I arrived at Kyle's just after lunch, dressed in dark blue jeans and my Timberwood Cubs jacket and cap. I proceeded to the side door and knocked a happy tune on the frame until an athletic woman answered.

"Oh hi—"

"Hey! You must be Gavin," she said as a big toothy smile broke across her face and she urged me inside. "Come in, come in."

"Thank you." I smiled, took off my cap, and entered the kitchen where bags and camping equipment was strewn across the counters.

"Such a pleasure to meet you," she said as she raced around the other side of the kitchen then started going through cabinets looking for something. "Kyle's just getting changed, I think. He's not feeling great. But we're just about to leave, we're late and—"

"Kennedy! Do you have those little plastic containers we need for the snack thing?"

The question came from another woman shouting from the living room.

"Looking now, babe!" Kennedy called back. "We have company!"

I heard a flutter of feet on the carpeted floor before a woman, who looked so much like Kyle that I almost did a double-take, rushed into the kitchen. She had dark brown, curly hair pulled back in a loose bun, and I spotted crystals, flowers, and thread in parts of her hair. She was wearing long, flowing fabrics with intricate hippie patterns, and a beautiful smile exploded on her face when she saw me.

"Are you *Gavin*?" she asked with a cheeky wink.

"I am," I replied with a short chuckle.

"I'm Britt, Kyle's sister." She held out her hand, and as I shook it bangles jangled on her wrist.

"A pleasure to meet you both," I said and gave her a genuine smile. I liked filling in the blanks in what I knew about Kyle and Brock's lives. I knew Britt and Kennedy had been there for Brock when he'd shown his wolf side, and they'd supported him. That was good enough for me.

"Got 'em!" Kennedy said, and she started shoving the plastic containers into an overstuffed hiking bag.

"It was a pleasure to put such a handsome face to the name, but we have to run," Britt said warmly.

"Don't let me keep you."

"We wouldn't." Kennedy hoisted her hiking bag onto her back, and then picked up most of the equipment in her hands.

"Bye, Kyle. Gavin's here," Britt shouted toward the hallway off the living room, then she turned back to me and gave me a quick hug. "He'll be out in no time. Bye." Then she and Kennedy headed down the porch steps and out of view, and then the door slammed shut behind them.

I waited in the suddenly quiet kitchen and took in the peacefulness of the house. I really felt at home here, and I wondered if it was because Kyle it was imbued with Kyle's scent, and that of my son's.

I spun around when I heard Kyle padding across the living room. He was wearing an oversized sweater and tight sweats, and he smelled like lemon and cinnamon. A little different from his usual scent, but it still desperately made me want to bundle him up in my arms.

"Hey," he said softly.

"Hi," I said with a big smile. "You, uh...ready?"

"I'm really unwell," he said, and I could hear the weakness in his voice. My heart dropped.

"Do you need a doctor?" I asked quickly.

"No it's fine, I think it's a stomach flu. I just can't do baseball today."

"What about Brock? Is he okay?"

Kyle looked up toward the stairs, and then nodded.

"Do you want some company? I could stay."

He shook his head, and I started to feel worried I was losing my chance with him and Brock. Kyle definitely looked ill, but was he using that as an excuse to fob me off?

"Brock is okay though, right?"

"He seems fine for now, he's just upstairs playing one of those games you gave him," Kyle said as he leaned heavily on the doorframe to the kitchen. "Britt and Kennedy are away for the weekend so it's just the two of us."

"I'll take him off your hands for a few hours, then," I said. "We can go to the game and you can get some rest." Kyle looked at me like I was crazy, but I held my ground. "The whole pack will be there. There'll be kids his age, probably from his school who he'll recognize."

"They go to the local school?"

"Yes, so I'm sure Brock will be fine. He won't feel out of place."

When Kyle still didn't look convinced I decided to force the issue. It was either that or let him push me away. "Go get him," I said firmly. "I can handle it."

He looked me over and seemed to be considering it for an eternity, and then he gave a small nod just when I heard Brock barreling down the stairs.

"Gavin!" he said, racing over to me. He threw his arms around my waist and I gave him a big bear hug.

"Hey, Brocky," Kyle said softly. "I'm too sick to go—"

"*Dad*," Brock whined.

"It's not my fault I'm sick, Brock, and you should have some consideration for that, but I was going to ask if you want to go without me?"

Brock let go of me and went to hug his dad. "Sorry. But I want you to come too," he said.

"I'd love to but I can barely stand up." Kyle brushed Brock's hair back out of his eyes then gave his son a comforting hug. "You want to go with Gavin?"

"Yeah." Brock nodded quickly.

"Alright," Kyle said. "Come home straight after, though, okay?"

***

Brock raced out of the house, sprinted across the yard, and bounced excitedly as he waited for me at my car. I unlocked it and he dove in, buckling up before I even got close.

"This car is so cool," he said. "It's like something out of a game."

I chuckled as I turned on the engine. "That's how I choose all my stuff. I think to myself, 'what would look cool in one of my games?'"

"Are you working on any other games?" he asked excitedly.

"Yeah, all the time. I don't think anything will be as successful as RuneMaze, but it's still really fun to come up with new worlds and stories," I told him as I started the engine. I pulled away from the house, with just a glance back to make sure Kyle hadn't changed his mind.

"I want to illustrate games and stuff one day," Brock said as he looked out the tinted glass of my car windows.

"Oh yeah?" I asked. "That's really cool, that's like, the most important part of building a game. The visuals either make it or break it."

"That's what I think! But kids at school think it's about the bad guys and the guns."

"Well those kids sound like they don't know what they're talking about," I said with a smile. "What do your friends think?"

Brock was silent for a moment, and I glanced over at him. His eyes were fixed onto the buildings as we passed through the densest area of town and came closer to the homestead, driving north where the houses got larger and the yards were bigger.

"I don't have any friends," he said so quietly I almost didn't hear him… But I did hear him, and the words broke my heart. I wanted to reach over and pull him into a hug. Instead, I looked straight ahead.

"You want to meet some kids today?" I asked. "There are a bunch who go to your school who you might not know."

"I guess," he said, and started fidgeting.

"If they're the idiots who think it's all about guns and bad guys, just give me a signal and we'll get the hell out of there," I said, and Brock let out a little laugh.

"Like a secret hand signal? Like this?" He threw his hand up on top of his head and waggled his fingers around.

I laughed and nodded. "Yep, just like that, very subtle."

"No one will know what it means." He giggled, and I had a good chuckle.

"Does your dad get sick very often?" I asked cautiously.

"Dad? Nah. He hasn't been sick for ages. Maybe his margarita pizza wasn't very good."

"Any idea what makes him feel better when he's sick?"

"Hmm… Peace and quiet."

I laughed again. "Well he's getting plenty of that right now."

"Oh! I know! Chicken noodle soup. He always makes it for me when I feel bad, and he says he loves it too."

"Great." I nodded and quietly formulated a plan.

I was about to pull in through the gates of the homestead when I realized I'd been driving on autopilot. We were supposed to be heading to the sports field in town. I quickly veered back onto the main road, but I caught glimpses of Brock's face as he saw the pack lands for the first time. His mouth was open and his eyes were huge as he sat up straight in his seat. I wound down the electric window and he took in a deep, instinctive breath.

"It smells amazing in this part of town," he said as he looked out of his window. The homestead was fenced but you could still catch glimpses of it from the road.

"It's pretty nice, huh?"

"Wow." He sighed as he took in flashes of the mansions, the intricate architecture of our houses, and the forested mountains that overshadowed the entire community and made it feel like home.

He slumped back into his seat when we turned south to head for the sports field. I could hardly wait to properly show him the homestead.

"Oh, those guys are cool!" Brock said as he spotted Cole and Liam outside on the field. "They're in the grade below me but I see them around and they're always nice."

"So, no hand signal?" I asked, and he laughed and shook his head. "No, they're cool."

I parked, and then we walked over to where the boys were stretching.

"Hey guys, this is Brock. Brock, this is my nephew Cole, and his friend Liam. They're like you."

"Like me..." Brock frowned.

"We're wolf shifters." Cole smiled and held out his hand.

"Oh! I'm not—" Brock glanced at me nervously, and I gave him a reassuring smile.

"It's okay," I said. "I am too."

His eyes almost bulged out of his head before a knowing smile spread across his face. "I knew it," he said smugly, then happily shook Cole's hand.

"Do you play?" Cole asked.

Brock hesitated. "Just video games."

"Cool!" Liam said as he shook Brock's hand too. "Do you play RuneMaze? We play that *a lot*."

"Yeah! I do," Brock said, still clearly shaken at this newly pleasant social interaction.

"Let's play together sometime," Cole said, and then he quickly turned around when Jaxon whistled for the team to gather up on the field.

"We'll see you at school!" Liam called over his shoulder as they ran off.

Brock stood completely still and watched as they left. "Cool," he said quietly as we made our way to the concession stand and stocked up on snacks for the game.

"Can I have one of those or do you have to be in the game?" he asked, pointing to a Timberwood Cubs hat.

"You can definitely have one of those." I put it on his head. He looked at me from under the brim with a huge, goofy smile.

As we watched the game, I decided Brock was a really great kid. He got fully into the game and cheered hard for the Cubs. I had to admit, I'd been a little worried he wouldn't fit in so well, but it really felt like he had always been part of the pack. And a part of my life.

The game was long and the Timberwood Cubs lost a fair fight. Cole flounced off the field when the out-of-towners scored their final home run, and Jaxon chased after him. We caught up with the two of them in the parking lot where Cole was staring at his feet, Liam had an arm around him in solidarity while Jaxon finished up a coaching lecture about hospitality and being a VIP.

I saw Nicole rushing over from the other direction and I waved to her. She smiled and waved as she spotted us. She reached my side at the same time Jaxon did.

"Hi there," Jaxon said, and he immediately looked Brock over.

"Brock, this is Jaxon. He's the coach of the Timberwood Cubs."

"Hello," Brock said politely and offered his hand. Jaxon gave it a firm shake and tipped his hat to Brock.

"You might recognize him from the back of cereal boxes or television commercials," Nicole added as she wrapped an arm around Jaxon's shoulder.

Brock just looked confused.

"I was a pitcher for the Timberwood Wolves," Jaxon remarked. "A little before your time maybe."

Brock laughed nervously and I gave his shoulder a reassuring squeeze. Realizing I needed to take attention off him, I introduced Nicole. "Brock, this is my sister Nicole. She's Cole's mom. Nicole, this is Brock."

"An absolute pleasure to meet you, Brock. Gavin has been telling me a lot about you," she said, ignoring the harsh look I gave her.

"He has?" Brock asked as he glanced from her to me.

"He said he met a couple of cool guys at the convention," she explained, then she quickly diverted her attention to her own son. "Cole, what was that about on the field?"

"Just didn't seem fair," he said.

"But it *was* fair, wasn't it?" Jaxon frowned to show his disapproval.

"Their kids were bigger than ours so they could hit the ball further," Cole grumbled.

"Well that just means we need to work on our batting game," Jaxon replied.

"Or we could get a big kid on the team," Liam announced. "Like Brock!"

"Yeah, I wish I was a big kid like Brock," Cole said, giving Brock a small grin.

Brock just stood dumbfounded until I squeezed his shoulder again and got us out of there. "Well, we need to get going. We have some chicken soup to make."

Chapter 8 - Kyle

The smell of chicken noodle soup woke me up from a long, deep nap in bed. I pulled back the covers and sniffed the air. It smelled too good for it to be Britt or Kennedy's cooking, and besides, they were out of town for the weekend...

As I sat up, nausea hit me again and my head spun.

"Oh god." I groaned and ran a hand over my face. I'd been feeling awful all day, and it had come and gone while Brock and Gavin were at the game. I'd been pottering around the house, organizing my music collection and trying to tidy up, until I finally admitted I had to lie down.

I hadn't really *wanted* Gavin to take Brock to the game alone... But I had to admit having an empty house was exactly what I'd needed. And *now* what I needed was some of that chicken noodle soup.

I threw on my sweats and an oversized Feather Boats hoodie then wandered toward the kitchen, bracing myself against the wall, the couch, and then the door frame in case the dizziness hit me again.

I stopped in the kitchen doorway and absorbed what was there. A handsome man in a tight baseball shirt and slim cut denim jeans, standing over my stove and blowing on a spoon full of soup he'd made for me. If I'd felt dizzy before, the giddiness of this moment just about knocked me out. I practically melted as I leaned into the doorframe. My heart was fluttering, and I could barely believe how happy I was to see him.

"That smells so good," I said quietly, and then laughed when Gavin jumped and almost spilled the spoonful of soup on himself. He chuckled as he spotted me, and then brought the spoon over.

"Try it," he said, and I obeyed. I opened my mouth and let him feed me.

"Mm!" I said as a strong umami flavor hit my tongue. "That's incredible!" I went to grab the spoon out of his hand but he held it out of my reach.

"Just wait, it's almost ready." He headed back to the pot to give it another stir.

I came up behind him and leaned my chin against his shoulder, looking over him at the simmering pot.

"You're making me chicken soup?" I asked.

"A little bird told me it's your go-to food when you're sick. Where do you keep your soup bowls?"

"Cabinet above the fridge," I said as I slumped into a chair at the kitchen table. "Where do you keep my son?"

Gavin laughed and motioned upstairs. "He's in his room. I thought he'd want to help me make dinner but I was wrong. He's playing games with Cole and Liam, some kids from the pack."

"There are kids here?" I just about jumped out of my chair before Gavin gave me a look to say *as if*.

"They're playing together on live," he explained in a very patient tone. I gave him a sheepish grin and shrugged.

"One day I'll learn all the game stuff," I promised.

He pulled three bowls down from the cabinet then placed them on the table before putting a soft kiss on my forehead.

"You don't have to be into video games just because I am."

"No, I know... But it'd be nice if I spoke the same language as you and Brock."

"How're you feeling?" he asked as he ladled out a bowl of soup and stole a few glances at me.

"Nauseous... Dizzy..." I tried to sound nonchalant. Maybe he picked up on it or maybe he didn't, but to me it was obvious was having symptoms of morning sickness. The exact same symptoms I'd had when I was pregnant with Brock. But I also knew it was *way* too early to start freaking out about it, when I *probably* just had a stomach bug. So I kept my eyes on the soup and changed the topic.

"Where'd you learn how to cook?" I asked as he placed a steaming bowl in front of me.

"Well, my sister Nicole and I kind of had to fend for ourselves most of our childhood, so we both learned how to cook early on. Plus, we're *very* critical of each other's cooking, so that spurred us on to get better."

I was just about to ask why he and his sister had to fend for themselves when he ducked into the hallway.

"Brock! Dinner's ready!" His voice was so deep and strong I almost jumped. It felt like the whole house was shaking. After a couple of minutes with no sign of Brock, I couldn't wait a moment longer so I started drinking my soup. It was packed with layers of herbaceous flavors and every mouthful seemed to make me feel better.

"What's in here?" I asked. "Is that heat coming from the ginger?"

"Yes, and an herb called galangal," Gavin said as he pulled up a seat. "It's from south east Asia."

I raised my eyebrows, truly impressed by his culinary skills.

"Brock seemed really happy to meet some packmates today. I think it'll be good for him to know some other shifters who go to his school. Especially some other alphas. It sounds like he's not having such a good time there without friends."

I stopped eating mid-spoonful as I felt my defenses rising. This co-parenting business was moving a little too fast for my liking. But as soon as Brock came bouncing into the kitchen, I relaxed. There was something about his demeanor that seemed different. For one there was a huge smile on his face. That was new; completely different to the usual sulky pout he stomped around the place with.

"Hey Brocky," I said.

"Hey, Dad." He slid into the chair next to me, leaned over, and gave me a kiss on the cheek. I looked at Gavin in shock and he produced a smug grin.

"Are you feeling okay?" Brock asked me with a look of genuine concern on his face.

"I...am! You okay?"

"I'm great. I just played a level with these kids from the baseball today, Cole and Liam. They're younger but they're really cool and pretty smart. Thanks for taking me today, Gavin."

"No problem, pal," Gavin said as he reached over and ruffled Brock's hair.

I stared in awe at the politeness, the affection, and the smile on Brock's face. I could barely believe it. Had I walked into an alternate universe? Maybe there really was some kind of alpha father power Gavin was using to turn my wild son into a nice boy.

We ate dinner and I downed two servings of soup. By the time we were done I felt so much better and my dizziness had disappeared. I was about to stand up to clear the plates when Gavin put his hand on mine and urged me to stay put.

"I've got this. You and Brock go relax on the couch. We picked up a movie on the way home. Start without me, and I'll be there once I'm done with the dishes."

I swallowed and glanced over his shoulder toward the living room. I hadn't signed up for a family night with a guy I'd really just met... But I guess he *was* family. Brock was already grabbing the DVD from the kitchen bench and making his way over to the television.

Brock and I cuddled up together under a blanket and watched the previews while Gavin cleaned up in the kitchen. It felt so good to have someone taking care of things while I felt unwell. Part of me wanted to keep building that wall, kick him out, and prove I could take care of everything myself. But a bigger part of me told me that I'd already done that. I'd shown the whole world I could be a capable single parent, a popular radio host, a kind brother, and a good friend. Where was the harm in letting someone else help out every now and then? After all, that's why here was here, wasn't it? Because I needed his help?

And besides, I was totally giddy about him.

I heard the kitchen sink draining and began getting ridiculously excited just from knowing Gavin was going to be joining us on the couch. A few moments later he snuck up behind me and held out a box of chocolates.

"I wasn't sure if you'd be well enough to eat these, but I thought I'd better get them, just in case..." he whispered in my ear.

Brock made grabby-hands at the box, but I quickly snatched the chocolates out of everyone's reach as we laughed.

"Your chicken soup did the trick. I feel so good I could probably eat this whole box right now!" However, when Gavin settled in next to Brock I shared my chocolates with both of them, and then leaned back on the couch to give Gavin a smile behind Brock's head.

"Thank you," I said softly. Gavin reached out and rubbed my shoulder.

"It's nothing," he replied.

"It's *something*," I insisted. "I really feel so much better."

He lightly squeeze my shoulder then turned back to the movie when Brock gasped and squealed. "Oh my *god,* look!"

We watched all two and a half hours of the movie, and I got through it by nibbling on chocolates and closing my eyes whenever I felt my dizziness coming back. But by the time the credits were rolling, I wasn't doing too great.

"I think your soup's magic is wearing off," I grumbled. "I think I need to go and lie down."

"Dad, is Gavin staying the night?" Brock asked quickly.

I glanced at Gavin, who glanced right back at me. I felt a flash of doubt, but it went just as swiftly as it came.

"If he'd like to, I think he should," I said, and watched as Gavin grinned at me happily.

"Yes!" Brock pumped his fist in the air.

"Bedtime, Brocky," I said. "I'll come get you tucked in."

We got up without too much grumbling from Brock, and I started up the stairs. I got all of three steps from the bottom before I got a head-spin and had to lean against the wall.

"Oh god."

Gavin rushed to my side.

"You okay, Dad?" Brock asked from the top of the stairs while I slid down the wall and sat heavily on a step.

"I'm okay."

Gavin crouched and put a hand on my forehead. "Get ready for bed, Brock. I'll be up in a minute," he said before turning all of his attention back to me. "Let's get you to bed, okay?" He looped an arm around my back.

"I'm fine, really, I can walk—" But Gavin easily hoisted me up in his arms then started carrying me to my room. "Oh, this is good too, I guess." I laughed and looped my arms around his neck.

"You ever felt like this before?" he asked cautiously as he lay me down gently on my futon.

"*Mhm*," I murmured, my lips shut tight.

"With Brock, huh?" He pulled the covers up to my chest. I cleared my throat and gave him a look to say *shut it*.

"It's way too early for that," I told him.

"I mean… Your heat did stop pretty much right after, right? I noticed your scent had changed."

I waved him off. "Even if I was… Even if I *am*… No need to have this conversation now, or for another few weeks, alright?" I knew I sounded kind of snappy and I grimaced, but Gavin gave me an understanding nod and ran a hand over my shoulder.

"I'm going to help Brock to bed. Anything I should know?"

"If you can get him into bed without playing video games, you'll be my hero."

"Consider it done."

***

As soon as he left the room I must have fallen right to sleep. I didn't know how long I was out for, but I woke up with a start. Gavin wasn't in the bed next to me. The house was silent.

I hauled myself out of bed and was gratefully not dizzy. I padded my way up the stairs and found Brock's bedroom light shining into the hallway.

Should have known better. I was sure I was going to walk in and find the two of them playing a video game, and then I'd look at the clock and find that it was four in the morning. Instead, what I saw when I stood in the doorway was Gavin sitting beside Brock who was tucked up tight in his bed, and two of them were laughing and telling stories.

Gavin held a sketchbook of Brock's, and Brock was pointing out the monsters and different types of plants he'd drawn in there.

"This one is a plant that gets all of its power from the wind instead of the sun."

"I love that one," Gavin said, pointing to a picture.

"That's a-a— That one's a Pegasus but with other kinds of powers," Brock stuttered in a way that meant he was equal parts tired and excited.

"Very cool. I hope I dream about that one tonight," Gavin said.

Brock chuckled, and I watched as his eyelids started to slip shut. "Hm, me too."

"Sleep well, Brock," Gavin said as he closed the book.

"I love you, Gavin," Brock mumbled.

My heart swelled, and then I physically began to shake as Gavin smiled down at our son and whispered, "I love you too."

I was shocked at how it sounded like the most natural thing in the world. The two of them seemed so in sync. Without meaning to, I cleared my throat and Gavin looked up. He smiled at me warmly, and motioned for me to come in.

"Sorry we took so long, we were talking about art and monsters," he said quietly.

Brock sleepily peeled his eyes open. "Goodnight, Dad. I love you."

"I love you too, Brocky," I whispered as I leaned down and planted a kiss on each of his plump cheeks.

As Brock closed his eyes again, Gavin reached out and took my hand. I gave his grip a little squeeze, then led him out, switching off the light and closing the door behind us.

"You alright with the stairs?" he asked as we padded down the stairwell.

"I'm feeling one hundred percent better, but if you're offering to carry me again, I won't say no." In one swift motion, Gavin lifted me up into his arms. I let out a loud laugh and he chuckled as he raced down the stairs to my bedroom. We fell into bed with a heavy *thud* and he immediately planted little kisses all over my face.

"I'm glad you're feeling better," he said. "I've been wanting to do this all day."

I tilted my head to the side and accepted kisses down my neck. He slid his hands up the inside of my hoodie and gently tugged it off. Before I could even think about kissing him, he trailed his lips down my torso, pecking sweetly at my collarbones.

"Still feel okay?" he asked gently as he looked up at me.

"Mmm," I moaned, too interested in running my hands over his shoulders and greedily squeezing his muscles through the thin fabric of his baseball tee.

"Good... Just tell me if you want me to stop," he said before tracing a line of kisses down my belly. I let out a deep sigh and relaxed back against the futon, feeling my whole body melting under his touch. As he flicked his tongue at the space above my belly button, my slick started to flow—nowhere near as heavily as last time, but he inhaled deeply, and then let out a satisfied moan.

My cock throbbed at the sound, thickening significantly as he reached for the waistband of my sweats and tugged at them. I lifted my hips so he could wriggle them off my body, and then I lay there in the dark, naked, watching his every move. His body was perfected silhouetted against the bright moonlight shining through the window, and I gazed hungrily at the outline of his muscular frame.

Gavin continued kissing where he'd left off, nibbling and licking around my belly button. The dark scruff on his chin scratched at my soft skin and I reflexively bucked my hips. With a grin, held me in place, my hip bones jutting into his meaty palms. I experimented with squirming around, only to find his grip was unwavering, and then I suddenly felt his lips pressing against the underside of my cock.

"Oh fuck!" I took in a desperate breath as he lapped with broad, warm strokes along my length. No one had ever done that before, and I couldn't believe how incredible it felt. "That's... Oh my god, that's..."

Gavin chuckled before taking the head of my dick into his mouth. I grabbed at the sheets, and without any thought tried to thrust more of my cock past those soft lips, but Gavin kept me pressed against the bed. I whimpered in frustration, ready to beg, but he chuckled again, and then started to suck.

"That's so fucking good," I managed to groan as he began bobbing up and down, taking an extra inch with every move. Soon enough, he was taking all of my cock into his warm mouth and I was desperately gasping for air. I grabbed at his hair with one hand while holding tightly to the sheets with my other. I moaned and writhed, going slightly crazy, but just as heat began to infuse my balls he pulled up, the head of my cock decadently popping free.

"Do you want to fuck?" I asked, thinking that was why he'd stopped.

Gavin grinned. "No. I just want to drive you wild."

I practically snarled at him, proving how wild he was already making me. Gavin laughed, and then took his t-shirt off before gripping my cock and slowly sliding his hand from base to tip. It wasn't his mouth but it still felt good.

"Faster," I whispered.

"Just wait." He urged my legs open, and then before I actually knew what he was going to do, he pushed his thumb into my slick hole. My muscles instinctively clenched, and I felt light headed again, but this time with a surge of pleasure.

"Oh god."

He jerked my cock with the same rhythm as he pushed his thumb in and out of my hole. Within seconds everything felt like one, warm massage, flowing from inside my ass, down through my balls, and up to the very tip of my cock. I strained for breath, feeling like I could come any moment.

"Do you want to come?" Gavin asked softly, as though reading my mind.

I gasped and nodded, and then stuffed a fistful of the sheets into my mouth, trying to muffle my frantic moans.

He groaned, obviously pleased with my response, and started to jerk me off faster while pushing his thumb deeper in and out of my wet hole. My stomach tightened and my legs started to shake, and I became one big mess of sensation.

"Come for me. C'mon, come for me, Kyle. *Come for me.*" The authority in his voice pushed me over the edge. I arched my back and closed my eyes as I struggled to hold in a deep, guttural moan. My cock throbbed in his hand and pulsed ropes of cum over my belly while a warm, sweet orgasm rolled through my body.

I gasped for air and fell back against the bed, arms and legs totally limp. But just as I was melting into the aftershocks of release, Gavin let go of my cock. I heard the sound of a zipper and glanced down to see that he'd pulled his dick out of his jeans and was jerking it hard and fast. In the shadows, I could see his grip was tight and strong around his thick rod. My cock twitched lazily and a small thrill ran through my body.

Gavin's thumb was covered in my slick, which shone wetly as he slathered it over his cock. He let out a gruff grunt of pleasure and started to pump his dick even faster. I bit down on my bottom lip and watched, transfixed, as he leaned forward and angled his cock so the tip was almost resting against my half-hard, completely satisfied dick.

"Fuck," he grunted. "Fuck yes!"

With a furious thrust of his hips, Gavin started to come. His cock shot load after load of creamy cum all over my dick, spraying my abdomen and mixing with my own ejaculate, and I moaned at the thrill of being covered in our molten juices.

Gavin shook out the last of his come and gave a satisfied groan as he sat back on his heels. "You're incredible," he whispered as he ran his hands over my legs.

"Uh, *you* did all the work."

He chuckled. "Trust me, it wouldn't be that good without you."

After we got cleaned up, Gavin slid into bed beside me and wrapped his arms around my body, pulling me into a warm embrace. I lay my head against his chest and let out a soft, satisfied sigh. All of my muscles felt heavy and relaxed, and I was ready to fall asleep. Gavin traced his fingers along my arm, soothing me even more.

"I could get used to this," he said softly.

"Me too," I said sleepily. "I'm really glad you found us. Or we found you."

"So am I."

"I think Brock is really glad too," I added.

"He's really a great kid. You did a good job on your own."

An oppressive sadness moved through me. I couldn't help but wonder what it would have been like to raise Brock with Gavin by my side...

"Do you think this is a mistake?" I asked, suddenly wide awake.

"What? No, I want to be in his life—"

"No, I mean, you and me. What if things don't work out between us?" I asked in a voice that was barely audible.

"We're fated mates," Gavin said gently as he smoothed a hand over my back. "I wish I could show you exactly what that means. How special it is."

"I wish you could too."

"I'm going to be here for you and Brock no matter what. Even if things didn't work out between us, I want to be part of his life."

"Mm." I nodded and started to relax again. "I suppose we should tell him *why* you'll be hanging around so much."

Gavin laughed and gave my shoulder a squeeze. He leaned down and pressed a kiss against the top of my head. "I'd love for him to know I'm his father. If you feel ready for it..."

"Mm." I nodded again as I started to drift off to sleep. "Soon."

Chapter 9 - Gavin

October slipped into November, and the weather instantly snapped. Cold winds rolled off the ocean and ripped through Timberwood Cove. The homestead was a little sheltered by the mountains to the north, but I still pulled my long, black overcoat tight around my body as I hurried from my car into my house. Nicole raced behind me and slapped my back to encourage me to hurry up as I fumbled with my keys at the front door.

We tumbled inside and I pushed all of my weight against the door to get it shut while Nicole unraveled all three of the oversized scarves she was wearing.

"That wind is *insane*," she complained as she hung her scarves on the coat rack and took the shopping bags out of my hands. "And *you're* insane. How much stuff did you buy?"

"Enough to let the kid know I care about him," I said gruffly as I hung my overcoat then brushed off the twigs and leaves that clung to the fibers.

"More like, enough to impress your mate that you're rich," she said as she hauled the bags to the kitchen table.

"I'm sure he's figured that out already," I said as I ran a hand through my hair and followed her.

"Yeah, I'm actually sure he knows everything about you, considering how much time you've been spending together these last few weeks." She started unpacking the games and consoles I'd brought Brock.

"Jealous?" I asked as I went to grab whiskey glasses from the cabinet.

"Of course I am, I miss you. And I can't believe you still haven't organized time for me to get to know *my* nephew!"

I sighed and placed the glasses heavily on the bar. "After tonight, Brock will know that this is his pack, and then you can smother him in all of the family-lovin' you want."

"Oh good, I can get back at you for all the ways you've corrupted Cole."

I laughed and raised my eyebrows at my sister as I reached for a bottle of our favorite whiskey. "*Corrupted*? Please, that kid is wild enough without my influence."

"Rude, but true. And this wind makes him ten times worse. Him *and* Paco. They've been running riot. I had to send them both to Linc's for the weekend just so I'd have the chance to clean the house."

I stopped pouring our drinks and looked at her seriously. "You are a really good mom."

Nic waved me off, but a happy grin twitched at the sides of her mouth.

"You are," I insisted as I finished pouring off her drink and placed it in front of her. "How did you figure it out?"

"Oh I didn't." She swirled her glass and waited for me to sit with her. "I just made it up as I went along."

"That explains why Cole is such a terror," I quipped with a grin.

"Rude!" She slapped my arm.

"But seriously, how did you learn how to do it? The parenting thing?"

"I *am* serious. I *did* just make it up as I went."

I looked down at my drink and frowned.

"Oh," Nicole said with clarity. "You're asking how can *you* learn to be a dad?"

I cleared my throat and nodded.

"Well, buying a shitload of presents to celebrate a big day is a good start," she said as she motioned to the stack of games. "Being consistent is important. Also having a sense of humor. Honestly, anything else is a bonus."

"That sounds like the omega basics, though…"

Nicole swirled her drink again. "I suppose it is. I never had to worry about the alpha side of things, not with Linc around. If I'd had to do it alone I would feel pretty lost since you and I didn't have an alpha role model."

"Right. It's intimidating. I need to show Brock how to deal with alpha issues, but I was never shown how to do that. I mean, I went off the rails for a bit as a teenager and a young adult. I drank to excess, fucked to distraction, and if it wasn't for Greer, I probably would have remained that way. I was a mess."

"You're not now. You've matured."

"If that's a dig at being old, just remember, you'll be my age one day."

Nicole laughed, but then shook her head. "No. What I mean is, you've turned out to be a successful entrepreneur who now has a head on his shoulders."

"I know, and most of the time I feel confident with Brock. But what if that changes when he knows I'm his dad? There's a bigger chance to fuck things up. More on the line."

Nicole put a hand on my arm. "You won't fuck things up. You're smart, and strong, and capable. And you have a whole pack behind you. Maybe Linc or Jaxon can give you pointers about alpha dad stuff?"

"Mm." I nodded, genuinely considering it.

"More importantly, you have *me*. And the sooner you organize some time for Brock and me to chill, the sooner I can help!"

I laughed and held up my glass. "To expanding our weird little family."

"Cheers to that!"

***

With a few glasses of whiskey warming my belly and a hot roast dinner in the oven, I was feeling confident when I heard Kyle's car in the driveway. Over the last few weeks of spending almost every day together, I'd become attuned to the exact sound of his car engine. My wolf's ears pricked up and I felt its happiness. This was Kyle and Brock's first time at my house, and I savored the way that the sound of his tires on the gravel in my driveway made me feel giddy.

"Come in, come in." I smiled at him and Brock from the front door as they hurried through my front garden, both of them bundled up in jackets and scarves. All I could see were Kyle's eyes crinkling as he beamed at me from between the beanie pulled down low over his eyebrows and a scarf that was bundled up as high as his nose. I stopped him in the doorway to kiss his cold, chilled cheeks, and Brock pushed past us into the heat.

"He's excited to see you," Kyle said quietly. "I told him we had some big news to share. He's going to be so happy."

"Does he have any idea what we're going to talk about," I asked as I started unwrapping scarves from Kyle's neck, as if I were unwrapping a gift.

"I don't think so," he replied, and I was caught off guard by how delectable his lips looked as I revealed them. I felt myself pulled forward, and I pressed a soft warm kiss against his cold lips. He moaned and kissed me back, until we heard Brock clearing his throat.

We chuckled and looked at him as he stood in the hallway with his hands on his hips.

"Are you going to give us a tour, or what?" he asked impatiently.

"I am. Just wait while I get your dad unwrapped."

"I *really* want to see your games room!" he exclaimed, shaking out his hands excitedly.

I gave them a quick tour, and sure enough Brock fell in love with my gaming console. Kyle was impressed with my sound system but didn't say much else, though he did spend a long time looking up at the high ceilings and at the ornate glasswork. Once Brock got set up in the games room playing the latest releases, I went into the kitchen to tend to the roast.

Kyle came up beside me as I was turning a hot pan of nearly-done roast potatoes.

"Mm, that smells incredible," he said.

"I hope you'll like it. It's not chicken soup, but it's tasty. How've you been feeling today?" I asked.

"Great. No longer dizzy, and my appetite is back."

"Hm, that's good," I replied quietly as a wave of sadness washed over me.

"I guess it was just a stomach bug after all," he said.

I was surprised by how disappointed I felt. It's not like I'd been counting on Kyle being pregnant, but the possibility of it had made me excited. My wolf had been on high alert for the last few weeks too, in ultra-protective mode over our possible cub, and it had felt good to have that kind of alpha energy pulsing through me. I sighed as I let that feeling go.

Kyle reached over my shoulder and snatched a piping hot piece of potato off the pan. I gasped and spun around to snatch it back, but he was already dashing off across the kitchen, juggling it between his hands and blowing on it.

"Thief!" I cried, and he let out a wicked cackle as he disappeared into the living room. I would have chased him if the timer hadn't gone off on the oven.

We settled in for dinner together, and Brock practically sucked down an entire plate of roast dinner before Kyle and I had even started on our sides.

"Hungry, huh?" I asked, ruffling his hair.

"*Mhm,*" he mumbled with a mouthful of potato.

I served him up more meat and vegetables, and as I was reaching to get him another helping of potatoes, Kyle shot me a look and kicked me under the table. I put down the tongs and left Brock with the food on his plate. I figured Kyle knew a hell of a lot more about the dietary needs of his kid than I did. And when I thought about it, I probably wouldn't want to feel too full when I got big news.

After dinner, I cleared away the plates and Kyle leaned forward and caught Brock's attention.

"We have something we'd like to talk to you about. It's pretty big news. Would you like to hear it now?"

I glanced over at Brock as I put the dishes in the sink and saw the serious look on his face.

"Yeah, I want to hear it now."

"Alright." Kyle looked at me. I wiped my hands on a dish towel and hurried over to sit by his side. Brock glanced nervously between us.

"Are you two breaking up or something?" he asked quietly.

"No, nothing like that," Kyle said quickly before looking at me again. I gave him a reassuring smile, and then looked at Brock. It was my first chance to show him how an alpha reacts in a serious situation, and I didn't want to fuck it up.

"This might sound scary, but I know you can handle it so I'm going to tell it to you straight," I said.

Brock swallowed nervously, but he sat up and pushed out his chest.

"I know your dad raised you all by himself, right? And you never knew your alpha father?"

"That's right," he replied bravely though he began to bite his bottom lip.

"Well, we just found out something about that." I glanced at Kyle, and then back at Brock. "I'm actually your alpha dad."

Brock winced. His eyes darted from me to Kyle, and then down at his hands. Kyle reached across the table. "Did you hear what Gavin said, Brocky?"

Brock just nodded a little as his chin started to tremble.

I swallowed down a lump of self-doubt. "I was really happy when I found out I'm your father, Brock."

He nodded again, still biting his bottom lip.

"Brocky?" Kyle asked quietly. "What's up?"

Brock looked up with tears in his eyes and a look of confusion on his face. "Why weren't you at my birthday parties?" he asked in a tiny voice that made my heart break.

"Oh, Brocky. He didn't know," Kyle said, rushing to his side. "When I got pregnant with you, we didn't know Gavin was your dad. We just found out. He would have been at your parties if he'd known."

"Of course I would have. Brocky, I'm here now, and I want to be in your life."

Brock stared at us, and then started to sob into Kyle's embrace. My chest ached with the strength of my wolf's protective instincts. I desperately wanted to hold my son in my arms. Instead, I stayed put and grit my teeth, giving him and Kyle the space to cry it out.

"Do you want Gavin to be your dad?" Kyle eventually asked. "You don't have to answer now, but you should think about it."

"Yes!" Brock wiped furiously at his tears.

"It's okay to cry," I told him. "It's okay for alphas to cry."

Kyle reached out and motioned for me to join them in their hug. I was over there in flash, wrapping my arms around both of them. I pressed a kiss against Brock's forehead and his sobs started to slow as he leaned his head against my chest.

"I'm so sorry I wasn't around. I'm going to make it up to you. I promise I'm here with you from now on," I told him as I kissed the top of his head over and over again.

My heart beat hard and fast, and I felt tears brimming in my eyes too. Kyle rubbed his hand over my back and his touch made my wolf sigh with relief. It was such a comfort to be so close to my mate and our son.

"Are you why I'm a wolf?" Brock asked as he looked up at me.

I nodded. "That's right. You're part of a pack of wolf shifters who live here in Timberwood Cove. You have a huge family who are really excited to meet you."

Brock's eyes widened in excitement and he sniffled. He bit down on his lip and I could tell he wanted to ask something.

"What is it? You can ask me anything," I said.

"It's just… I don't think I'm a very good wolf."

Kyle let out a sigh and looked up at me.

"Why don't you think you're a very good wolf, Brocky?" he asked our son.

"I can't always control him. He's always there, prowling, and I'm often scared to let him out, but I also want to so badly. And when I shift, he wants to run, but I'll only shift in my room, and sometimes he gets angry."

I heard Kyle moan as if he were in pain. I gripped his hand and gave it a reassuring squeeze.

"That's because he's a young wolf, and you're a young alpha, but I can show you how to control him."

"You can?"

I laughed. "Yes. Of course. That's what alpha dads are for, right?"

"Can you show me right now?" he asked, bouncing excitedly.

I looked at Kyle who gave me a nod and a huge smile.

"Let's go to the backyard, it'll be easier out there."

***

The moon was waxing and almost full, and my backyard looked silver under its light. The western redcedars and mountain hemlocks danced dramatically in the harsh wind that howled and rushed through the woods. Brock stood in the center of my lawn, bundled up in his hoodie and scarf, looking up at me with his whole attention.

"First lesson. Listen to your wolf. You can trust it," I told him.

"But what if it wants me to do naughty things?" he asked.

"Naughty? Like what?"

"Sometimes I can feel it wanting me to snatch food or go running after cute omegas at school… Or hurt someone who's being mean to me."

I didn't hesitate. "*Listen* to your wolf. It's always right. Those instincts mean you're hungry, or attracted to someone, or you need to defend yourself. You don't have to *act* the way your wolf tells you to act. But you should listen to it. You can trust it."

Brock nodded and shoved his hands in his pockets. "Okay. Trust my wolf. Okay… I can do that."

"The best way to control him is to let him out. You were right to shift in your room if you weren't being supervised, but if you don't let your wolf run free, he will keep pushing, and you don't want him to get the upper hand. So, here, with me watching you, you're safe. I won't let anything bad happen to you. And I won't let your wolf do anything naughty."

Brock nodded again. The wind howled through the trees and I heard branches cracking. Brock looked around, like he worried someone else might see him shift.

"It's okay. You're safe here," I said again. "The only people who are here are wolf shifters like us."

My wolf dug at my chest, wanting to meet Brock's wolf so badly. I warned him to calm down, not wanting Brock's wolf to sense how frantic mine was and decide to retreat.

"Ready?" I asked. Brock glanced up at me, and then grinned.

Suddenly, a handsome young wolf stood in front of me with a long snout and bright, curious eyes. I stood back and my heart soared with pride as I admired my son in his wolf form for the first time. His fuzzy fur looked adorable, with light and dark patches of brown mingled with white. He was lit by the moon, and his pink tongue flapped excitedly out of the side of his mouth. He looked past me, back toward the house. I turned and saw Kyle on the back balcony, wrapped up in a blanket, tears of wonder and joy in his eyes.

Brock let out a happy yelp and I spun around to find him bouncing back and forth on the lawn. I chuckled, and shifted into my wolf.

My nose was full of the scent of my kin, his smell both strange and familiar. If I hadn't already known him in human form, my wolf would have instantly known who he was, and in both recognition and delight, I lifted my muzzle and howled. Brock immediately joined me, his voice coming out broken and jagged at first, as if he had never howled in his wolf form before, but by the time we reached a crescendo, he was able to hold a strong note. I barked happily and bounded forward to play with him. I nipped gently at his forelegs and he sprung back before dashing forward and biting at my haunches. He bit down a little too firmly, and I let him know with a short yelp and a soft growl. He cowered and lowered his head in apology. I dashed forward and licked at his face before I bounced back and encouraged him to keep playing with me.

The wind dropped, and I heard the sound of canine paws sprinting along the forest floor heading toward us. I smelled them before they appeared; our closest pack members. Jaxon broke through the tree-line and bounded straight over to us. Right on his heels was Nicole, Linc and Cole, with Liam sprinting up behind them.

Brock looked at them with cautious eyes as they encircled him. Each one slowly approached and sniffed him over as he sniffed them back. When Cole's wolf came near, Brock let out an excited bark and bounded forward. Cole jumped back in a fake-out and then dashed forward and tackled Brock to the ground. Brock let out a playful yelp, and then Liam was on him in an instant. Brock's larger wolf knocked them both off without a problem, and he reared up on his back legs before pouncing and roughhousing with his new friends. He again landed a bite that was a little too hard, but Cole didn't make a big deal about it, he just bit back.

Nicole came up beside me and rested her cheek against my shoulder. I let out a happy sigh and lovingly licked her face. It felt incredible that our pack was growing...

I looked over my shoulder and found Kyle still watching, with equal measure of adoration and amazement on his face.

Something inside me opened, flowering in my chest. Kyle was my fated mate, the one meant for me, but he was so much more than that. He was kind and generous, loving and incredibly sexy. He'd already made me want to be a better man, and he'd given me the opportunity to have a family of my own. He was a great father to Brock, and I knew he'd be a great father to more pups. My heart surged at the idea, and I knew then, with all the clarity of my wolf's instincts, that I wanted him as my chosen mate. I wanted to claim him. And I didn't want to wait.

Chapter 10 - Kyle

Watching Brock romping with Gavin and the pack of other wolves in the yard felt shockingly normal. I brought the blanket closer around my shoulders as the wind whipped through the yard, and I admired how beautiful all of their coats looked under the moonlight.

Suddenly, Gavin's wolf turned and stared at me with an intensity I'd never seen in my life. I swallowed nervously and brought a hand up to my heart. I felt something there, tugging me forward. I desperately wanted to be with him.

I raced down the stairs and by the time I made it to the backyard, everyone had shifted into their human forms. I felt disoriented, like what I'd just seen was a dream.

"Dad!" Brock cried as he raced forward and threw his arms around my waist. "Did you see that? Did you see how I was a wolf?"

"I did!" I laughed as I walked with him toward Gavin and the others. "You looked *amazing*. Much bigger than when you did it as a little pup." I wished I'd had the opportunity to see him shift more often, but Brock had always been too scared to shift in front of me again, so it was good he felt comfortable now. In such a short time, Gavin had already given Brock so much confidence. I couldn't help but be grateful for that.

"Duh. I'm older now. And it's *so* cool not to be the only one!"

As I stopped in front of Gavin he held my gaze, and then he held my hands. I had an inkling something serious was about to happen.

"This is Nicole," he said, as his sister stepped forward. She looked like the absolute feminine form of Gavin. Where he had brawn, she was slight and slim, but they shared the same plump lips and angled facial features.

"I have been *dying* to meet you," she said as she pulled me into a tight hug. "Sorry we couldn't meet earlier, it seems my brother was keeping you all to himself."

"So greedy of him!" I liked her already.

"Oh god, that *voice*," she said as pulled back and fake-swooned. "I listen to your show all the time, but your voice is even better in real life! Oh, and this is my son Cole, Gavin's nephew."

"Does that mean we're cousins?" Brock asked Cole, who smiled and nodded enthusiastically.

"*Cool*!" Brock said, looking up at me. I smiled down at him and ruffled his hair.

"And this is Jaxon, our pack alpha, and his son Liam," Gavin said, urging me to meet their leader.

"Nice to meet you," I said pleasantly, shaking everyone's hand. Liam smiled at me, and I instantly knew he would be a calming influence on Brock.

When I turned back to face Gavin, my breath caught in my lungs. He was down on one knee and looking up at me with a surprising seriousness. He reached out and took my hands in his as he wet his lips. His hands were soothingly warm, and I melted under his touch.

"Kyle... I want you to join us," he said. "You're the father of my child, and you are the most beautiful man I've ever met, and I've met... *Never mind*. But you... You are the love of my life. I told you I wanted to show you what it means to be fated mates. So, Kyle Shannon, will you let me claim you so you can mine forever?"

A harsh wind blew so hard it almost knocked me over, and I suddenly remembered I needed to breathe. I dragged in a deep breath and looked at the faces of the pack surrounding me. I'd literally just met them, but there was no denying they already felt like family...

I closed my eyes and shook my head to clear my thoughts; and felt Gavin's grip tighten.

"That wasn't a no," I told him as my eyes shot open. Relief washed over his face, followed by a slight frown.

"Is it a...yes?" he asked hopefully.

"Please say yes, Dad!"

My heart was pounding so hard I could barely hear the gale that whipped through the trees. This was insane. This was *insane*!

"Can I call my best friend before I answer?"

***

I was an idiot. I should have just said yes the moment Gavin had asked because the second I'd hesitated I could tell I'd seriously hurt his feelings, not to mention disappointing Brock. But I'd been too overwhelmed to think straight.

Gavin had graciously nodded, given me a soft kiss and told me he would still be Brock's father whatever I decided. Brock had sulked, and it had taken Gavin's assurances that nothing would change between them to drag a smile out of him. We'd headed back to Gavin's house, and while Gavin and Brock went to play video games, I sat in Gavin's bedroom with the door closed.

My hands trembled slightly as I dialed Trevor's number, already knowing what he was going to say, but needing to hear it. After all, he'd been my best friend for years and had helped me so much with Brock, not to mention we'd sworn a blood oath to be at each other's weddings. So one way or another, Trevor needed to know what was going on.

"Gavin just asked me to...kind of marry him," I said the second Trevor answered.

"Oh my god! When's the wedding? I need to get my suit cleaned! Was it romantic? Oh this is going to be so good for Brock."

"Look, I haven't said yes, I wanted to ask you—"

"What? Kyle! Say yes! *Obviously*! What the hell are you thinking? Say yes! Go and tell him right now."

I laughed and ran a hand over my face. That was the exact response I was expecting from him but... "Don't you think it's too soon?"

"No! Why? Do you?"

"Well, I've only known him—"

"Do you love him?"

"I—"

"Have you ever felt this way about anyone else ever before?"

"No, but that's—"

"Can you imagine your life feeling fulfilled *without* him in it?" Trevor asked, his voice softening now as he realized he was asking me questions *he* wanted to answer for himself one day.

I felt my throat closing, and it took me a few seconds to respond. "No, I can't." Being in love with Gavin wasn't my issue. I think I fell in love with him almost as soon as I saw him again.

Why else would I have agreed to go out to dinner with him? Why else would I have allowed him into my life? What worried me was that final step…

"So?"

"He wants me to become a wolf shifter. To give me a claiming bite."

"You're his fated mate, of *course* he wants to claim you. It's only natural. Is that why you didn't say yes?"

"Do you think it's a weird thing to do?"

"Oh, honey, no. I've wanted to become a wolf shifter since, well, for *ever*. It just means he loves you and wants you to be together the way his wolf's nature intended."

"So you think it's a good idea?"

"Yes!"

I smiled, relaxing for the first time since Gavin asked me.

"I'm so pleased for you, Kyle. Now, go and tell your wolf he can claim you!"

I nodded even though Trevor couldn't see me. "I will."

After hanging up I sat on the end of Gavin's bed for a moment, collecting my thoughts. I wasn't sure what had spooked me. Gavin was perfect for Brock, perfect for me. There was no real reason why I shouldn't accept Gavin's proposal.

I got up and slowly walked to Gavin's games room. The door was open and I heard both Gavin and Brock laughing as they argued over who was winning whatever race they were playing.

"Hey, no cheating," Brock said.

"That's not cheating, it's being smart."

I poked my head into the room, and I suppose it was enough for them both to know I was there. They both stopped playing and looked at me, a mix of hope and apprehension on their faces.

"Well?" Gavin asked.

"Yes," I said.

* * *

Two days later I watched the full moon rising over the horizon before the sun had even set. I was getting claimed tonight, and I'd planned a special show to celebrate even though I wasn't going to be here to actually play any records. My producer had agreed for me to pre-record the show, so as soon as I'd made my own personal dedication to Gavin, I'd pressed play, and then started giggling as the airways filled with wolf-themed love songs. Who knew there were even that many made.

Gavin was waiting for me when I got home, and I felt like a giddy teenager when I saw his car parked in the driveway. I raced inside to see him sitting in a large chair in the living room while Britt and Kennedy fawned over him, giving him different accessories that would match his deep red suit.

"Here, try my yellow bow-tie," Kennedy said as she nudged Britt aside.

"That is ochre, not yellow. And it does *not* look good with the burgundy suit. Here, wear my black scarf," Britt said, nudging Kennedy back.

"I think you should wear them both," I said. Everyone turned to look at me, but my gaze was locked on Gavin. He was caught mid-laugh, and the creases beside his eyes were deeper than ever. He smiled at me lovingly, then started folding the scarf. As he stood and made his way over to me, he placed it into his jacket as a pocket square, crimping the corner to it sat straight and flush against his broad chest.

"You look amazing," I said, straightening the bow-tie.

A high-pitched squeal of excitement came from the women in the living room, and I rolled my eyes at them over my mate-to-be's shoulder.

"Go and get ready," Gavin said. "I'll try and keep these two off you."

I grinned as I headed to my bedroom. I had intended to wear an old suit I had tucked away in my wardrobe, but when I opened the door I saw a deep blue suit laid out on my bed, complete with a tie to match the color of Gavin's suit. I gasped, realizing he must have bought it for me. I was about to go back out there and thank him before I realized I didn't have enough time. *And* I'd be putting myself in Britt and Kennedy's clutches.

I dressed quickly, and then admired myself in the full-length mirror while trying not to allow the tears that had formed in my eyes to spill over. I was getting married, claimed, *whatever*. I was going to be Gavin's.

Taking a deep breath I managed to pull myself together, and then with little more than a final glance at my thirty-year-old no longer to be single self, I went to join the only man who was ever meant to be mine.

"Ready," I said as I entered in the living room. Both Britt and Kennedy were nowhere to be seen, and only Gavin stood waiting for me.

"I noticed," he said with a light smile. "And very handsome you look too."

"I would say it's not traditional to see the groom before the wedding, but I guess this isn't a traditional wedding."

"It's better. It's where I make you mine."

I shivered at the possessive quality of his voice, and he smirked before planting a soft kiss on my lips. "Let's go."

***

As we drove toward the homestead, I could see the Wolf Lodge in the distance. It almost seemed to glow under the light of the full moon. I glanced out the windows of Gavin's car and wondered if this was the last time Timberwood Cove would look like *this* to me… Would anything look the same ever again? I bit on my bottom lip and tried to keep my nerves at bay by stealing glances at Gavin as he drove. He was confident, centered, and focused—and being around him made me feel a little bit of the same.

Gavin and I had insisted the ceremony wasn't to be a big affair, but when we arrived at the Lodge the place still looked stunning, with fairy lights strung from all the rafters and a buffet feast being served along tables that spanned the hall.

I spotted Brock playing with Cole and Liam, and I found that most of the pack had arrived along with Trevor, Britt, and Kennedy. The three humans were all dressed to the nines and talking with Jaxon. I caught the tail end of their conversation as I walked over.

"Top secret, okay," Trevor said with wide, wild eyes. "A complete secret. Not to be revealed to anyone. Got it."

Jaxon pointed at him with a stern look on his face. "Seriously."

"I wouldn't!" Trevor declared. "I've been keeping your kind a secret for years."

I nodded as I wrapped an arm around his shoulder in solidarity. "He has. He's the one who told me about shifters in the first place, and he's kept Brock's identity quiet for over ten years. So has Britt and Kennedy."

Jaxon looked at all of us, then he seemed to accept his pack wouldn't be in any danger from my friends and family because he gave us all a brief nod and Trevor a pat on the shoulder before he walked away.

"He's cute," Kennedy said, waggling her eyebrows.

"They're *all* cute," Britt retorted as she rolled her eyes at her girlfriend.

"That one is especially cute," Trevor whispered to me, and then he motioned to a member of the pack who had his back to us as he arranged flowers in vases by the banquet table.

"How can you tell?"

"Oh, you know…"

The guy turned to the side, and I gasped. "Trevor! That's Jason, the guy from the flower shop, the one who drives you crazy."

"Oh, is it?" he asked in an all-too innocent voice. "I couldn't tell, I'm not wearing my glasses."

"You don't wear glasses."

Suddenly, I felt Gavin put his hands around my waist. I instantly leaned back into him and released a soft sigh. He chuckled, and then pressed his lips to my ear. "Are you ready?"

I smiled "Yes, I am."

***

We stood outside in the manicured gardens of the Lodge, under the bright full moon. The pack crowded in and created a protective circle around us.

Nicole stood by Gavin's side, while Britt stood beside mine. Gavin took my hands in his and gave me a reassuring squeeze. In contrast to his steady, warm hands, I realized I'd been shaking like a leaf. His touch immediately helped me relax.

Jaxon held up his hand, and everybody fell silent.

I could hear my heart beating heavily as he spoke. "By the beauty of the moon, we accept a new member to our pack. Kyle, fated mate of Gavin and father of Brock, please join us as our brother."

I looked into Gavin's eyes. He looked right back at me.

"Gavin and Kyle," Jaxon said. "By this claiming bite, you will be bound together for eternity. In spirit, body, and wolf. May the moon forever guide you back to each other, to take refuge in your love."

I took a breath and closed my eyes. I exhaled and leaned my head to the side, exposing my neck. My next breath was sharp and short as I felt Gavin sink his teeth into my neck, and I jumped, but Gavin steadied me. I heard the roar of the pack cheering, and I felt Britt put her hand on my shoulder. And then I felt nothing, saw nothing, until I glimpsed a pair of green eyes shining in the moonlight. I wasn't afraid, but I was cautious, and then a wolf came padding out of the darkness. Almost immediately I knew who it was. I was him. And he was me. I was a wolf.

I remembered what Gavin had said, to remain in control but to allow my wolf free, but when I tried, nothing happened, and then all of a sudden, he was gone.

Where the wolf had been there was now Gavin, gazing at me with intense worry etched all over his face. Behind him, the moon shone straight down into my eyes. It was so bright I had to squint. That's when I realized I was lying on my back in the cold grass.

"Kyle?" Gavin gently placed a hand on my cheek. "You kind of fainted. I was worried. Are you alright?"

"Just a little woozy." I groaned as I propped myself up and looked around. The whole pack was staring at me. "I saw my wolf," I whispered to Gavin. "Doesn't that mean I should be able to shift now? Like you and Brock?"

"Well, it might take some time to learn, but you can try. Just relax and think of your wolf, accept him."

"I did. I tried, like you told Brock." I didn't mean to sound concerned, but if I couldn't shift, then what kind of mate could I be to Gavin?

"It's okay, it doesn't come naturally to you. It may take some practice."

I nodded, but as Gavin helped me to my feet I heard whispers in the crowd. A man came forward, and I remembered him being introduced to me as Bryce, Jaxon's mate. Beside him stood another man, and they both glanced at each other before Bryce grinned.

"There could be another reason why he can't shift," he said.

Gavin frowned. "Oh?"

The other man, who I thought was Shawn, Linc's mate, looked at me. "Yeah. The same reason Bryce and I couldn't shift when we were claimed. You could be pregnant."

"No," I said in denial.

"Oh my god, yes. You were dizzy and slightly nauseous a week or so ago," Gavin said, starting to grin.

"And that stopped."

"Still…"

I shook my head. I couldn't be. I mean, I could be. I went into heat, and we didn't use condoms, and then my heat stopped, and I felt lightheaded like I did with Brock… I glanced around at the shifters all gathered around me. Technically I was a shifter now too, except I couldn't shift because… I swallowed hard, and then looked at Gavin who was still grinning. "I don't suppose anyone has a pregnancy test, do they?"

I didn't even see who pressed one into my hand a few minutes later, but I found myself being ushered into the Lodge's toilet by Gavin, with Trevor, Britt and Kennedy close behind.

"No. I'm not going to have an audience. You can all wait outside."

"But…"

I glared at my sister. "Outside." But at the animated shimmer in Gavin's eyes I relented. "Okay, you can come in." I waited until the trio of busy-bodies had sat down at an abandoned table, and then I gripped Gavin's hand in mine and closed the door behind us.

"It's going to be okay, sweetheart," Gavin whispered.

I simply nodded before opening the little box and taking out the plastic stick. I remembered having to do this once before, and how frightened I'd been, how sick with worry. I didn't have to worry so much now though because I wasn't doing this alone. I wouldn't have to try and raise another baby with no one to help me. Yes, I had Britt and Kennedy, and even Trevor, but I had to admit it wasn't the same. Being with the man I loved, my *mate*, made all the difference in the world.

"Well, are you going to just stand there looking at it or are you going to pee on it?" Gavin asked as he looked over my shoulder.

"Well, I don't think I can actually pee with you staring at me, so if you wouldn't mind turning your back a little..."

Gavin laughed but did as I asked.

I did my part, and then placed the stick on a little shelf below the window.

"How long..."

"Um, three minutes, but it's probably best to wait a little longer because you're supposed to do this in the morning."

Gavin nodded, but kept his gaze glued to the stick. I put the lid of the toilet down and sat on it.

"Nervous?" Gavin asked, sparing me only the slightest of glances.

"Yes, and a little excited."

"Me too." I looked up at him, and he smiled softly before crouching in front of me and holding my hands. "Whatever happens, we're mates now, together, and I will always look after you, be there for you, and I promise to be the best father I can be."

"I know. You've already proven you're a good father to Brock. I couldn't ask for better."

I expected Gavin to offer up some cocky reply, but he only squeezed my hands, the light in his eyes fading just slightly. Then he stood.

"Times up."

I stood as well, my legs slightly wobbly. I reached for the test but didn't look down at it. I simply watched Gavin's face and the incredible joy that slowly graced it.

I was pregnant.

Chapter 11 - Gavin

The first snow broke on the day Kyle and Brock officially moved in to my house a few weeks after the claiming ceremony. Kyle had an armful of records while I was leveraging part of his gigantic display cabinet through the living room door when Brock came screaming inside.

"You guys!" he shouted.

"Oh my god," Kyle said as he nearly dropped the records. "What is it, Brock?"

"Snowing!" Brock squealed. "It's *snowing* for the holidays!"

Kyle shook his head, and then put his bundle on the coffee table before he shot Brock a look. Brock just gave him a cheerful grin and clapped his mittens together, sending a spray of half-melted snowflakes all over the hardwood floor.

"Go spread your Christmas cheer somewhere else," Kyle said, waving him off.

"Not a fan of the holidays?" I asked Kyle as Brock happily skipped outside.

"Are you?" he raised his eyebrows, tensing the tiniest bit as if worried about my answer.

"We may celebrate the moon, but we would never deny the kids the same joys as human kids, so the holidays are just as important to us for their sake," I admitted. "I haven't picked up a tree yet. I was hoping you and Brock would want to, and we could do it together?"

Kyle smiled and relaxed. "Oh, yes, thank you. Brock is obsessed with Christmas. He knows Santa isn't real, but he keeps pretending like he is to keep the holiday spirit alive."

"Cute," I said with a grin. I finished positioning the display cabinet to Kyle's liking, and then slid a box of vinyl across the floor to him. He happily ripped it open and started to unpack the multitude of records. I was about to open up another box when I caught a flash of worry on Kyle's face.

"Oh." He stopped short and put a hand on his belly.

"What's wrong?" I asked quickly.

"Nothing. I think... It's nothing," he said. He shook his head as he frowned. My wolf whined and I started worrying that something was seriously wrong.

"Do you need to see a doctor?"

Kyle laughed and shook his head. "If we go to the doctor's office every time something weird happened during a pregnancy, then we may as well move in there together instead of here."

I chuckled, but couldn't help feel worried, and I guess Kyle noticed. He smiled reassuringly.

"I'm fine. Let's get the rest of the cases," he said as he turned to leave.

"Hm. We'll mention this to Dr. Reed when we see her, though," I insisted as I walked beside him out into the freezing cold yard.

"Mention that I keep getting indigestion? I'm sure she'll be riveted to hear about it. Seriously, Gavin. Don't worry so much. I know what I'm doing."

It was a small comment, but it felt like a slap. I couldn't *help* but worry. It wasn't Kyle's first time being pregnant, but it was my first time being around for it.

* * *

Kyle insisted he wanted to keep working, not just through the holidays, but through his whole pregnancy. That meant I was home with Brock in the evenings while Kyle was on air.

"Hey, switch on the radio," I told Brock as we got set up in the games room. "It's my tradition to listen to your dad's show while I play at night."

"Seriously?" Brock looked at me like I was a loser, and I looked right back at him like I was the coolest guy who had ever lived. "Ugh, alright."

Brock settled in beside me, and the opening credits to the game started to roll as Kyle's voice joined us by introducing the next love song, dedicated to Shawn from Linc.

"Hey, that's Cole's dads!" Brock exclaimed.

"See? It's a cool show. How's school going?" I asked.

"Hm." Brock shrugged and pressed the start button on the game to skip the rest of the credits.

"Are you hanging out with Cole and Liam?"

"Yeah, they're cool. But they're not in my grade so I don't get to see them all the time or anything."

"What about other shifters from other packs? Any in your grade?"

"I dunno. Everyone kind of stays away from me," he mumbled.

"Why do they stay away from you?" I asked, sitting up and looking at him. Brock just shrugged and started playing, so I joined in and focused on the game. As Kyle spun another soft tempo love-song, I thought about how I could get Brock to open up about what was happening.

"When I was in school, I didn't really have any friends," I said quietly. "Just a few from the pack. But like you I was older than them and in a different grade, and I got picked on by my human classmates *a lot*."

"*You* got picked on at school?" Brock sounded completely unconvinced.

"I really, really, really did," I said as I pushed the right combination of buttons to get us through to the next level of RuneMaze.

"But you're so cool now," Brock said.

"I was cool then, too. Even cool people get picked on."

"No they don't. Only nerds like me get called names and get pushed around."

My wolf let out a deep growl. *I knew it.*

"What do you do when people call you names and push you around?"

"I just walk away," he said in a small voice. My wolf growled again.

"Why?"

"You can't win with bullies, so…"

"But how does that make you feel?" I asked, almost gritting my teeth. My son was being bullied. I was pissed, and could only imagine how he felt.

"Angry," Brock said, smashing his buttons hard to get through a blockage in the maze ahead of us.

"Yeah, I bet. It makes me angry, too."

Out of the corner of my eye I saw Brock glancing at me like he could barely believe what I was saying.

"What do you do when you're angry?" I asked.

"I count to ten. And then I play video games. Or I go crazy and I feel like I can't keep it inside. That's when my wolf would become harder to control, and…"

"And…"

"I'd go out and run through the woods. In my wolf form."

He said the last like it was a bad thing, and once again my wolf growled. "Well, that's a great way of releasing some energy, but what if you stood up to them?" I asked.

"What do you mean?"

"What if you stood up to the bullies? If you spoke back or pushed them around a bit? Give them a taste of their own medicine?"

Brock was quiet, and I watched as his character on the screen got more aggressive and tactical in breaking through the puzzles.

"You're an alpha, right?" I asked him.

"Yeah," he said sounding a little unsure.

"Alphas fight. Bullies will only remain bullies if you don't stick up for yourself. You need to make a stand at school without showing your wolf, and then you might not feel so angry. If the bullies *still* keep harassing you, then your dad and I can visit the school—"

"No! I don't want you to do that. That'll only make it worse."

I didn't think it would, but I wasn't going to argue with him about it right now. "Okay, well let's see how it goes. In the meantime, whenever you feel frustrated or angry, you can take a run as your wolf, and I'll run with you."

"Yeah?"

"Of course, that's what dad's do."

Brock smiled, but then dipped his head, and I prayed I hadn't just set him on a path to mess up his school and social life forever.

School term ended a couple of days later without any incidents, which I took as a good sign. To celebrate, I suggested taking us all out to pick a Christmas tree on Christmas Eve. Brock dressed up in his most Christmas-y outfit, complete with Santa hat, bright green and red gumboots, and an ugly hyper-colored Christmas sweater that Britt had tried to knit him years earlier. It looked more like a squashed pudding on acid than a reindeer, but he said that was part of the charm.

Britt and Trevor met us at the tree farm, both of them bundled up in brightly colored ponchos.

"Why can't we just get a tree from the woods at the back of the new house?" Brock asked as we walked through the aisles of trees.

"All of the trees in the woods are valued by the pack," I told him. "Each one has a story, and a spirit. Also, if we take one, it throws the whole ecosystem out of balance. It's better to get one of these trees that have been grown for this one purpose. It's like they've agreed to be Christmas trees."

"Hm, that's kind of cool," he said, and I couldn't help but smile. It felt good to be educating my alpha son about pack lore.

Kyle picked out a big, symmetrical pine, and Brock and I got to work cutting it down.

"Hm, but it's kind of saggy on the ends," Trevor said as he pointed to the far branches.

"And the center spike isn't very spikey," Britt added.

"Oh my god, you two!" Kyle snapped. "You're so critical. We can trim the ends and make the spike more spikey. This is the one!"

"Oh, pregnant much?" Trevor pouted at him, and made Kyle laugh.

"Yes," Kyle agreed as he put his hands on his barely there belly. His gesture warmed me from the inside out, and I grinned at him before continuing to fell the tree he wanted.

Once we got the tree home, Kyle and I strung up lights while Brock decorated it with his huge collection of video game-themed ornaments. I loved how the house smelled like pine, but what I loved most was the joy on Brock's face as I put on some Christmas carols then pulled his dad into my arms and danced with him in the middle of the living room.

I'd been happy to spend the whole evening like that, but eventually, Kyle insisted Brock went to bed otherwise "Santa" wouldn't be coming the following morning. Brock had cheerfully agreed and rushed upstairs to his bedroom.

"Well, that's different," Kyle said, shaking his head. "He'd normally protest or have some sort of hissy fit, and I'd have to coerce or beg him to go."

"Things are different now. He's got me." Kyle thumped me on the arm but grinned good-naturedly, and for the first time I truly began to believe I might have what it takes to be a good father.

The following morning, Brock woke us up early, barging into our room with presents. I could only assume Britt or Kennedy had helped him, but as Kyle unwrapped a limited release vinyl, and I tore open the box of a new game controller, I couldn't help feel proud that Brock had been so thoughtful in his gifts.

"Gosh you're a good kid," Kyle said, pulling him into bed with us. We snuggled for all of two minutes before Brock got impatient and demanded to open his presents *now*.

We all raced down to the tree to see what "Santa" had left for him, which turned out to be more video games than he could possibly play in a year, a bunch of new cool clothes, and a lot of art supplies.

I presented Kyle with some pajamas because he complained he was cold at night even with me wrapped around him, and a gold pendant in the shape of a wolf with amber for eyes, and he surprised me with a thumb drive. At my raised brows, he laughed.

"It's a compilation of all the songs that remind me of you. You can listen to it when I'm not here."

"I listen to you every night."

"Yes, well, I've interspersed some of the songs with special messages for you. For your ears only."

Then he'd grinned, and the mischief I'd fallen in love with shone bright in his eyes. If it wasn't for Brock and the promise I'd just made him to play one of the new games, I would have taken Kyle up on the unspoken promise *he* was making *me*. Instead, I'd dipped him, making him giggle before I placed a hot passionate kiss on his lips, which told him in no uncertain terms I would be taking him up on his x-rated Christmas gift that night in bed.

Later, as Kyle was packing up the wrapping paper into a big box, he paused and spread his fingers over his stomach. I raced over to his side.

"Kyle?"

"It's nothing."

"It's not nothing. You keep doing that. I really want you to tell Maddie when we see her," I declared.

"And I want you to let it go. It's no big deal."

***

But I did bring it up with Maddie, the pack's obstetrician, when we had our first sonogram appointment with her the following week on New Year's Eve. After the nurse took his vitals, Kyle lay on the bed and held my hand tightly while Maddie read over his chart.

"How are things going?" she asked. I glanced at Kyle and noticed how relaxed he looked. Completely at peace. In contrast, my leg was bouncing and I was gripping his hand so tightly I was probably hurting him.

"Everything is fine," he said.

"Kyle has been getting pains," I blurted.

"What kind of pains?"

"Nothing, really," Kyle insisted. "It seems like indigestion."

"Hm." Maddie looked him over. "I'll be checking for signs of any trouble, but from what the nurse has written here, it looks like everything is probably fine with the pregnancy."

"Should he be eating anything in particular for the baby?" I asked.

"Anything nutritious. But really, whatever he can keep down between the morning sickness and the indigestion." Maddie gave Kyle a warm smile. "Try eating less but more often. So five small meals a day instead of three larger ones. Drink plenty of water, stay hydrated, especially if you do throw up."

"Is it okay for him to have a bath? Should he only be having showers?" I asked, remembering something I'd read on a blog.

Maddie turned her attention to me. "Whatever he feels comfortable with. There's no right or wrong."

I nodded, but I didn't feel like I'd got the answer I wanted.

Normally, a sonographer would do the sonogram, but because Maddie was a shifter and specifically dealt with all the shifter omegas in town, she always did these exams. She pulled over the machine and started preparing it as she patiently replied to my numerous questions. Kyle must have realized how nervous I was. He gave my hand a reassuring squeeze as Maddie lifted up his shirt. I caught a glimpse of his small baby bump and felt a little embarrassed at how turned on it made me.

Kyle hissed as Maddie squirted lubricant on his tummy, and my wolf became on edge and protective.

"Sorry. I always forget to warn people how cold it is."

"It's okay," Kyle said with a small laugh. "Nothing I haven't felt before."

Two minutes of prodding and pushing the ultrasound wand into Kyle's tummy, and Maddie let out a happy sigh.

"There it is," she said, pointing to the monitor. My wolf started pawing at my chest as soon as I saw the tiny bean-shaped blur that was wriggling around on the screen. Kyle gasped and grabbed my hand tightly. There it was... Our new cub.

"Wow," I whispered.

Kyle shot me a huge smile, and my wolf frolicked, on such high alert I felt like I was going to shift at any moment.

"Does everything look healthy?" I asked quickly.

Maddie nodded. "Looking good. Let's see if we can hear a heartbeat."

She turned a dial on the sonogram machine and pressed harder into Kyle's belly.

"Ouch. If you press any harder, I'm going to wet my pants."

Maddie chuckled. "Sorry. Wait, there it is."

She turned up the volume, and suddenly our little one's heartbeat echoed through the speakers. It was fast, like the fluttering I felt when I looked at Kyle. But it also sounded weak, and fragile. My wolf whimpered.

"Does that sound right?" I asked.

"Yes, good pace and a strong percussion for about ten weeks. Seems like a fast growing, healthy shifter cub," she reassured me.

"Can we get a recording of that?" Kyle asked. I looked at him and saw his wonderful smile. It should have relaxed me, but I couldn't shake off the worry or the guilt that I hadn't been there when Kyle had to do this the first time. All alone.

On the way out of Maddie's office, Kyle wrapped an arm through mine and leaned against me. When we stepped outside, the frigid wind ripped across my face and stung my cheeks.

"Cold?" I asked Kyle, ready to offer him my jacket.

"At little."

I peeled off my jacket and wrapped it over his shoulders. "You can't be getting cold."

"I'm pregnant, not sick." Kyle laughed, the sound light. It would normally have made me smile. Instead, I frowned, not liking how incompetent I appeared. Kyle was carrying my child—had already carried one child of mine. I should know how to look after him.

We drove home in silence, and I thought Kyle was looking out the window and happily watching the snow-covered town go by. But when we pulled into our driveway, he sighed loudly and turned to face me.

"Why are you being so distant?" he asked.

"I'm not—"

Kyle's eyes were locked onto mine, and instead of accusation, all I saw was compassion. I wanted to be the strong alpha, the man who had all the answers, but I didn't have any. All I had were questions.

"I'm scared," I admitted with a great degree of difficulty.

"Of what?" he asked quietly as he reached over and squeezed my knee.

"Parenthood. It's all happening so fast and I don't know how to be a *dad*."

"You already *are* a dad. Brock is much calmer now we live here, all because you're being a *dad*."

Was I? A *dad* didn't abandon his son and cause him to become anxious in the first place.

***

"Did you *see* it? The baby?" Brock asked. He and I had decided to stay in and play video games instead of going to a pack party for New Year's Eve. I'd already dropped Kyle off at the radio station, and I thought this might be a good opportunity for more bonding time with Brock. To be the dad Kyle thought I could be.

"Yes, we sure did. Your dad has the photos, I'll show you when he gets home. It just looks like a little, blurry jellybean."

"A jellybean? It that all?"

"It will grow." I said as I got us through a tricky level on the game to keep my thoughts away from how sexy Kyle was looking now his baby bump was just starting to show.

"How are you feeling about having a new baby brother or sister?" I asked after some time.

"Good. Maybe like...excited? Scared? I don't know *what* to think."

"You and me both. Hey, let's call in a song."

"For dad?"

"Yeah, and the new baby."

"Yes!" Brock raced to get my phone and dialed the number before I'd had a chance to even think of a good song to request.

"This is Gavin—"

"And I'm Brocky!"

"We want to dedicate this song to our favorite radio host, the man who brings us joy every day."

"And to the new baby!"

Kyle left the microphone on and we could hear him laughing with joy as our dedication played.

"Nailed it," Brock said as he gave me a high five.

Psyched about it, we kept playing and chatting. We talked about Brock's responsibilities as an older brother, and how he'd have to look out for the baby even if they turned out to be an alpha as well because he'd be the older brother. Between the conversation and the gameplay, time got away on me. Kyle was wrapping up his show, and it was time for me to go and pick him up... It was almost midnight.

I glanced at the clock, and then at Brock. "You should have been in bed by now."

He shrugged. "I can go to bed now."

"No, I can't leave you alone. Why didn't I think to get a sitter?"

"Um, it's New Year's Eve, no one would want to take care of a kid on New Year's Eve. It's okay, I can stay here by myself."

"Nope." I got up and helped him up too. "You'll just have to come grab your dad with me."

As I drove us into town, each mile made me more nervous. Brock's eyes were heavy and I could tell that he was barely able to stay awake. I kicked myself over and over for forgetting about the sitter, for keeping him up late, and for driving him in now. I really had no idea what I was doing with that parenting stuff.

He's not your gaming buddy. He's a kid and needs you to take care of him.

If you can't even think about getting a babysitter for New Year's Eve, how bad are you going to be at taking care of a newborn? Or raising Brock to be responsible?

A dark, plump figure waddled out from the radio station. I got nervous as they started to make their way straight toward our car—until I realized it was Kyle. He was wearing so many layers it looked like he was already nine months pregnant.

I unlocked the door for him and he slid into the seat beside me with some difficulty.

"It is *cold*." He pulled the door shut behind him, and then twisted around to put his jacket in the back. "Brock!" Kyle covered his mouth when he realized the kid was sleeping.

"Sorry. I know he shouldn't be out this late. I forgot a sitter," I mumbled.

Kyle stared back at Brock and a frown twitched across his forehead before he looked at me and gave me a reassuring smile.

"It's fine," he said as he rubbed my shoulder. "I'm sure he'll just sleep in later tomorrow."

Those were nice words, but as we drove home in the first minutes of the new year, I couldn't help but feel that Kyle was thinking the same thing I was—that it was becoming obvious I wasn't going to be a very good dad after all.

Chapter 12 - Kyle

Gavin was acting more like Brock's best friend than his new dad. Their late-night gaming habit grated me the wrong way at first, but I had to admit something about it was working. Brock was actually excited to go back to school after the holiday break. On the first day back, I picked him up after school and found him in the schoolyard with friends. He walked over to the car with confidence. No sign of his hunched shoulders or bag pulled up high onto his back.

And in the meantime, our newest pack member was growing at a crazy rate. As the next three months went by, my belly got *huge*. Like, jumbo. I was twice as big as I thought I should be. By the first week of April, I was already waddling around the house with difficulty. Partly because it was tricky to maneuver my body through tight corners, but mostly because Gavin couldn't keep his hands off me.

"Aren't you supposed to be working on developing a new game?" I asked, slapping his hands away when he grabbed me in the nursery while we were putting the final touches on the furnishings.

"*Mhm*, but you are so much more fun," he growled as he nuzzled his nose into the crook of my neck and bit down gently.

I moaned and melted into his arms, but then my phone buzzed in my pants. Gavin pulled it out of my pocket and tried to hide it behind his back, but I gave him an epically pouty face until he gave in.

"It was Britt," I said before calling her back.

"Coffee and vinyl?" she asked as soon as she answered.

"Um, hello? I'm pregnant? No caffeine allowed."

"Duh, I'll get you decaf. Meet you there in ten."

When I hung up I looked at Gavin apologetically. "Britt wants to meet me. I won't be too long."

Gavin sighed and shrugged. "That's okay. Enjoy and I'll see you when you get home."

***

Britt was waiting for me, coffee in hand, in front of the pop punk section. She was wearing a gorgeous spring scarf and looked radiant.

"You are looking *big*!" she said as she threw her arms around me, almost sloshing coffee all over my back.

"Right? I'm fearing twins. Could the doctor have missed that in the first ultrasound?" I asked, only half-joking.

"When's your next scan?" she asked as she handed me a coffee.

"Next week, can you believe it? Oh wow, *coffee*." I moaned and took a sip. "Are you sure this is decaf? It's so good. Holy shit."

Britt laughed and guided me over to the records. We browsed and joked around, and I was just thinking of how nice it was for things to feel so *normal* when she started putting her hair up into a bun.

"So, I'm throwing you a baby shower," she said.

"A *what*?" I raised my eyebrows. "Uh, that is *not* my kind of thing."

"C'mon, Kyle. You never got to have one when you were pregnant with Brock. Most importantly, *I* never got to throw you one when you were pregnant with Brock..."

"So it's for *you*?" I asked.

"*Mhm*. If that makes it easier to say yes." Britt nodded frantically as she looked at me with hopeful, pleading eyes.

"That's unfair, you know I can't say no to you." Britt gave me the same pouty look I'd given Gavin, and I laughed. "Fine. What do you need me to do?"

"Just take your gorgeous man shopping and add stuff to a registry. That's it."

"Like a wish list?"

"Exactly."

"Hm… Alright, I'll drag him there after our appointment with Dr. Reed."

"How *is* Gavin doing with everything?" Britt asked quietly as she turned back to flick through records. I stood beside her and dragged my fingers over the spines of pop classics as I considered what she was asking.

"With suddenly being a dad?"

"Yeah, that," she said.

"He's coping. I'm trying to keep him involved in everything as much as possible since he's bummed he missed out on so much when Brock was little. But he seems to be completely on edge pretty much any time he's in charge of something. And I think he's getting more stressed out, the closer the due date comes. The other day he packed Brock's lunchbox, but after Brock left for school, Gavin realized he'd forgotten to pack a piece of fruit and got super upset about it."

Britt snorted. "As if Brock would care."

"Yeah, one less thing for the garbage can, right? That's what I told Gavin, and then he started freaking out that he wasn't taking care of Brock's nutrition. I just hope he isn't right… Like maybe I'm not seeing that he *is* actually a bad dad? Fuck, I don't know."

I let out a heavy sigh and realized how much tension I'd been carrying because of it. Britt rubbed a hand over my back.

"He'll calm down. He probably just needs an opportunity to get it right on his own," she suggested. "Without your help."

"God, I hope so… Help me pick a record for tonight's show. I want to do something to celebrate the warmer weather."

***

Britt was right, Gavin *did* start to calm down… But that was before my second sonogram. As I was lying on the table with sticky lube spread all over my big belly and a wand pressing hard against my organs, Gavin fell completely silent.

"Yep, it's a girl!" Maddie announced.

I grabbed Gavin's hand and watched a look of overwhelming fear spread across his face.

"Are you okay?" I half-laughed and put a hand against his cheek. He snapped out of it and took my hand before kissing my fingers and smiling at me.

"I'm ecstatic, but having a girl is *really* going to put my alpha skills to the test."

His joke landed flat, like, belly-flopped right onto my chest where a deep sadness began growing. "Your alpha skills aren't being *tested*."

"I know. I just mean that Brock and I will always be her protectors. We'll make sure she'll never be hassled by boyfriends."

"She could have *girlfriends*," I said sharply. Gavin looked at me with wide eyes, and then lowered his head in apology.

"Well, the same rules will apply no matter what." He laughed, still trying to lighten the mood. I wasn't buying it.

We left the hospital and headed straight for the Baby Boutique where we created a registry then walked around the store. Well, Gavin walked. I waddled.

I looped my arm through his and took him through the aisles, pointing out the ridiculous things babies need, even though they seem completely pointless.

"See this?" I picked up a box. "It's a nose sucker."

"A *what*?"

"You heard me right. A nasal sucker. It's an aspirator, to get the mucus out of—"

"Oh, I got it." Gavin's eyes widened. "Is that really…necessary?"

"Believe me, the moment this little girl gets a cold, you're going to be thanking whoever gets us this for the baby shower."

"What about that?" He pointed to another box I was carrying.

"A mirror."

"For…"

"If we get that rear-facing baby seat, we're going to go crazy not being able to see her. So you strap this onto the back seat and angle it so you can see her."

"Huh… I never would have thought."

I squeezed his arm. "Sure you would have."

We racked up a huge registry, and I filled a basket with cute toys and accessories for the nursery. As we were checking out, I struggled to get my wallet out of my pocket thanks to my oversized belly, and Gavin swept in with his credit card.

"Put it all on here, thank you," he said to the clerk. "And everything on the registry, too."

I slapped his arm. "That's not how a registry works."

"There's no way I'm letting anyone else provide for my baby," Gavin said in the gruff, alpha voice I hadn't heard from him for months. It stopped me dead in my tracks. I stared at him, half annoyed and half aroused. I loved it when he became all *alpha*. Part was because of the wolf inside me naturally submitting to dominance, part was because I simply got a kick out of Gavin showing me he wanted to take care of me. However, there were times when he always wanted to be in control, like now, but having kids, raising them, wasn't about control, it was about compromise, respect and unity.

By the time we got into bed that night, I couldn't stop remembering the way Gavin had started to panic when he'd learned we were having a baby girl, and when I'd shown him some items at the baby shop how he'd insisted we only got the best, and then nitpicking about the quality or effectiveness. I understood he was worried, and I knew it was hard to be a parent, but I had a sinking feeling that if he couldn't put things into perspective then maybe he wasn't cut out to be a parent.

I didn't want to think like that, and when Gavin pulled me into his arms to cuddle me, I put my worry down to pregnancy hormones blowing everything out of proportion. *Of course* Gavin would be a good dad.

***

Everything arrived from the Baby Boutique a week later. The packages filled the hallway and I spent all morning opening boxes while Gavin was out at a meeting for his next game design. I was blasting some Feather Boats on the stereo when I felt someone reach around my waist and grab my belly. I almost jumped out of my skin, and I felt my wolf surge in my chest.

"Sorry!" Gavin shouted over the noise. I caught my breath and grinned up at him as I leaned back into his strong chest. I melted into his arms when Gavin leaned down and kissed me softly. My wolf faded into the background.

"I thought you'd be out all day," I said loudly.

"What?"

"I thought you'd be—oh hang on." I peeled myself out of his arms and turned down the stereo. "I thought you'd be out all day."

"I hated the idea of you doing all of this on your own," he said, looking around the hallway.

"Oh, you came to help?"

"Is that so unbelievable?" He frowned, and my stomach clenched. He was taking my ribbing too seriously these days.

"No, it's not. I could use your muscle. Here, carry those boxes of baby books."

We moved most of the stuff out of the hall and into the nursery, unpacked and set everything up. We finished by unrolling a play rug, and I sat down on it with a heavy thud as my butt hit the floor. Gavin joined me and wrapped his arm around my shoulders. I shimmied closer so I could lean against him, and he happily brought me into a warm hug.

"This room is looking good," he said as we took in all the work we'd put into it. I smiled at the pale blue walls we'd decorated with golden hand-painted wolves, woods, and the moon shining down on it all. I loved it in here. The colors were so peaceful, and I wanted nothing more than to bring our little girl into this beautiful world.

"I've been thinking about something," I said quietly. "I want to give birth here."

Gavin's body immediately tensed. I waited for him to respond, but he didn't say a thing.

"I want to do a water birth. My experience with Brock was so traumatic at the hospital. I didn't have the kind of support I have now, and I've heard great things about water births. We can get a special tub, and there's plenty of space in the family room—"

"No way," Gavin said, pulling his arms away.

I sat upright and turned to look at him. "What do you mean, *no way*? We have a beautiful environment here."

"No. Too many things could go wrong."

"Why would you say that?" I asked as calmly as I could. I felt a mood swing looming, but I wanted to stay as logical as possible to get my point across.

Gavin just shook his head and looked at the wall.

"Gavin! *Why* would you say that? What is going to go wrong?"

"Everything! Anything! I don't know, and that's the problem. *We* don't know what could go wrong, that's why there are hospitals full of doctors to help you give birth."

"But you don't know how horrible it was when I was having Brock in the hospital—"

"Okay, you're right, I don't know anything." He threw his hands up in the air.

"That's unfair, that's *not* what I'm saying—"

"Why would we put our new baby in danger because of a past experience?" Gavin's face was fierce, and I knew I'd upset him.

My bottom lip trembled and I bit down on it, determined not to cry. After a few minutes of tense silence I hauled myself up off the floor. "It's time to pick up Brock. I'm going to get him."

"Kyle."

I paused in the doorway and looked back at Gavin.

"We can talk about it more later," he said softly.

"Sure." I nodded, and then hurried out of the room before the tears I'd tried to hold back started to trickle down my cheeks. I took deep, calming breaths as I drove to Brock's school, and by the time I got there, my mood had swung from sadness and anger all the way back to composed. When I spotted Brock laughing with kids I didn't recognize, I smiled, delighted he was now getting along with his peers. He looked really happy.

"Are they your new friends?" I asked him when he climbed into the car.

Brock shrugged. "Yeah, kind of. They saw me stand up to the bullies, and I guess they realized I'm not such a nerd."

"Bullies?"

Brock sighed. "I told you about them, remember? But it's alright now. Dad told me not to back down, to stand up to them but not let my wolf out."

"Your dad?" I couldn't help my grin as Brock called Gavin "Dad," but I wondered what he was talking about in regard to bullies. He'd mentioned them before, but I thought it had just been an excuse not to go to school because he wanted to play video games.

"Yeah. He helped me."

I nodded, but as I pulled out to drive us home a huge ball of embarrassment formed in my stomach. I hadn't believed him, and my son was being *terrorized* at school. What kind of father did that make me?

"Well, I'm glad Gavin… Your dad, has helped you, and I'm sorry I didn't believe you when you told me about the bullies."

"Nah, it's okay. Dad said I was being kind of bratty with you, and it wasn't your fault. We weren't communicating properly, and relationships are all about communicating."

"Your dad said that?"

"It was while we were playing one of the games. He's cool like that, explaining stuff in a way that doesn't make it boring."

Boring? Was that how Brock saw me?

I kept thinking about what he said, and knew I would have to thank Gavin, and I would also have to revise my opinion about how he was coping with being a parent. He was being a great dad, and our little spat earlier was only because he was worried, not because he wasn't willing to compromise.

Later that night, as we were eating dinner, Gavin put a hand on my knee under the table. I instantly scooched a little closer to him. He gave me a squeeze, and my affection for him flowed as strongly as ever. He was right—we *could* talk about the home birth plan again later. We still had nearly four months to figure everything out.

Brock cleared his throat, taking me out of my thoughts.

"Um, I've got a little bit of news to share."

He sounded so edgy, I quickly put down my fork. "What is it, Brocky?"

"Well it's just, um, there's a gaming contest."

"Oh yeah?" Gavin asked, sounding very interested.

"It's for kids at our school and other schools close by, and it's in town at the video game store, and I just think it might be really fun!"

"Nice!" Gavin said. "Sounds like something you could win."

"That is *very* cool," I said. "When is it?"

"It's next Wednesday, but it's at seven o'clock." Brock sighed, glancing at Gavin and then me again.

"I'm working," I said as I realized why Brock had looked so edgy before he said anything. He knew I wouldn't be able to take him, but there was a perfectly capable dad who should be chomping at the bit to do so. I raised my eyebrows at Gavin. This would be the ideal time for him to step up.

"Guys, *I'm* the one who plays games. *I'll* take you," Gavin said to Brock. He winked at me, and I smiled. If there was a perfect opportunity for Gavin to hone some of his parenting skills, it would be where kids were playing games.

Chapter 13 - Gavin

Gaming conventions and competitions were things I knew a thing or two about. Finally, there was something about raising a kid I felt completely confident about. The game he would be playing at the contest was a new release, so we couldn't practice on it, but there were plenty of other games that would build up the skills Brock needed. For the next few days, Brock and I camped out in the games room whenever we had free time, until Kyle had enough of it and insisted we were turning into gremlins.

"If you stay in there a moment longer, you're going to get a vitamin D deficiency and end up as sad, withered, old men. Don't your wolves want to *run*?" he asked us, exasperated.

Admittedly, our wolves were dying to get some fresh air. So I sighed and put down my controller.

"Come on, Brock. Let's get out before we send your dad utterly barmy."

Brock didn't argue, which I counted as a plus. He'd been definitely getting better lately, and whenever I could see he needed to let off steam we went out for a run, and this was a good a time as any.

Mid spring in Washington State could sometimes be cold, but we were lucky as we stepped outside. I took in a lungful of clean, pine scented air, and then shifted, loping through woods with Brock at my side.

I kept my pace slow so I didn't get too far ahead of him, but I shouldn't have worried— he was right at my heels, and he soon passed me. His young, spritely wolf sprinted ahead on the track and took sharp corners like he knew they were coming. I was impressed and had to push myself to keep up as he bounded through the brush and scrambled over fallen logs. It felt damn good to be running with my kin, and I couldn't wait to share the same experience with Kyle.

We broke through the tree-line and raced back into the homestead right near Nicole's house. I showed Brock where to squeeze through gaps in fences and how to open up holes near hedges so we could take a shortcut to her backyard.

As we padded across the yard, the back door suddenly banged open and Cole came bounding out of the house toward us in his wolf form. Brock let out a happy bark that was cut short when his cousin tackled him. They romped together in the sunlight as I shifted back and watched them. Nicole waved to me from the kitchen window, and I headed up the porch steps to join her where she was washing the dishes.

"A gaming contest, huh?" she said after I filled her in on what was up.

"Well, Brock's really excited," I explained as I dried off a mug with a dish towel.

"Just Brock?" She started scrubbing a pot with a laugh in her eyes.

"Okay, *we* are really excited, but Kyle has had enough of us hiding out in the games room. He says the sound leaks into the rest of the house, even though I *swear* it's noise proof."

"Well he's pregnant, and he's just become a wolf. So he's sensitive as hell and he probably *can* hear it," she said, using her sponge to emphasize the point.

I let out a sigh and grabbed another plate to wipe dry. "It's just the first time I've felt like I knew how to be a *dad*. I have a feeling these opportunities will be few and far between."

Nicole paused and frowned at me. "There's really not much to it, Gavin. Just make sure they don't die. Tell them you love them. Don't disappear. Do that, and you're considered a good dad."

I grunted and fell silent.

"I bet Brock is loving the extra time with you, though," she said kindly as she gazed out the window.

"I think he is. Man, I'd love for him to win," I said as I looked over her shoulder and watched as Brock and Cole rolled over and over and over, each trying to pin the other.

"Winning isn't everything," she said in a cautious tone.

"It is when you're being bullied at school and have low self-esteem."

"Bullied? You never told me that?"

"Well, Brock seems to have it under control right now, but that's not to say someone else won't pick on him. He's a really sensitive kid who could do with proving to others he won't allow himself to be pushed around anymore."

"And you think winning will do that?"

"It certainly won't hurt."

She was silent for a moment, and then said, "You can practice here if you want. Give Kyle some peace. Just don't rope Cole into the contest, I *don't* want him getting worked up about it."

So, we practiced in Nic's living room from then on. Kyle seemed to be in a much better mood every time we got home, having had the house to himself. And Brock said the runs we took on the way to and from Nic's helped to clear his head and kept him focused in the game.

On Wednesday, after dinner, Brock put his dishes in the sink and then faced Kyle.

"Can we *please* use the games room, I need to practice."

"I think it's better if we *don't* practice tonight, Brocky," I said. "It would be better to distract yourself with something else instead, so your nervous system has a chance to relax before the big game."

"Distract myself? With what?"

"Oh, maybe homework," Kyle said.

"Good idea," I agreed.

"Um…" Brock looked at us like we were crazy, a habit he'd definitely picked up from Cole.

"Homework. Now," I said. As Brock stomped up the stairs, Kyle took my hand and gave it a firm squeeze.

"Very good parenting."

"Thanks," I said with a grin, but I couldn't help but feel he was being a little patronizing.

I brushed off the thought, and after Brock and I dropped Kyle off at work we then headed straight to the games store where the contest was being held. As we entered the doors, I had a potent flashback to the gaming convention when I'd first met Brock and reconnected with Kyle… I wrapped an arm around my son and gave him a squeeze. Who would have thought I would have my son, my mate, and a baby on the way, all because of a nerdfest?

I thought back to who I'd been then and how much more of a *dad* I was now. I might not have any real idea what I was doing, but I'd come a long way since then.

My phone buzzed, and I opened the screen to see a text.

Good luck! X Nic & Cole

I showed Brock, and he grinned. "I don't need luck, though. I've got you."

I laughed and clapped him on the back, then steered him toward the registration table.

"Welcome to the Regional Championship, Brock. And *hello*, Gavin!" The young registration clerk stood and held out her hand.

"Erm, hello." I tried to place where I knew her from. I didn't recognize her at all. *Did* I know her?

"Longtime fan," she explained as I shook her hand. I heard a gruff grunt coming from behind us and I turned to find a family standing nearby. The dad was watching our interaction, his arms across his chest and a dark frown on his face. Before I had a chance to ask him what his problem was, Brock tugged on my sleeve and pointed to the lanyard the clerk was offering me.

"VIP access, for competitors and family. It means you get access to the snacks. Nothing very special. But the lanyards make you look important."

"Cool," Brock whispered as he looked at the holographic sticker on his lanyard.

"Thanks," I hurried Brock to the area where the snacks were laid out before any other fans spotted me.

After we'd loaded up on sugar we took our seats in the crowd to watch the heats. Soon enough, it was Brock's turn. He stood up, but I noticed he was shaking like a leaf.

"Brock, you are a gaming *machine*. You have been training for this your *whole life*. And besides—you have gaming success in your blood."

Brock laughed and stopped shaking. "Okay. Okay I've got this. It's in my blood!"

Of course he absolutely blitzed his competition. I stood up and cheered as he accepted his entry token for the semi-finals.

"Calm down, it's just the first heat," someone in the crowd groaned, but I wasn't going to let them kill my buzz. My son had just won his first contest!

"I did it! You were right!" Brock was all smiles as he came back to sit beside me. "I wish Dad was here to see it."

"I'll record the next one," I promised, feeling a bit stupid for having forgotten to take photos of the first heat.

"Yeah but only if I win."

"Uh, *when* you win."

"But I might not."

"Or you might. Positive thinking."

He nodded, and of course, he *did* win. I caught the winning fighting sequence on my phone and sent the video straight to Kyle.

AMAZING! Good luck for the final!!! - Dad

Brock just beamed and bounced happily in his seat, and we watched the other semi-final between two amazing gamers.

"This is taking so long because they're so good," Brock whispered to me as the game stretched out.

"They're pretty good, but you can see their weak spots, right?"

"Yeah, the guy with the canon doesn't check his blind spots, and the guy with the tennis racket is slow with his aim," Brock replied.

"Impressive," I told him, genuinely amazed at how much he'd picked up.

As the heat ended, Brock started shaking again.

"It's in your blood," I said to remind him.

"I was born for this," he said as he nodded.

I cheered as he made his way up to the stage. The crowd erupted into applause as the two finalists took their places in front of their personal screens. "Go Brock!"

"Go Dennis!" a loud voice bellowed from the back of the crowd. I turned and clocked it as the same guy who had grunted at me at the registration table earlier. We all took our seats, and I set up my phone to record it. The game began. Brock took some heavy hits at first, and I bit down on my lip to stop myself from panicking. He could come back from that. I'd done worse to him in training and he'd always bounced back.

Sure enough, he sprung a surprise attack on his competitor that almost completely demolished him—but not quite. Dennis quickly recovered and started in on a new attack, but Brock had something else up his sleeve. *Bam*! He hit Dennis with another surprise attack.

"Yes, Brock!" I watched as his character did a happy dance. The crowd cheered and yelled for him to finish the game, but he dragged it out a little, maybe to give Dennis more of a chance.

Dennis half-recovered by the time Brock's character was back to full health and running circles around him, collecting points and earning extra bonuses. Dennis mounted a frantic retaliation against Brock's character, but it was too emotional and not well thought out at all. Brock saw it coming a mile away. He dodged the attack and landed the finishing blow.

"Whoooo!" I leapt to my feet to cheer as the game ended. Huge letters appeared on Brock's screen spelling WINNER! Brock jumped up and grinned at the crowd as the judge raised his hand in victory.

A rumbling *boo* came from the back of the crowd and I spun around to face the same guy again.

"Hey, c'mon! He's a kid. It was a fair win."

"Fair? Yeah right!"

I turned back and did my best to ignore him as I applauded for Brock. He was still grinning and looked so excited. My heart swelled and I felt my wolf spinning in circles with happiness for my cub. I clambered across seats into the aisle when Brock bounded down the stairs of the stage and raced over to me. I embraced him in a huge hug then gave him high fives until our hands hurt.

"Can we have the winner on stage?"

Brock gave me one last high five and raced back to stage to collect his trophy and his prize.

"Cheat!" the guy in the back called.

"Hey!" I turned around to glare at him. "Shut up, man. That's my kid."

"No shit that's your kid. How'd he get so good at the game before the game was even released? Got some insider contacts?"

I glanced at Brock on stage with the trophy and the game in his hands—and a frown across his brow.

"Shut the fuck up or I'll shut you up," I growled just loudly enough for the guy to hear me. He shot me a filthy look, but he did shut up.

Though Brock's excitement was a little tempered by the rude reception from the back of the crowd, he was hugging the trophy close to his chest and had a huge smile on his face as we headed out of the convention center. We got all of three steps before the jerk from the crowd blocked our path.

"Okay, cheater, give the prize back," he said to Brock.

"Shut up and back off," I said, trying to hold back my temper.

"Or what? You'll use your *fame* to get me chucked out?"

"I'll do worse than that," I muttered under my breath as the guy looked me over. I noticed that Brock's opponent, Dennis, was standing off to the side, trying not to watch the altercation. He must have been this guy's son.

"Give that prize back. You shouldn't have been allowed into the contest in the first place. You were obviously *groomed* by this nerd," the heckler said to Brock.

"Do *not* talk to my son." I narrowed my eyes, unable to believe this guy's accusations.

"It's okay, I don't mind giving it back." Brock started to hand the guy the trophy before I shook my head.

"Absolutely not. You won that fair and square, and you know it. Don't let bullies win."

"Bully! You're calling me a bully after *your son* cheated and humiliated my son up there?" The guy took a threatening step forward, but I grabbed Brock's arm and urged him toward the front door.

"C'mon, Brock. We have to get home." Once outside I made a beeline for the parking lot while keeping an eye on the ignoramus who was still spitting bullshit lies at us, but we were stopped by a group of young girls and guys, all about Brock's age.

"Hey, wait. Can I get your autograph?" one of them asked as she held out a copy of the game and a sharpie.

"Me?" Brock asked, turning a bright red.

"Yeah…" The girl laughed nervously.

"Sure, I guess." Brock laughed too and scribbled on the case of her game.

"Me too, please," the next person said, smiling sweetly at him.

"Um yeah, okay." Brock did another autograph that looked nothing like the first one. The spoils of fame… I let him chat while I kept an eye out for Dennis's dad.

Once the small group were satisfied, we continued to the car.

"I'm so proud of you," I said as I gave his shoulder a squeeze.

"Thanks." He looked at his trophy. "I could have landed a few more moves or ended it sooner maybe…"

"I noticed. You could have. I'm proud you made it fun for your opponent, though. And I'm proud you're *so good* at this."

He laughed. "I am really good, huh? Thanks for sticking up for me. I didn't really want to give the trophy back."

I was reaching for my keys when the same gruff voice from earlier came from behind us.

"Oh, here's the cheater and his rich wolfy daddy!"

I twisted and caught a flash of bright amber in his eyes. His son was nowhere to be seen, and neither was anyone else. It was just us and him. My wolf was on high alert and it started to bare its teeth. I quickly unlocked the car door and nudged Brock to get in. He didn't move.

Suddenly, the guy's neck began to pulse and scales sprang up through his skin. He opened his mouth and let out a warning roar. My wolf howled, and I only just resisted the urge to shift and lunge at him. He was a fucking dragon shifter!

"Brock! Get in the car *now!*" I insisted, shoving him back.

"Filthy cheating dogs! Your pack's days are numbered!" Claws sprung from the man's fingers, and before I could react, a ball of fire shot out of his mouth and roared right toward me. I barely dodged it, and it landed beside my car, smoldering on the asphalt.

"Fuck! Brock! *Get in the fucking car! Now!*"

Brock was already running. I heard the door open then shut. I let out a deep, guttural growl as a warning to the dragon shifter, then quickly ran after Brock.

"I will *end you.* I will end your whole filthy stinking dog pack!" the dragon shifter shouted as I sprinted around the car to the driver's side where Brock had thrown open the door for me. A bigger ball of fire burst through the air and just missed me as I ducked into the car. The smell of singed hair followed me as I slammed the door and turned on the motor.

Brock was whimpering and growling, squirming in his seat.

"Hold back your wolf," I demanded as I put a hand on his chest and pushed him back against the seat. I turned on the car and hit the accelerator. A bright orange light flashed, and a splattering of fire rained across the hood. I raced as fast as I could, burning rubber and screeching out of the parking lot. More fire rained down on the trunk, and I had to fish-tail along Pack Lane to shake it off.

"Call Jaxon and get him on speaker phone," I told Brock as I found my phone and chucked it into his lap.

I looked over and found him shaking like a leaf.

"Brock! Call Jaxon right now!" He snapped out of it, and quickly dialed the pack leader's number.

***

By the time we got through the homestead gates, Jaxon had called an emergency pack meeting at Wolf Lodge. We pulled up to find a group of shifters waiting for us. Nic raced forward and opened Brock's door then wrapped a blanket around his shoulders and pulled him into a big hug.

I got out and nodded to Jaxon who came to check on me.

"I'm alright." I ran a hand through my singed hair.

"No signs of an attack on the homestead, but we've posted scouts and made it clear we're on the lookout. If he was coming here, we might have scared him off."

I nodded, relieved. My wolf started to settle down, and bloodlust stopped pumping through my veins. I turned to find Brock still in Nic's arms, looking pale and completely freaked out.

"That was scary, huh? We're okay though. We're home, and we're okay."

"I want Dad," he whispered.

"He'll be at work for a few more hours," I told him as I ran a hand over his forehead. "But maybe we can call him?"

He nodded quickly, but his eyes remained wide in fear. He still had my phone so Nicole took him off to a quiet place to talk with Kyle while I gave Jaxon a more thorough report of what had happened.

"You did the right thing," he said.

"Maybe not. I should have let Brock give the damn trophy to the other kid. I shouldn't have insisted Brock stand up to bullies. Look what happened because I told that guy to back off. Brock looks traumatized. Fuck."

"Kids bounce back," Jaxon said. "And you had no idea the guy was a dragon shifter. You were defending your son's honor, and then you defended his life. You stayed in control, that's the most important thing. That's how you kept him safe."

I wasn't so sure. I'd made mistakes tonight, and because of them Brock had been a target of a dragon shifter. Of all the creatures on this planet, why did my *son* have to end up in their sights. Wasn't it enough they took my father?

Brock tugged at my arm and held up my cellphone. "Dad wants to talk to you," he said in a small voice.

"Thanks, Brocky," I said, taking the phone and walking a small distance from the crowd.

"Hey babe, I—"

"Are you *fucking* kidding me? You put my kid in serious danger and you start the conversation with *'hey babe!'*"

My heart started racing. "Kyle, we're safe, it's okay—"

"No it's *not* okay. Come and get me from work. *Right now.*"

Chapter 14 - Kyle

I stood outside the studio with my arms crossed, scouring the traffic for Gavin's car. The night air was cool, but I was hot with rage.

Dragons? Seriously? Why the hell hadn't Gavin told me about dragon? What was he trying to hide? I should have known getting involved with a wolf shifter would bring more problems than it was worth. Why did I trust him? Why did I think this could work?

As soon as I spotted Gavin's car, my wolf started clawing at my chest. I inhaled and held back the urge to rush into an altercation. I'm glad I did because as soon as Gavin parked, Brock flew out of the car and came running straight into my arms. I held him tightly and closed my eyes as he burst into tears and his body shook in my embrace.

When I opened my eyes I saw Gavin walking closer to us with his eyes down, refusing to meet my gaze. His sheepishness just made me angrier.

"I want to go home," Brock said between sobs. "I want to go home to Aunty Britney's and Kennedy's. The dragon said he'd-he'd-he'd attack the homestead."

"Shh, it's okay." I kissed the top of his head. "We can stay with Britt and Kennedy, it's okay. That's a good idea."

Gavin looked visibly hurt, but just shoved his hands in his pockets and looked at the ground.

"I'm never going to play video games every again, I promise!" Brock buried his face in my protruding stomach and continued to cry. I shot a look at Gavin. Still no reaction.

"Are you happy now?" I asked, almost spitting the words out. I immediately regretted it, but it did shake him out of his silence. He grimaced and looked at me.

"No, I'm not. Kyle, I'm sorry, I'm so sorry. I need to tell you what happened—"

No. I didn't want to hear his excuses, and I didn't want to fight around Brock. I held up a hand. "Take us to Britt's where we can feel safe."

"I'm so sorry," he said again, but nodded and headed back to the car.

I sat in the backseat with Brock and ran a hand over his back as his sobs started to slowly recede. Gavin was silent. By the time we got to Britt's house my rage had tempered, but it was still a sharp anger. Brock and I clambered out of the car, and I closed the door behind us. Brock ran straight into the house, and I heard Gavin getting out of the car. I turned and glared at him.

"Please, just hear me out. You don't have the full story," Gavin begged.

"No. And I don't want the full story. I don't need it. You didn't tell me about dragons, that they were going after your pack."

"They're not. Not really. There are just a few rogue—"

"I told you, I don't want to hear it. You should have told me. You should have given me the choice of knowing before you turned me into a—" I shook my head. I couldn't disparage being a wolf. That wasn't fair to Brock. I certainly wouldn't dream of degrading what was his fundamental nature. I shook my head again, staring at Gavin as he barely made eye contact. I could smell smoke, burnt hair. My stomach roiled.

"This is the *exact* reason why I didn't want to rush into things with you. I needed the time to know Brock would be safe with you. You told me he would be. You *promised* Brock he would. Now look what happened."

"Kyle, it's not like that—"

"Isn't it? Brock could have been seriously hurt or *killed*. You get that, right?"

Gavin swallowed and nodded.

"What if the flames had hit the gas tank? *You* could have been hurt or killed. And where would that leave me?" I asked, my voice thickening as my throat began to close. "I'd be a pregnant, single widow who just lost my son and my mate because of who—what you are. Do you get that? I don't want to put my son or my unborn daughter in any more harm. You need to give us space to feel safe again."

Gavin nodded again, his gaze on the ground.

I waited.

He didn't speak.

I turned, and followed Brock into the house, slamming the door behind me.

***

Britt and Kennedy fussed over us with hot chocolates, blankets, and tried to get us to pick a movie to take our minds off things. Brock squished up his nose and shook his head when Britt held up a rom-com, and did the same for comedies, dramas, and even cartoons.

"Want to play some games?" I asked as sat beside him on the couch and rubbed his back. Though he said he'd never play them again, I knew my son and I knew he'd never stay away from them forever.

"I don't know," he grumbled.

"We could play something you don't usually play. Maybe something I'd be a good at."

Brock let out a light laugh and forced a smile. "Okay," he whispered. "Let's play an easy game."

We messed around with a game where you had to match colors and patterns, depending on what music was playing. Brock started to relax pretty much right away, and I was also happy to find it was helping me to calm down too.

"Do you want to talk about what happened today?" I asked quietly when Britt and Kennedy left for bed.

"It was really scary," Brock said softly.

"It sounds really, *really*, scary. I'm glad you're okay."

"Gavin was really brave," he said, and I felt my hackles rise. Had Gavin bribed Brock to say that or something?

"Was he," I said, rather than asked.

"He really was, Dad," Brock insisted. "He tried to get the dragon guy to calm down, even before the parking lot. He was in the crowd and booing me and calling me a cheater. He wanted me to give the prize back, and Gavin told him to calm down. And then in the parking lot, Gavin just got me in the car as fast as he could and got us out of there. He couldn't have done anything better. You would have done exactly the same thing."

"I would never have put you in that position in the first place, if it wasn't for Gavin taking you there—"

"Kennedy would have. She likes games too, and you know you would have let me go with her. Honestly, Dad, it wasn't Gavin's fault. And Gavin hates dragons on account of his dad, and Cole's mom said the dragon was lucky Gavin didn't rip his throat out."

That was a little more gory than I believed Brock should be exposed to, but I was intrigued by what he'd just said about Gavin's father. "What did you mean Gavin hates dragons because of his dad?"

"Oh, well, Cole told me his alpha grandad was killed by a dragon. It set his grandad on fire, and Gavin and Cole's mom had to grow up without an alpha dad. That's why Gavin hates dragons."

I noticed Brock had stopped calling Gavin "Dad" and a little bit of my heart ached, but maybe it was for the best… Maybe Brock needed to get used to not having Gavin around.

I bit down on my bottom lip. As angry as I was, as hurt, I wasn't really ready to think of not being with Gavin. I just needed to space to think, to put Brock's mind at rest that he was safe; that dragons were not going to come after him. Only then would I consider my future with Gavin.

After Brock and I finished our game, we dragged ourselves upstairs to his bedroom, both of us almost tripping on the stairs from exhaustion. We'd moved most of our stuff to Gavin's, but his room at Britt's still had most of its furniture. I guessed Kennedy hadn't started on her plan to turn the room into a personal gym. I was grateful to find that Britt had made up Brock's bed with fresh linens.

"Alright, Brocky," I said as I tucked him in and kissed his head. "Sweet dreams, okay?"

"Okay," he said, his voice a little broken. I put a hand on his chest and rubbed it softly.

"Just call out if you wake up, okay?"

"Okay…"

"Do you want the nightlight on?" I asked.

"Yeah…"

I switched on his old nightlight and he smiled when the video game character lit up. But when I looked at him again, I saw he was still shaken.

"Want me to read you a story?"

He bit his lip and nodded quickly. I grabbed a book from the half-empty bookcase, and then settled in next to him on the bed. I'd read almost half of a short novel before I heard his breath even out and felt his head grow heavy on my shoulder.

I slowly peeled myself out from under him and gave him a soft kiss on his cheek before I snuck out, leaving the door ajar. I'd almost put myself to sleep with the story, and I stumbled down the stairs even more clumsily than I'd climbed up them.

When I walked into my old bedroom I saw that Britt had started turning it into her home office. Where my wardrobe had been was an oversized desk, and where I'd had my desk was a bookshelf full of her crystals. At least my futon was set up with fresh bedsheets, but it was smooshed into a corner. I let out a sigh and collapsed onto the familiar surface. I missed my big, soft bed I shared with Gavin, but I had to admit it felt good to get back to my old bed. I kind of felt more like myself.

But when I inhaled deeply I realized I my sense of smell had changed. The futon smelled differently to how it used to… It smelled like a version of me from the past, before I'd been bitten by Gavin. My stomach turned… *I* was different now. There was no going back. No matter what, I was joined with Gavin in a real, deep way. This was the "real me" now.

I groaned and covered my face with a pillow. I was way too exhausted for this kind of existential crisis. I put a hand on my big belly and fell asleep, praying I'd feel better and more clear-headed in the morning.

Chapter 15 - Gavin

I grit my teeth and watched as Kyle walked away with our son and our unborn daughter. My wolf snarled and whined in an attempt to make me stop Kyle, but I remained stoic, pushing down my anger until he was safely inside, and then I got in my car, slammed the door, and smashed my hand against the steering wheel.

"Fuck!" I cried as I hit it again and again. "Fuck this!"

When my palm started burning, I slumped back in the seat, forcing myself not to completely lose it. It was okay. It was going to be okay. It had to be—I couldn't lose my family because of a dragon shifter. Not again.

Once my wolf stopping snarling and simply went back to pacing and growling, I drove back to the homestead. I hated driving home without Kyle and Brock. I didn't want to go back to an empty house, and I sure wasn't going to get any sleep that night. I drove straight to the Wolf Lodge where Jaxon, Linc and Greer were still lingering after the emergency meeting.

"Any sign of him?" I asked.

"Linc and Jason have just reported a few scorched trees on the western border by the cliffs, and Steve has gone back to the police station to see if he can get his officers to do a patrol of the streets," Jaxon stated.

"What about talking to the dragon shifters who live on the mountain? He might be one of theirs," I said.

Greer seemed to think for a moment. "Dragon shifters generally have a strict code of conduct—each code is different between each clan, of course, and though many don't adhere to our rules, most conventional clans certainly don't go around starting fires or attacking innocents. This sounds like a renegade."

"You said there was just the one, didn't you, Gavin?" Jaxon asked.

"One adult, yeah, but his son was also in the gaming contest. About the same age as Brock."

"So possibly able to spit fire as well. And there were too many scorched trees for there to be only one dragon shifter. There may be a group of renegades. If they're getting closer to Timberwood Cove and attacking its residents... You may be right, Jaxon. We may need to run them off," Linc said.

Run them off? I swallowed nervously, and Greer caught my eye.

"An opinion, Gavin?" he asked.

"I think it will cause more harm than good," I said honestly, though my wolf didn't want to hear it. It wanted vengeance, but I needed to speak from experience. "Retaliating might stir things up. Last time wolf shifters went after a renegade dragon..." I didn't really need to add that my father had been killed, they all knew the story. "If the dragon who attacked my son is part of a bigger group, ones who don't seem to have any trouble in attacking a child, then it could end badly for our cubs if they turned on us."

"And if we don't do something to let them know we won't tolerate their tactics, they could still attack us," Jaxon said.

"I agree with both of you," Greer said. "But until we know who we're dealing with, I think we should simply remain vigilant. Maybe take a few more runs and spread our scent through the trees to show a united, strong front. If they realize our pack and the others in

Timberwood Cove are going to come together, then maybe the dragons will think twice before causing any more trouble. In the meantime, I can go and talk to Marco Shannahan of the Spitfire Clan. He might have some knowledge on who these renegades are."

"Yeah, good idea, Dad. You okay with that, Gavin? Linc?"

Jaxon didn't actually have to ask our permission to make a decision, but it proved he was a willing and compassionate leader who wanted to do right by his pack.

"Yes, thanks. I just don't like the idea of starting a fight with a creature who can fucking spit fire."

"I get where you're coming from," Linc said. "So yeah. Whatever you think is best."

I released a breath, and then headed back across the homestead, walking fast with pent-up energy. I heard Jaxon as he caught up to me.

"Are Kyle and Brock safe?" he asked.

"Yeah. I dropped them off at his sister's place."

"And you? Are you okay?"

I clenched my jaw. "No."

"Will they be coming back to the pack soon?"

"I don't know. Kyle doesn't want to put Brock in harm's way."

"And he thinks he won't be safe here?"

"*I* don't think he'll be safe here. That dragon said he'd come after us, and he knew where I lived."

Jaxon grabbed my shoulder, bringing me to a halt. "So why did you vote not to retaliate?"

"Because technically it's the right thing to do, but..."

"But..."

"That bastard went after my son, my family. I can't just let that go."

"And what did you intend to do about it? You heard what Greer said, don't engage."

I glanced off into the woods. My wolf growled and threw itself against my chest, desperate to get out and find the dragon I wanted to destroy. Jaxon must have seen the look on my face.

"I'll run with you. But if we find the dragon, you let me deal with him."

It was an order, and one I couldn't disobey. I nodded, actually relieved he was going to be at my side. I honestly didn't think I could trust myself if I went out there alone.

We shifted together and bolted off into the woods. Jaxon raced ahead and followed an ancient, worn path our forefathers had used for centuries. I loved how it felt to run these old tracks. I always felt closer to my pack and the paranormal magic that made us who we were. However, I didn't feel the calm I usually associated to these paths. Instead, anger pushed me to run faster, harder.

At the base of the mountain we caught a scent and dashed off through heavy scrub. Brambles dug deep into my fur and pricked my skin, but I was determined to get through, and I pushed hard. A trickle of blood ran down my foreleg as we stepped out of the brambles and into a burned out clearing. I glanced around and saw the bark of the trees scorched black, and the undergrowth reduced to dark black ash. I lifted a paw and shook off the soot.

The trees were still hot, but there was no scent or sign of where the dragon shifter who'd caused this fire could be. A growl escaped my throat and I let out a frustrated yelp. Jaxon looked at me, and then raised his snout to the sky. He took a deep breath and let out a sad, solitary howl of compassion. I joined him, singing out my pain into the night.

We sniffed around and scoured the area for any hint of where we could find the dragon shifter but came up with nothing. Discouraged, we loped back to the homestead, my head down, my thoughts on Kyle, on Brock and my unborn baby girl. At the edge of my house Jaxon and I shifted.

"We can look another night," Jaxon said. "We'll set up a schedule with our alphas and some from the other packs to keep combing the area."

I nodded, but I couldn't hide my despondency. Though part of me was glad we hadn't found the dragon, another part of me was still fantasizing about what I'd do if I ever came face to face with him...

"Maybe they've gone. That attack on you and Brock would certainly have put them on edge. Let's hope they've realized they've gone too far."

"Yeah." I doubted it though. The look on that dragon shifter's face, the vile hatred he spewed... No. I didn't think our conflict with the dragons was over. I said goodnight to Jaxon and headed inside my house.

The house was dark, cold, and empty. Without Kyle and Brock to fill it with love and laughter, the house now felt depressing and sad. As I switched on all of the lights I wondered how I'd ever managed to live alone before I'd met Kyle. I missed Kyle's music and Brock's loud yelling. I missed the sound of them as they danced or ran from one room to another. I missed just knowing they were *there*.

I headed straight for my gym, changed into a pair of shorts, and strapped on my boxing gloves. I gave the bag a few hits before my wolf saw the opportunity for release and took it. I'd just proven how unworthy I was to be a father, how unreliable, dangerous... What possessed me to think I could ever raise a child? Kyle had believed in me, but now he'd finally seen how pitiful I was. He'd never trust me again. He'd take Brock off me, my baby girl.

I growled in both grief and rage.

You don't know how to be a dad.

I smashed my fist into the bag.

You've never had an alpha father to model yourself on.

I hit the bag again, harder, feeling the pain shooting up my arm.

Because you lost your father in an attack by dragon shifters.

"Fucking dragons!" I yelled, and then I pounded the bag relentlessly. I huffed and grunted, smashing it again and again, unable to stop—not *wanting* to stop. Kyle would never come back to me now. I'd effectively lost my family, my mate.

Without really thinking about it, I shifted and lunged straight for the bag with my teeth bared. I sank my jaws around the thick leather as I landed, and I yanked at it until it split. I bit it again and again, my claws scratching at the bag and ripping it until I eventually stood among a pile of shredded leather and stuffing.

Panting, my body shaking, I let out a pained, furious howl, my heartache and anger so overwhelming it was almost ripping *me* apart.

Chapter 16 - Kyle

When I woke up Monday morning I checked my phone, just like I had every morning, and every night. Nothing from Gavin, but I had told him to stay the hell away from us. What did I expect? He was giving me the space I'd asked for. Even so, I thought I'd hear from him, even if it was just to ask me if I was okay.

Nausea rolled up from my stomach and heartburn kicked in as I sat up. My baby girl was letting me know she was growing. I groaned and dragged myself out of bed and into the kitchen to find Brock dressed and his school bag on his back.

"What time is it?" I asked, rubbing my eyes and peering at the clock.

"It's almost time to leave," he said as he tied his shoes.

Kennedy was rinsing dishes at the sink and she gave me a look that said, "I know, weird right?"

"You're uh, going to school today, Brocky? You know you don't have to, right?" I asked. We'd agreed he didn't have to go on Thursday and Friday. I'd wanted to make certain the dragon shifter wasn't going to hassle Brock at school, and a quick text from Jaxon on Thursday morning had told me they were keeping a watchful eye on both the school and the homestead. Still, I wasn't certain.

"What else am I going to do? Stay home and play video games all day?" He shook his head.

"Um… Yeah? That isn't appealing to you?"

"I'd rather see my friends," he said as he grabbed an apple off the kitchen bench and stuffed it into his backpack.

Kennedy caught my eye and raised her eyebrows.

"I don't know who this kid is," I whispered to her and she giggled.

"Well, I like him," she said.

"Me too. Alright, Brocky. I'll drive you to school."

"Um, okay? But you're in your pajamas?" He pointed to me, and I looked down at the pajamas Gavin had gotten me for Christmas, the ones with the wolves printed on them.

"Give me ten minutes." I laughed and hurried to get dressed.

On the way to school I noticed Brock was particularly quiet. I gave him a side-eye. "Sure you feel ready to go back to school already?"

"I'm sure," he said shortly.

"Then what's up?"

"Nothing." He sighed and looked out the window.

I was getting the silent treatment from two alphas in my life. Great. Luckily, this one had less patience… When he started to rub his fingers and bite his bottom lip as we crossed Pack Lane, I knew he was going to burst at any moment.

"It's just…When can we go home? To the pack?"

"I don't know," I said honestly.

He let out a heavy sigh and slumped into his seat as we pulled into the line of cars dropping off kids at the school. "Why can't we just go back to the homestead tonight?"

"We need to stay safe. It isn't safe there right now with the dragons."

"Then why is Gavin still there? Is he safe?"

"He is. Listen, Brock. Gavin and I need some time apart," I said, leveling with him.

He sighed again, and we moved up closer to the gates.

"Can you just…"

"Trust me, Brocky. I'm doing the best I can, and so is Gavin."

Another sigh as we rolled up to the drop-off zone, but this time he didn't have anything more to say until he opened the door and was halfway out of the car.

"Dad," he said as he turned back to look at me. "Can you *please* think about how we could go home soon?"

"Sure, Brocky. I will," I promised as I gave him a reassuring smile.

I pulled away and immediately headed for the best place to work out my feelings—Pampered Paws Doggie Daycare. As I parked I spotted Jason, the florist from our claiming ceremony standing on the street with his hands on his hips, staring at Trevor's shop. He was frowning.

I got out of my car and was about to ask what he was doing when he turned on his heel and stomped up the street toward Petal Pushers without noticing me.

"Your neighbor has been checking you out," I told Trevor as I pushed open the door to his shop. The moment I stepped inside, a blast of smells hit me—dogs, dogs, dogs.

"Who? What? What are you saying?" Trevor came over and gave me a big, warm hug, leaning over my bump.

"Jason, he was standing outside and staring at your shop."

Trevor pulled away and held me at arm's length. "Something's wrong."

"With the florist?"

"Yes, *obviously* there's something wrong with that infuriating idiot, but there's also something wrong with *this*," he said as he traced a finger in the air over my entire being.

"Hm, well…"

He placed his hands on his hips. "What is going on?"

"Do you want the short version or the long version?"

"I want every detail in technicolor. Come here and get comfortable," he said, walking behind the counter and thumping one of the bright pink stools there. "I'll put on some Taylor and you can tell me all about it."

He put on "Trevor's Tay" mix and I told him the basics of what had happened on Wednesday.

"Have you heard from him since you walked away?" he asked.

"No." I looked down at my bump and placed a hand there. "I might never hear from him again."

"Oh please." Trevor rolled his eyes. "Those pregnancy hormones are making you dramatic, girl."

"I told him to give us space. He's an alpha, he might not know that means *just a bit* of space…"

"And if he took you back right now? Would you go?"

"No," I said honestly. "I need to keep Brock and the baby safe. It's not safe up there right now, and obviously I can't trust Gavin to keep us out of harm's way."

"Hm…" Trevor gazed over my shoulder, and from years of experience I knew he wasn't looking at anything in particular.

"What do you want to say, Trevor? I've known you long enough to know what you look like when you're trying to hold back from saying something mean."

"What? No..."

"Spit it out. Just say it. I can take it," I said, sure I could handle whatever he had to say.

"Maybe you could have been a little nicer during that conversation with Gavin," he suggested in his most diplomatic tone.

I'd been wrong. I could not handle it. "I don't think so," I said sharply.

"Even after Brock explained to you what had really happened?" Trevor looked at me with piercing eyes. "Even after you found out Gavin had done his best to keep Brock safe, and had actually acted very intelligently to try and diffuse the situation? You still don't think so?"

"Well I didn't know that *then*, did I?" I crossed my arms over my chest.

"*Mhm...*"

"Sure. Okay. Fine. I might have been a little emotional. But I still don't want to see him yet. I still need some space." I let out a frustrated sigh and ran my hands over my face. "Is that terrible?"

"No, it's not. It's probably healthy, given what you've been through. Just don't leave it too long, okay? You're fated mates, and fate doesn't mess around."

"If you ask me, fate is conspiring against me. First with Brock and now with this baby girl. I'm destined to be a single father."

"Oh get over yourself," Trevor said, slapping his hand against the counter and making me jump. "The moment you're ready, go and talk to that man of yours. Get it worked out. You're boring me with this self-pity, it's ugly on you."

I burst out laughing and Trevor gave me a warm smile before leaning forward and giving me another big hug.

"I'm sorry you're having a hard time," he said genuinely. "And I'm sorry I have to be so honest with you."

"It's what I come here for." I leaned into his embrace. "You're my best friend."

"And you're mine. Now, tell me why you think Jason was standing outside my shop."

***

The next six days went by with a snail's pace. Instead of simply checking my phone each morning and night, I was now checking it every hour. Not a peep from Gavin, and I felt sick from the silence even though I'd been just as uncommunicative.

I'd lost count how many times I started to text him, but I couldn't bring myself to send anything. I knew Gavin and I needed to work things out, but I just wasn't ready to talk yet, and as the weekend rolled around, I started to worry I might never be ready...

"Aquarium day!" Brock shouted as he came storming into the kitchen on Sunday morning wearing a t-shirt with a neon blue whale on it.

"Aquarium day!" I shouted back. Britt shot me a look of disdain through her curtain of messy hair from where she sat at the kitchen bench, nursing a hangover.

"Want to come to the aquarium, Aunty Britt?" Brock asked as he started raiding the pantry for snacks. I grabbed an apple and started slicing it up for our snack pack.

"Not today, Brocky." She groaned quietly and took a sip of her black coffee. "Not...today..."

"Would Kennedy want to come, do you think?" I asked.

"She's dead to the world. You're on your own," she grunted at me.

I sure was. I got Brock into the car and headed down Poplar Road toward the ocean. We hit the coastal highway and headed south with the ocean to our right, and I wound down the windows to let in the fresh, salty air. It was a warm day, and Brock was in a great mood, grabbing my outdated cassette tapes out of the glove box and DJing what we listened to. It was almost contagious—I almost felt happy.

At the aquarium we hit up the penguin enclosure first and caught the end of the feeding session. Brock squealed and clapped his hands as the smallest fairy penguins toddled up the ramp to accept fish from the feeder.

"Too cute," I said with a laugh.

"They are *so* cute."

"I meant you." I winked at him, and he rolled his eyes and poked his tongue out at me.

We rushed to get through the biggest exhibits and were so excited to see the free roaming dolphins coming in off the ocean for their feeding, followed by whale-spotting out on the horizon where they breached and splashed their tails. We stopped for a snack break by the otter enclosure and laughed at how quickly they scurried through their burrows. By the time we made it to the dimly lit nightlife exhibition, we were dragging our feet a little.

"This has been a really fun day," Brock declared.

"I'm glad you've had fun, Brocky," I said, ruffling his hair as we stopped to look at a tank of seahorses. I smiled at how much I resembled the pregnant ones with my big belly.

"I wish Dad was here though," Brock said quietly as he leaned against the barrier near the tank.

My heart softened a little at Brock's confession and the fact he was now calling him "Dad" again. "It would be nice with him here, wouldn't it?"

"Do you think he misses me?" he asked in a tiny voice.

"Of course he does," I said, putting my hand on his back.

"I hope I can see him soon. I feel bad about how much we missed when I was little and I feel bad I can't see him now."

I swallowed down my emotions and gave his shoulder a squeeze. I just didn't know what to say to that.

***

That night, Brock finished all of his dinner and asked if he could play Runemaze on live.

"Sure. Just make sure you get ready for school tomorrow, okay?"

"I will!" he shouted back, already halfway up the stairs.

A few minutes later, as I brought up a plate of dinner for Kennedy and Britt, who were still brutally hungover, I heard a familiar voice coming from Brock's room. I stopped in my tracks. My wolf lunged forward and I barely kept myself from rushing into the room. It was Gavin's voice.

"I miss you too, Brocky," he said. "Are you taking good care of your dad?"

"Yeah, I took him to the aquarium today," Brock said proudly, and I bit down on my bottom lip to stop myself from laughing.

"Nice. That place is cool, huh?"

"I wish you could have been there."

"Me too. I miss you and your dad a lot. So, so, so much," Gavin said.

"Do you think we can come home soon?"

Gavin went silent for a moment, and then I heard the sound of an explosion in the game. "Woah look out," he cried.

I hurried down the hall and delivered the meal to the two sleepy, cranky women before I stumbled down the stairs and collapsed onto the couch. My heart raced, and my tummy felt tight.

I automatically put my hand on my bump, and immediately felt a kick. I yanked my t-shirt up then gasped when I saw a lump pushing up through the taut skin of my belly. It slowly moved left, and I knew it was the baby moving her foot. When she began shifting her foot again I grabbed my phone and immediately started recording.

"Hey, baby girl!" I zoomed in on our cub exploring the boundaries of her home. She pushed harder and slid her foot to the very top of my belly where she kicked me once more.

Before I could have second thoughts, I sent the video to Gavin. I let out a sigh and dropped my phone beside me. He should have been there with me to see that…

My phone buzzed. I looked at the screen and a smile broke across my face when I saw he was thinking the same thing.

WOW. I should have been there… - G

I held the phone tightly wanting to reply, but I couldn't bring myself to type anything. The phone buzzed again.

I want you to know I'm only honoring your wishes. I want to be there. I'll talk as soon as you're ready - G

If only I knew when that was going to be.

That night, in bed, I wrapped my arms around a pillow, pulled it against my body, and thought about Gavin's big, broad shoulders, his scent, his smile, his laughter. I missed him so much. I hated being away from him, and I hated being the one who had to do something about it. I felt completely lost, scared, and alone.

Hot tears soaked my pillow, and then I began sobbing… And couldn't stop.

Chapter 17 - Gavin

Life without Kyle and Brock was more than just miserable, it was like living in darkness. I spent the last eleven days in an absolute fog. I'd woken up on the floor of my gym, among the debris of my boxing bag and wished I could just go back to sleep. That feeling had followed me through to now. Nightmares about dragon shifters attacking my family had plagued me every night, but they were short and fast—better than my waking days, which were slow, long, and dark.

I stopped working on the game I was designing and spent my time at home, watching television and eating. My wolf desperately wanted to run, but I ignored it until it curled up and sulked. I tried to play games, but the games room just reminded me of Brock and of training him for that competition. I tried to listen to music, and of course that just reminded me of Kyle and how much I missed his radio show, which I couldn't bring myself to listen to. I was missing the nicest parts of my life—Kyle and Brock, but I was also missing things I'd enjoyed *before* I'd met them. Losing them meant losing more of myself than I thought possible. And I had nothing to fill the hole that was left.

Sitting in the kitchen, staring blankly at the wall, I was broken out of my reverie by a knocking on the front door. I jumped up, raced to a mirror to check I looked okay, and then hurried to answer the door.

"Oh," I said sadly when I saw who it was.

"Well, good morning to you too," Nic said as she looked me over. "This is an interesting look to greet your sister with."

"You like my underwear?" I asked gruffly as I stepped aside and let her in.

"I like it more than I like this," she said as she came inside and reached up to tug on the scraggly goatee that was growing from my chin. "What the fuck have you been doing in here? Losing yourself completely?"

I grunted and closed the door behind her before I slouched my way over to the couch. I sat down on the cushions with another grunt and pulled a throw blanket over my lap.

"You want a cup of coffee?" she asked from behind me in the kitchen. I heard water running and the kettle going on the stove. I didn't have to give her an answer. I stared into the middle distance of the living room until Nic came over and put a cup of strong, black coffee in my hands. That's when I realized I was really looking at Kyle's cabinet of vinyl records, cassettes and CDs. I released a deep, melancholy sigh.

"So, this is a fun pity party," Nic commented as she sat down beside me then tugged at the blanket, pulling some onto her own lap. "I like how you've got the AC on so it's freezing cold in here, like a real cave you can just die in."

I grunted again and took a sip of the coffee. It burned my tongue, but I didn't care.

"Has this been going on all week? Why wasn't I invited?" She nudged me with her elbow, and I moved over to get out of her way. She let out a huffy sigh and leaned back against the couch, nursing her own coffee.

"I'm here to cheer you up," she said after some time.

"No one asked you to."

"Jaxon did, actually," Nic said as she looked me over. "He noticed you haven't been around lately, and he's been worried about you."

"But you haven't been." I was being snarky and I knew it was unfair, but I felt as bitter about the world as the coffee tasted on my tongue.

"I have been, of course I have. But I know how you get," she said, waving her hand over my general state of disarray. "I know you need time alone."

I nodded then swallowed another gulp of coffee. I started to feel a bit of a buzz, and my wolf stuck its nose out of the dark hole it had crawled into.

"But Jaxon was specifically worried because he thought you might have gone out looking for that dragon on your own. He would have come to see you himself but he thought I might be able to connect with you better. So here I am." Nicole then slapped my thigh for emphasis.

"Now what?" I asked, turning to look at her.

"Now we have a deep and meaningful talk about your emotions," she said with a smirk.

"Um…"

"Just kidding." She laughed. "C'mon, when are Kyle and Brock coming back to the homestead?"

"I don't know." I shrugged and looked back at Kyle's music collection. "Maybe never. It's up to Kyle, and he hasn't shown me any indication he wants to come back. Ever."

"Bullshit." My eyebrows shot up and I looked at her in shock.

"*Bullshit*?"

"Yeah, total bullshit," she said, meeting my gaze directly with no fear in her eyes.

"He's not talking to me, Nic. I fucked up. He told me to stay away," I said gruffly.

She frowned at me. "Big fucking deal. We all fuck up. That's what relationships are about. You fuck up, you make up. And then you fuck."

I snorted and gave her joke a consolatory chuckle. "I don't think I can come back from this one, Nic."

"Uh, what exactly did you do *wrong*?" she asked as she turned to face me more directly.

"I put our son in harm's way. I didn't take care of that dragon shifter the moment he started shit." I swallowed hard as I, once again, remembered the look of terror on Brock's face, heard his tears, felt his disappointment…

"What do you think would have happened if you'd reacted differently?"

"The guy would have backed down, and Brock wouldn't have been attacked."

"Uh, maybe in some weird alternate universe where dragons are passive as fuck. Think about it, Gavin. You didn't lose your head. You showed your son the best way to stand up for himself. You demonstrated when it's time to just get the fuck out of there. You didn't use violence like that dragon. You even had the presence of mind to warn the homestead about the dragon threat. What do you think that does for Brock?"

I shrugged, not quite ready to shift my perspective and end my self-pity party, even though everything she was saying was logical and true.

"You showed him how to take care of other people in a responsible, thoughtful way. Just like an alpha does," Nic said as she pointed to me. "That's what alphas do, right? They take care of others?"

"I wouldn't know, I didn't have a—"

"Oh shut up, my darling brother!" Nic laughed and slapped my arm. "We didn't have an alpha dad, *I know*."

"It's never bothered you as much as it's bothered me," I said quietly, shifting my gaze and staring at Kyle's display case again.

"No shit. Do you know why that is? Why I wasn't so fucked up about losing our alpha dad?"

"Because you're younger," I said.

Nicole waited for me to look at her, then said softly, "Because I had you."

I swallowed down a wave of emotion but didn't stop looking at her.

"Because I had you, Gavin. My big alpha brother who always took care of me *and* Dad, and literally everyone you've ever come in contact with. You keep saying you don't know how to be a good alpha example for Brock, but that's just not true. *You* are the example he needs. Exactly as you are. Gray hairs and all."

I let out a short laugh that turned into a sob as my sister ran her fingers over the patch of gray hair by my temples. I quickly wiped away the tears that pricked the corners of my eyes.

"Alphas take care of people, right?" she asked as she took my hand. My wolf whimpered, urging me to listen.

"Right," I agreed, squeezing her hand.

"And who are you taking care of now?"

I swallowed. She was the queen of emotional manipulation…and healing.

"Brock. And Kyle. By giving them space," I said stubbornly.

Nicole scoffed, and then gripped my hand so hard it hurt. "You need them as much as they need you, which is an infinite amount. Get them back here."

"How exactly do you think I'm going to do that? Just demand it?"

"Oh god, Gavin. I don't know." She let go of my hand. "Did you fight for him to stay, when he threatened to leave?"

"No," I admitted as regret settled deep in my guts.

"Well. How about you be a fucking alpha and fight for him?"

I laughed again and ran a hand through my hair.

"You know how to do that right? How to be an alpha?" she asked, punching my arm with each syllable.

"You know I do," I growled, and Nicole let out a pleased laughed.

"That's more like it. Now get up, we're going for a run," she said as she jumped up.

I groaned and leaned my head back on the couch. "Nic, I just don't feel like—"

"I said *get up, we're going for a run,*" she repeated as she kicked my shin.

"Ouch! Fuck! Stop it!"

"What're you going to do about it?" She kicked me harder until I grabbed at her foot. She jumped backward out of my grip and stuck her tongue out at me.

"I'm going to beat you to the top of the mountain, is what I'm going to do." I threw the blanket off my lap then stood.

"In your *dreams,* you pity party loser!" Nic sprinted to the door, threw it open, and then shifted in the yard. I was right on her tail, leaping over the coffee table before bounding down the steps and shifting as soon as my feet hit the grass. It felt incredible to sink my paws into the warm dirt as the smell of spring flowers flooded my senses.

My wolf took over, and it shook off all of the last few days misery as it bounded through the forest after my bratty little sister. I lost her when she jumped over the creek and took a sharp turn through dense brush we didn't usually cover, but I caught her sweet bergamot scent and followed it until I found her clambering over a boulder. I nipped at her heels and we both fell over the other side of the boulder, sliding before our paws got a grip on the loose earth and we ascended up the final section of the mountainside.

My muscles stretched and relaxed with every push of my legs, and every contraction of my lungs felt like I was letting out old, musty emotions while bringing in new, fresh energy.

As we mounted the crest and reached the rocky plateau at the top, I felt so alive... And then angry when Nic kicked her back leg and shot dust into my eyes, buying herself just enough time to bolt forward and make it to the top before me. I let out a bark, blinked the dust from my eyes and dashed right after her. I gave her a nip on the haunch, but she just looked at me like the smuggest wolf I'd ever seen.

We panted to cool down as we looked out over the scene before us. The town of Timberwood Cove stretched out below, surrounded on three sides by dense, verdant forest, and the ocean to the west.

Nicole shifted into her human form and carefully sat on the edge of the overhang. I followed her lead, and we both laughed out loud when we realized I was in my pity party outfit—underwear and nothing else. But the sun was warm on my skin, and we swung our legs like we'd been doing ever since we were kids when we'd first discovered that rocky outcrop.

She sighed as we took it all in. "What a place to live, huh?"

"We're so lucky, aren't we?"

"We have a lot to be thankful for." She moved closer and rested her head on my shoulder.

"You're right," I agreed.

"Oh, what's that?" she asked slyly. "*I'm* right? Did I hear you correctly? Did you just say '*Nicole is right*?'"

I growled and wrapped an arm around her shoulder while she chuckled. We sat together in silence and watched as the shadows of the forest moved with the sun's track across the sky, and as waves broke across the big blue ocean. I thought I could see whales breaching, but from that high up they just looked like white splotches against a deep blue background.

When Nicole pulled away from my embrace, I realized just how relaxed I'd become. We stood and stretched out our limbs.

"Pity party over?" she asked as she patted my chest.

"Yeah, I'm back." I took her hand and held it over the top of my heart. "Thank you. You got me back to myself."

I saw tears welling in her eyes and I gave her a warm grin. She inhaled sharply, then pulled away and wiped her eyes.

"Want a real challenge? Want to walk down on two legs?" she asked with a grin.

"In my underwear?"

"What are you, a chicken?"

I pushed past her and hurried down the trail in my bare feet and my tighty-whities, hearing the beautiful sound of Nicole's laugh echoing behind me the whole way back to the homestead. We parted ways at the Lodge after a long hug.

I got home feeling more like myself, and decided to stretch my alpha muscles a little more. I headed straight for my games room, kicked back with my dirty feet up on a big ottoman and turned on RuneMaze. I raced through the hardest levels to get myself psyched, and then logged onto the live version. I spent the next few hours helping out kids who were stuck in puzzles, and then took a break to order a pizza from Tony's.

I was halfway through a slice of pepperoni and pineapple when I felt a familiar tugging in my chest. My wolf was alert, and it was guiding me to a certain part of the game. I put down the pizza and followed my intuition until I found Brock. I don't know how my wolf knew, but I guess it had something to do with our bond.

"Hey, Brocky" I said excitedly into my headset as I sat up.

"Gavin? Hey! I was hoping to find you."

"Want to run through some levels?" I asked.

"Hm... Nah, let's just mess around with this level and talk. If that's okay?"

"It sure is." My heart was racing and my wolf pranced, so excited to hear our son. "Hey, you'll never guess what I'm having for dinner," I said with a grin.

"What is it?"

"The best kind of pizza."

"Pepperoni and pineapple!" he exclaimed excitedly, making me laugh.

"Yep, the one and only."

"The best."

"Isn't it? Man, it's so good."

"Ugh, I'm jealous! I wish I could come over for pizza..."

My heart ached at the thought, but I stayed silent.

"Hey, how'd you find me?" he asked.

"My wolf showed me where you'd be," I told him as we dashed through the maze and solved puzzles together. "How's your wolf feeling lately?"

"Hm... Kind of sad."

"Yeah?"

"I miss you, Dad," he said quietly. I took a sharp inhale and closed my eyes as my heart felt fit to bursting. It was the first time I'd heard him call me "Dad", though Kyle had told me Brock had referenced me as such. I prayed it wouldn't be the last.

"I miss you too, Brocky. Are you taking good care of your dad?"

"Yeah, I took him to the aquarium today," Brock said proudly.

"Nice! That place is cool, huh?" I smiled as I wondered if we'd been looking at whales at the same time.

"I wish you could have been there," Brock said quietly.

"Me too. I miss you and your dad a lot. So, so, so much."

"Do you think we can come home soon?"

I fell silent. I wish I knew the answer. I wish I could tell him to get his things, get his dad, and come back right now. But that was a conversation to have with Kyle...

Suddenly, a puzzle in the game went wrong and a water cannon shot out from the wall, almost eviscerating Brock's character. "Woah look out!"

We played for a few more minutes before Brock said he had to go to bed, and I realized how tired I was too. The hike up the mountain had been easy enough but coming down on two legs sure was hard on the body.

When the video from Kyle came through on my phone, I was lying in bed looking at photos of Brock and Kyle goofing around in the kitchen a few weeks earlier. I was so surprised to see Kyle's name on my screen I thought I'd accidentally taken a screenshot and it was just a photo. I gasped when I realized it was an actual text from him.

I took a moment before I opened it. I knew it was going to be something confronting. Something emotional. I was right. The moment I saw Kyle's big swollen belly, I felt tears pricking my eyes. And then I saw a little lump moving across his taunt skin... I heard myself sobbing before I even realized what was happening. I held a fist to my mouth to break the sobs and ended up biting down on my fingers as I replayed the video over and over.

With shaking hands and tears running down my cheeks, I typed out a text.

I miss the three of you so much. Please, please come back to me.

I hesitated, hovering my thumb over the send button. I backspaced and started again.

I'm broken. Please, Kyle. I can't be without you and Brock and I want you to come home.

Backspace, backspace, backspace.

WOW. I should have been there... - G

That would have to do for now. I hit send, and lay back on my bed, clutching the phone to my chest as my sobs subsided. I remembered Nicole's words like she was whispering them in my ear.

"So be a fucking alpha."

I waited for a reply from Kyle... And I didn't get it.

"Be a fucking alpha," I said aloud as I unlocked my phone.

I want you to know I'm only honoring your wishes. I want to be there. I'll talk as soon as you are ready - G

I knew that it wasn't enough to win him back right away. I knew I'd have to do more. But it was a start.

Chapter 18 - Kyle

The next day, I woke up feeling horrid. It was the worst I'd ever felt. I could barely believe it, but my belly was even bigger and had really started to pop—but worst of all, it was *itchy*. I couldn't stop scratching my belly and it was driving me crazy. And then, as soon as I rolled over, heartburn flared up and made me feel like I'd swallowed fire. I groaned and rolled my way out of bed, cursing at how low the futon was, and deeply missing the comfort of my bed at Gavin's. The moment I took a step, I felt dizzy again.

"Great..."

I steadied myself, and once the dizziness cleared I showered, and then tried some soothing lotion on my belly. Hoping that would work, I dressed in clean clothes. But the itching wouldn't stop. The heartburn was going off like crazy too, but at least I knew what caused that—my baby girl pushing my digestive organs up into my throat.

I hurried out to find it was already late morning, and there was a note from Britt on the fridge.

Hi sleepyhead! Taking Brocky to school on my way to work. We love you!!!

I scratched at my tummy, and then hissed as my nails cut the skin.

"Fuck."

I called Britt and she answered on the first ring.

"Britt, I think something's wrong," I said as I rubbed my hands over my belly, trying to get some relief from the itch.

"What? What's wrong?" she asked quickly.

"I can't stop itching."

"Um...where..."

"Oh my god, not down *there.* My belly. The skin on my belly. There's no rash but it's so itchy, I literally can't stop scratching it." I wrapped my hands in the hem of my t-shirt to stop myself from using my nails.

"Okay, hang on, I think I've heard of this. Wait a sec, I'm going to do a search," she said.

I heard her typing and I grit my teeth as I paced through the house, barely stopping myself from rubbing my belly against every surface I saw.

"Okay, good news, it's totally normal," she said.

"Um, no it's not."

"Yes, it definitely is. It's a very common symptom that expecting parents get at the six-month mark. It happens because the skin is stretched and your immune system is whacked out."

"That didn't happen with Brock. What the hell am I going to do?"

"This site says it's worse with stress."

"Everything is," I retorted.

"Do you have dizziness? Swollen ankles? Heart burn? Backache?"

"Yes, no, yes, now that you mention it, yes."

"All common symptoms, but according to this, stress is the link. You need to take the day off."

"Uh, I can't just call in sick to the station."

"Yes, you can. Just because you never *have* doesn't mean you *can't*." I could practically hear her putting her hair up in that know-it-all bun.

I glanced down at my now very red stomach and groaned. "Okay, but you can call them, and do *not* tell them I've got itchy skin. I'll never hear the last of it."

"Great. I'll call them now. Oh, also, this site says to put your hands in socks to stop yourself from scratching. Like cute little mittens," she said with a girlish giggle before hanging up.

"I hate this," I mumbled aloud, but I did as she said. I shoved my hands into a pair of socks, but they were flapping around at the ends, so I switched them for Brock's smaller, superhero socks and wandered around the house, trying not to scratch myself. I did my best to relax, pottering around the house, listening to records from Kennedy's collection of soul music, and even taking a bath. It slowly started to work...

I took a walk with my hands shoved in my pockets, and eventually found myself at the park. I sat on a bench, closed my eyes, and let the warm spring sunlight kiss me all over my face. I took a deep breath and loved how I could smell jasmine and cottonwood flowers on the cool breeze. Everything was so peaceful, but despite my surroundings I couldn't get rid of the tension pulling me in all directions. I needed to let go of my anger, but where did I start? With forgiving Gavin? With accepting I'd made a mistake by not putting my trust in him?

After a while I wandered home, taking the long way through the prettier streets of Timberwood Cove. As I turned the corner to Poplar Road, my wolf appeared and began whining. I walked a little faster toward the house but stopped in my tracks when I saw Gavin's car parked out the front. My heart sped up, and for long moments I didn't know what to do, but then I began walking again.

As I got closer, I noticed his car was empty. I looked up and saw him at the door, knocking firmly on the frame. I could only see him from behind, but his broad shoulders looked even bigger than usual in a tight white t-shirt, and his hips and thighs looked spectacular in dark denim jeans that hugged them perfectly. I took a breath to calm myself, and reminded myself how mad I was at him...

Didn't you tell him to stay away? To give you space?

Maybe I didn't want so much space anymore...

I shuffled up the garden path to the porch, and then stood at the bottom of the steps. I cleared my throat. My belly started itching like crazy as soon as he turned around, and I felt my wolf surging upward, making me dizzy. I just held the banister and smiled.

"Hi," I said softly.

Gavin said nothing. He flew down the stairs until he reached the bottom. Then he softly ran his fingers down my cheek. I let him. I practically melted into his touch.

"How are you?" he asked.

"Itchy," I replied honestly, and he frowned in confusion. "It's a...pregnancy thing."

Gavin sighed and put his hands on my shoulders, squeezing them gently. My stomach churned, and a flush of heartburn flared before quickly fading. I wanted him to say the right thing... I didn't know what it was, but god, I wanted him to convince me to come home.

"Kyle," he said, his voice rough as his eyes met mine. "I'm sorry for putting Brock in danger. I will be more careful. But I wouldn't have done anything different that night. I tried to defuse the situation. I kept him safe. I warned the pack about the dragon shifter. I set a good example for your son, for *our* son. I was a good father that night. And I'm a good father now."

Heat rushed to my cheeks. I nodded and felt my wolf pushing hard to get closer to Gavin. I'm sure if I could shift my wolf would have tried to force me to do so. I let go of the banister and let Gavin hold me up with his big, strong hands. It felt so good to allow him to bear some of my weight, physically and metaphorically. I really needed his strength even if I didn't always want to admit it. To try and raise our two children on my own would have been hard, but I didn't have to make it hard if I could accept that Gavin really did what *any* father would do; protect his child.

"I—"

"I don't want to argue. I need you to come home," he said.

I flinched and frowned reflexively as my stubbornness flared.

"It's not a question," Gavin said gruffly. "I need you and Brock to come home. We're meant to be together. We can work out whatever problems we have later, *together*. But you're coming home. I'm not taking no for an answer."

I could see he meant it. His alpha nature was certainly coming to the fore, and once again I felt my submissive wolf capitulate. I shook my head, and Gavin drew his brows together.

"Kyle—"

"No. Let me say something... I understand what you did that night was because you thought it was the right thing to do under the circumstances, and it was, so for that I apologize for not listening to your explanation. But you should have told me about dragon shifters in the first place. You should have told me Kyle really *was* being bullied and you were teaching him to stand up for himself. You need to talk to me, you need to let go of your crazy control. You need to understand that being a dad isn't easy and you're going to make mistakes, and *I* need to learn that you're still learning."

"Yes."

"That's it? Yes?"

"Yes I know I'm still learning, and yes I need to be less anxious about what may happen with Brock and our baby girl. And yes you were right to apologize for not listening to me."

A smile crept across my lips as I gazed up at him. My doubt and hesitation evaporated. It was obvious what I should do.

"Then...yes," I said, before he planted a firm kiss on my lips.

***

We pulled up outside Brock's school in Gavin's car before the end of the school day to get a spot at the front of the pick-up line, and then spent the next half an hour making out. I was so hungry for his mouth I literally only stopped kissing him to pull back and rub my still itchy belly.

"I missed you so fucking much," I groaned as he gently scratched my bump.

"I missed you." Gavin leaned in for another soft kiss, and then cradled my cheek in his hand.

We glanced at the school doors as they flew open, then looked back at each other with a grin. We climbed out of the car then leaned against the hood while we waited for Brock.

"Dads!" Brock screamed when he glimpsed us. He bolted down the stairs and sprinted across the yard so fast I was almost surprised when he slammed into us. He wrapping his arms around both of us and brought us into a tight group hug.

"Hey, Brocky." Gavin laughed and squeezed us all tightly. "It's good to see you."

"Dads!" Brock laughed so happily he sounded almost manic. "Are we going home?" he asked as he looked up at us.

"Yes, we are." I smiled down at him and felt tears stinging my eyes when I saw how happy he was.

"Yes!" he cried.

A car honked and we realized we were holding up the line, so we dashed into Gavin's ride and got the hell out of there.

"Need to pick up anything from Britt and Kennedy's?" Gavin asked as we approached the intersection of Pack Lane.

"Not me. Brocky?" I looked over to the backseat where Brock was swinging his legs and beaming.

"Nah, I have everything I need right here," he said with a cheesy grin. Gavin hit the indicator and took us straight up Pack Lane, driving north toward the homestead. Toward our home.

"Brocky, Cole said he's been missing you," Gavin said, looking at Brock in the rearview mirror.

Brock sighed. "Yeah. We hardly get to see each other at school."

"I was talking to his dads earlier... Do you want to go for a sleepover at Cole's house tonight? It sounds like Liam will be there too."

Brock gasped and practically jumped out of his seat. "Yes! Can I?"

Brock asked me, but I just motioned to Gavin. Frankly, I was impressed he was putting in so much effort and thought to organize something like that for Brock.

"Of course you can," I said. "It sounds like Dad has it all organized."

Gavin glanced at me, barely able to contain his smile.

"Yes!" Brock fist pumped the air and quickly got on the phone to Cole to tell him the good news. Gavin reached across the console to take my hand and squeeze it gently.

"You better tell Britt you won't be home," he said.

"Oh shit, you're right."

Guess what? You were right. Feeling very relaxed... Now we're back on the homestead. Will catch up tomorrow xo K

As we drove through the gates of the community, my wolf settled down and let out a happy sigh. I settled down as well, and felt the rest of my tension dissolve from my shoulders. We dropped Brock off at Linc's beautiful wooden home, and then headed straight back to Gavin's house. To our home.

I waddled up the steps of the porch, straining with every step.

"God, you got so big." he commented, putting a hand on my belly. He moaned in what was decidedly a sexual nature and rubbed my stomach gently before helping me up the steps. As soon as he threw open the front door I could smell something sweet. Rose petals. I gasped when I saw a trail leading from the door through the living room. I looked up at Gavin and he just gave me a big grin as he put a hand on my back and urged me forward. I followed the trail, getting more and more excited as it led me through the living area, past the kitchen, down the hallway…

A genuine apology… An explanation… And now a romantic gesture. This was what I had been looking for, without even knowing it. To feel special to Gavin… To feel like he heard me and wanted to show me he understood what I was saying.

I almost fell over when I reached the end of the trail. It didn't lead to the bedroom like I thought it would. Instead, it turned down the hall and led right into the family room where a birthing tub was sitting in the middle of the room with an oversized bow on its side, amid a huge display of bouquets.

I covered my mouth with my hand.

"I want you to know I'm listening to you," Gavin said as he appeared behind me and put a hand on my shoulder. "I respect you, and I respect your choices. And I always want to compromise. I've been stubborn because I've been scared. But I trust you, and most importantly, I trust myself now. I'm a good dad to Brock, and I'm going to be a good dad to our baby girl. I want her to come into this world in a fear-free environment where I'm confident, and you are too."

Tears trickled down my cheeks as I looked from him to the birthing bath and back again.

"I can have a home birth?" I ask in a quiet, squeaky voice.

"Yes. We can have Maddie here the whole time to make sure everything is safe. But you better bet that if anything goes wrong, I'm taking you straight to the hospital," he warned.

I laughed and nodded as I wiped tears off my face.

"Thank you," I whispered. I pressed myself against his broad chest and let out a relieved sob. "It's so good to be home."

Gavin simply held me for a little while, and then he took my hand and gently led me to the bedroom. I crawled onto the bed, sinking into its perfect softness. I moaned happily and watched as Gavin stripped off in front of me. He slowly peeled his t-shirt up, revealing his abdomen and then his sexy chest with its pert, dark nipples. He shook off the shirt then started plucking at his belt buckle as he gave me a cheeky grin.

"Take it off," I ordered. I wet my lips as he threaded the leather through the buckle, clicked the steel, and then whipped his belt off in one smooth move before dropping it onto the floor. I giggled, and then bit my bottom lip as he slid his hands over his hips and down to his crotch. He covered the outline of his cock with his palm and made a show of slowly grinding into it.

It was too much. I greedily grabbed for him, urging him to join me. He obliged, kneeling on the bed before me and leaning down to press a soft kiss against my mouth. I ran my hands over his back and shoulders, moaning at how good he felt. God I missed this. I missed him. He slipped his fingers under the hem of my t-shirt and rubbed his palm over the taut skin of my big pregnant tummy. I lifted my arms as he tugged the shirt off over my head, and he immediately planted kisses all over my belly. I was about to relax into the tickly sensation when I felt a kick. I looked down and saw a little lump forming.

"Gavin, look," I said, pointing to it.

"Oh my god." He fixated on the lump as it moved across my belly and then disappeared.

"That's…*incredible*," he said before leaning forward and kissing me all over my face. I laughed and ran my fingers through his hair. Eventually, he pulled back and looked at me with deep affection.

"I love you," he said softly.

"I love you too."

Gavin kissed me softly and with such gentleness I felt like I might float away from the thrill of it. I slid my hands down his back and grabbed his ass, pulling him closer to me. He moaned into the kiss, which sent a vibration straight down into my cock. It hardened almost immediately, and I was reminded it had been so long since Gavin had made love to me.

He tugged off my pants then sat back on his heels, looking me over, seemingly admiring my body. I felt a little self-conscious about how big my belly was, but the look on his face made me feel wanted and sexy. He slowly ran a finger from my belly button down over the curve of my tummy. When he reached my cock he grinned. The head of my cock pressed up against the underside of my gut, dribbling precum, and he started smearing the fluid across my belly.

"Mmm, I love your cock. You are *so* fucking sexy."

I bit back a moan as I felt my cock and ass twitch. I couldn't believe how much he made me want him with such wanton need.

"Fuck me," I whispered, and then I rolled over to my side.

Gavin helped position my leg, gripping my thigh tightly to keep it lifted. I arched my back and pushed my ass against his stiff dick, and the way he growled with desire made me need him more. My slick came in thick and wet, and Gavin sniffed at the air then issued an animalistic grunt. I braced myself for the hard fucking he usually gave me. Instead, he pressed the tip of his cock against my tight, wet hole then leaned over and gently kissed my neck. A shiver ran straight down my spine, and I whimpered.

"I love you," he growled as he thrust an inch of his cock into my hole. I clenched around him and he moaned, reflexively pushing in a little deeper until, inch by inch he was all the way inside, and then he began to move back and forth with slow, smooth thrusts as he kissed my neck, my jaw, my mouth. I breathed between kisses and reached back to hold his hip, guiding him to fuck me deeper. We moved together, not pushing for orgasm, simply happy to just enjoy a slow, warm arousal and a deep, sweet love… Until I felt his cock start to expand at the base and a frisson of cold, electric pleasure raced through my body. Gavin grunted and pushed in deeper. The swelling grew slower than it usually did, allowing Gavin to move a little, but instead of him gaining speed to quickly bring us both to that cascading edge, he continued his slow momentum, and every tiny movement felt like an injection of pleasure, deep inside. If it hadn't felt so fucking good, I wouldn't have been able to bear it.

I moaned when the knot eventually expanded to its full size and Gavin was no longer able to move.

We lay panting, completely knotted but not yet coming. I writhed desperately as my orgasm sat just out of reach, right on the edge. Gavin dug his fingers deeply into my leg that shook from the intensity of my upcoming orgasm.

"Gavin… Gavin I can't…"

Suddenly, he pressed his lips against mine, and the sweetness of his kiss sent me soaring. My ass clenched down hard around the knot. Gavin moaned into my mouth as my ass milked his orgasm out of him, and I shuddered as he spilled his cum into me. My cock shot off a load, smearing the underside of my belly, and my whole body spasmed with the force of my release.

I saw stars.

I felt nothing but bliss.

Slowly I came down, back into the room, back into my body and into the arms of the man I loved and would love forever. I finally felt at home.

Chapter 19 - Gavin

"What's the hold up?" I grunted as I tapped the steering wheel and watched as Brock helped Kyle to the car... Except Kyle kept stopping and squinting up at the sky, looking around at the garden, and generally taking his sweet time. It was the middle of August and Kyle, being due any day now, had been complaining about how hot and uncomfortable it was, so I was confused about why he was dawdling in the morning sun.

By the time he made it to the car, Brock was already late for school and we'd be late for our appointment with Dr. Reed if we didn't hurry up. Brock jumped in the backseat but Kyle bent down and looked at me through the open window.

"I don't want to go," he said.

"Why?"

"My feet are swollen, I'm sweating buckets, I'm in a horrible mood, I'm a balloon..."

I nodded and listened to his complaints, then offered a counter argument. "I'll rub your feet when we get home, there's great air conditioning at Dr. Reed's office, you can be as grumpy as you want to be, and you look gorgeous."

Kyle let out a pouty huff and frowned, looking downright pathetic.

"Come on. Get in. You've gotten this far. May as well come with me to drop Brock off at school."

"Yeah! C'mon, Dad, let's *go*," Brock said in encouragement from the backseat.

Kyle kept grumbling, but he did get in the car. I helped him buckle up over his gigantic belly then gave him a kiss on the cheek before we drove into town. Kyle stayed in a bad mood for the entire trip to the school, but after we dropped off Brock I simply navigated us toward Dr. Reed's office without any further discussion.

"I feel like I'm just going to *pop*," he grumbled to me, and then again to Maddie when we got into her office.

"Well, that's good. That's what's meant to happen," she said as she gave him a kind smile, and he just pouted in response. "Alright, let's have a look at you."

I helped Kyle up onto the examination table while Maddie collected her equipment then snapped on her latex gloves. He held my hand tightly as I stood by his side. I gave his grip a supportive squeeze and watched over him during all of the checkups.

"Well, alright," Maddie said as she stood back and looked at us.

"Alright?" I asked. "What does alright mean?"

"What's alright?" Kyle sounded very annoyed.

"Your symptoms are a sign of early labor."

"What?" we asked together, and Maddie chuckled.

"You're already three centimeters dilated."

"Oh my god," I said, squeezing Kyle's hand firmly to brace myself against falling over.

"Well, that explains this awful mood."

I did a double-take. He seemed so calm. "Oh my god," I said again.

Maddie laughed and gave me a pat on the back. "Nothing to panic about, Gavin. Just get that birthing tub set up and call me when you need me."

"Uh, wow. Okay." I felt like I'd dropped into the twilight zone. My mate was in labor, and no one seemed bothered!

At Maddie's instruction I helped Kyle up off the table. He started to shuffle out of the room, and I was about to follow him when Maddie put her hand on my shoulder. I thought she was going to tell me some secret about being an ideal birthing partner. Instead she winked.

"You have been an excellent father through this whole pregnancy. This will be easier than you think."

I smiled and felt a little better, almost convinced everything was going to be just fine when Kyle let out a yelp.

"Kyle!" I rushed to his side.

"Oh fuck. Bad contraction. Oh it's bad!"

"Breathe through it," Maddie said, and Kyle started huffing like a maniac. Just as I thought it was passing, he let out another cry and then gasped.

"My water just broke!"

The seat of his pants darkened, and then spread down his legs.

"Alright, here we go," Maddie said with a happy laugh. She rushed off to get supplies while I uselessly rubbed Kyle's back. When she came back she loaded me up with towels.

"Get him home, get him in the tub, and I'll be there shortly. The second baby usually comes faster than the first," she said as she gave me a shove and walked off down the corridor.

"Wait. Can't we… Can't we just do it here?" I asked desperately.

Kyle let out a guttural groan and glared at me. "Get in the car, Gavin."

I got the car.

* * *

In the birthing tub, naked and wet, I wrapped my arms around my mate and took him through his breathing techniques while he groaned through the pain of his contractions. We'd prepared the family room to be a dimly lit, peaceful haven, decorated with salt lamps and a thousand crystals from Britt's collection, with the water in the bath soothingly warm. But Kyle's desperate cries cut through all of that and sent my heart racing. My wolf whined constantly as it paced back and forth, all of its senses trained on our mate and unborn cub.

I was so focused on Kyle I barely noticed when Maddie arrived. She set up a lamp to see what was happening, confirmed Kyle was fully dilated, and it was time to push.

"Okay, alright, oh fuck." Kyle gripped my hand and brought it up to his mouth.

"You can do this," I told him, and pressed a kiss against his temple.

Through half an hour of grunting, crying and extreme swearing, Kyle pushed. I mopped his brow with warm towels as sweat flowed off him, and I let him bite down on my hand as hard as he needed to. In the end, I was holding him from behind as our baby was born into the warm water, captured securely by our doctor's waiting hands.

I watched as she lifted our little girl out of the water where she took her first breath and immediately wailed.

"Good lungs," Maddie said as she placed our baby on Kyle's chest.

My heart, my wolf, and every part of my body ached when I saw her up close. Kyle relaxed back against me and I cradled him in my arms.

"Raina," Kyle whispered. Our little cub instantly stopped crying but continued flailing her tiny arms and legs, scrunching up her fists and kicking.

"Raina." I looked down at her and a huge grin broke across my face. I'd never felt more proud or more capable.

***

Maddie helped me cut the umbilical cord, and we got cleaned up before she escorted us to the bedroom then left us to it, promising to be on call for anything we needed. We napped on and off with Raina all afternoon, until we heard a gentle knock on the door.

Brock poked his head into the room with Jaxon right behind him. "Is she here?" Brock asked quietly.

Jaxon had picked up Brock for us and told him that he had a new sister waiting at home.

"He was so darn excited I thought he was going to jump out of the car and sprint home," Jaxon said as he put a hand on Brock and urged closer.

"Thanks for getting him home, Jaxon," Kyle said sleepily.

"Oh wow," Brock whispered when he saw his little sister resting in my arms.

"Come say hi to Raina," I said, and he hurried over to my side of the bed. He leaned over and smiled down at his new sibling.

"She looks like…"

"She looks just like *you*, buddy." Jaxon smiled down at our newborn. "Welcome to the pack, little Raina," he said, smoothing a finger over her cheek. My pack alpha connecting with my newborn cub had something deep and ancient tugging at my heart.

"There are a few other visitors here, if you're up for it?" Jaxon asked, motioning back into the hallway.

I looked to Kyle who looked downright exhausted, but he smiled and nodded. "Send 'em in."

Our bedroom was quickly filled with most of the pack's eager faces looking down at our new baby. Nic knelt down at my bedside where she kissed Raina's face over and over again until she was distracted by Jason entering the room with an oversized bouquet. She went to help him arrange it in a vase by the dresser. The rest of the pack popped in and out of the room, mingling in the hallway and all through the house. Trevor stood by Kyle and leaned over him to get a good view of our baby girl, holding his face in his hands and squealing.

"I'm declaring myself an honorary uncle," Trevor stated.

Kyle grinned and told him, "Hey, you'll be next to have a baby, Trev."

"Oh, please. No one will ever be interested in me," he mumbled.

Jason turned, glanced at Trevor and frowned. His gaze lingered on him for a moment, but when he noticed me looking he quickly glanced away.

Not long after, Britt and Kennedy pushed their way into the crowded room. "Aunties coming through! We need to see the baby!"

They scooped Raina up out of my arms and took care of her for the rest of the evening while Nicole entertained our guests so we could get some rest. When we woke up, only Brock, Britt, Kennedy and Nicole were still here, tidying up and taking care of Raina.

"Thank you, aunties," Kyle said as he gathered Raina up from Nicole's arms so he could feed her. "We can take it from here."

"You need more rest," Britt said, pointing Kyle back in the direction of the bedroom.

"I have something else in mind," Kyle said before smiling at me.

Once the aunts had left, we found ourselves in the games room. Kyle relaxed back against the couch with Raina in his arms, while Brock leaned back against me as he played a game.

I looked over at Kyle and smiled as he reached out to take my hand.

"I love you," he said softly, sending a flutter to my heart.

"Thank you for all of this," I said sincerely. "You've given me two beautiful children, and a life that's even better than I ever could have dreamed for myself. I promise you, I'm not going to miss a moment of it from now on."

"I know," Kyle said with a smirk. "I won't let you."

I laughed and gave him a playful shove, which woke up Raina. The whole room instantly filled with crying until we got her settled down again. I kept laughing and shaking my head at the mistake—without any shame, fear or guilt about it. Maybe I was getting the hang of this parenting thing. Maybe I was good at it, after all.

Chapter 20 - Kyle

Two weeks later, our little girl was feeding well and hadn't lost too much of her post-birth weight, but she was also causing serious mayhem. I had barely slept, and my whole body was still sore after giving birth.

"Did you get the you-know-what from the you-know-where?" I asked Gavin as he hauled in three overflowing bags of games, sports equipment, and other last-minute presents for Brock's birthday.

"Yes, I got the I-know-what," he said as he hoisted the bags onto the kitchen counter. "How has the little miss been?"

"The same." I sighed and ran a hand over my face. I felt downright exhausted and could not wait to get back into a normal routine. I was even day dreaming of going back to work.

"Still demanding?" he asked, calling after me as I headed into the other room.

"Oh yes," I said as I came back carrying three rolls of wrapping paper. "That one is so spoiled."

""There's no such thing as spoiling a baby," Gavin replied with a smirk.

"Oh, so you're an expert on babies, now?"

"I've been doing my fair share of research, but no, I'm not, but you can't give a baby too much loving."

I couldn't argue with that because Raina was just too beautiful not to spoil. Granted I'd probably regret it later on, but now... I nodded, and then unrolled the sheets of paper on the table and motioned for Gavin to hand me a present. He peeled a price sticker off and passed me a video game called "Horror Car Crash Wars!"

"Well this looks appropriate for an eleven-year-old boy," I muttered, but I wrapped it anyway.

"It's rated for a general audience," Gavin said. I just grunted, feeling myself slipping into another exhausted, bad mood, but then Gavin wrapped his hands around my waist and pulled me back against him.

"I love you, you wonderful, protective father," he said before planting a kiss on my cheek. I laughed and arched my back so I could look at him, then I reached up to run my hand through his hair. Even when I was so tired he still managed to make me feel better.

"I got you something." Gavin put a small gift-wrapped present in front of me.

"What? What is this?" I smiled and picked up the gift. I gave it a shake and instantly knew what it was. I gave him a sly grin and he laughed.

"It's hard to disguise that kind of thing..."

I ripped off the gift wrap and beamed when I saw he'd bought me a vintage cassette. I turned it over and gasped. A rare edition of Feather Boats' first album.

"I noticed there was a space in the cabinet, and you don't have that album, right?" he asked.

I nodded, suddenly too overcome with emotion to answer. My throat closed up and my vision swum with tears.

"Oh, Kyle." Gavin wrapped his arms around my waist and I instantly leaned into his warm embrace. My hormones were still all over the place, and we hadn't had full sex since the birth yet, and I was still learning to shift and—

Gavin tilted my face up and feathered soft lips across mine. I moaned, my body sparking to life. I slid fingers into Gavin's hair and pulled him closer, parting my lips to deepen the kiss. When he lowered his hands to grip my ass I pulled away and smiled.

"Bed?"

"God yes."

I laughed and grabbed his hand, ready to drag him to our room…

"Hey dads," Britt said as she and Kennedy arrived with Nicole, all helping to carry an oversized cake between them.

I groaned, not hiding my disappointment. I really could have done with Gavin's soft tongue lapping at my—

"She's sleeping! And mind her tummy!" I shouted as they disappeared down the hall after putting the cake on the kitchen counter. I trusted them, but I still turned up the volume on the baby monitor. Gavin chuckled and kissed the top of my head, before we got back into wrapping presents.

We'd just finished tying the last of the bows when we heard tires on the gravel in the driveway.

"Already?" I asked, glancing up at the clock.

"Birthday boy coming through!" Brock shouted as he stormed into the house followed by a huge crowd of his friends from school and a bunch of parents from the pack. Dishes of food were spread out through the dining room and snacks found places in the living room where a bunch of pre-teen boys started making loud mayhem. Trevor hurried in at the rear of the group and stopped to give me a big hug before disappearing to find Raina and the aunts.

"Love you, but I gotta see that *baby*!"

"How was your birthday at school, Brocky?" I asked as I gave our son a big hug.

"So cool!"

Cole came up beside him and pointed to a big button on Brocks' shirt that said "11 TODAY!"

"I got him that," Cole said proudly.

"Very cool," I said.

Jason and his little girl Stacia, Linc, Shawn, Liam and baby Samuel came in, followed by Jaxon, Bryce and Lori, all carrying big plates of food. The rest of the pack and the cubs filled the house and soon enough the whole party was taking care of itself. People were dishing up their own food, putting on music from my collection, and most importantly, Brock was having a good time.

I sat back and took in all in. How had I gone from living a quiet life as a single dad to suddenly having the biggest, loudest, sweetest family in less than a year? It was too loud to tell Gavin just how much it meant to me, but I smiled at him and he nodded like he knew exactly what I was saying.

The night went on beautifully with no problems until Jaxon and Steve Daniels pulled Gavin and I aside.

"There've been some more reports," Jaxon said quietly.

"Of…" I glanced between the three of them. Gavin was frowning, as if he already knew exactly what it was about.

"Dragons," he said sadly. My stomach flipped and I sucked in a sharp breath.

"What's going on?" I asked.

"They seem to be causing more problems in town. There have been reports of small fires at the back of Kay's diner, and Tony's pizza… And a *lot* of burned patches in the woods, getting closer to the homestead. There has even been a break in at another pack omega's house."

I swallowed and glanced at Gavin. He stared at Steve. "How bad is it?"

"Let's just say I'm worried," Steve stated.

Gavin shook his head, and my heart raced. I gripped Gavin's hand, unable to hide how my fingers trembled.

"We have to do something," Jaxon said. "Before they do."

CPSIA information can be obtained
at www.ICGtesting.com
Printed in the USA
LVHW052250281019
635543LV00001B/324/P